Chapter 1

"Over there Granda!" Goldie shouted as she pointed to a spot in the choppy ocean waters, with Mack, her ring tail coon on her shoulder who was getting antsy with anticipation.

Granda tipped his old brown, flat cap at her and turned the helm where her long, slender finger pointed out into the unknown depths. Goldie had been his lucky charm on the shrimp boat since arriving in America and making the purchase of the 28-foot boat. The white boat with its single green shrimp net out to drag, chugged along slowly.

Goldie ran to one side of the boat with Mack still on her shoulder to watch as the net did its job in the water. She knew that it was skimming right at the bottom like it was supposed to. You could see the ropes and winches strained but not over strained. Her eyes glittered with excitement. She loved when the net came in. She felt like it was Christmas. You never knew what would come up.

"Look out there now Goldie. We are going to pull the net in my Charm," Granda hollered at her with his heavy Irish accent over the sound of the running motors and working winches.

Goldie ran back to stand by her grandfather as he pulled a lever and handed the helm off to her while he went to pull ropes and wrestle the net to the middle of the boat where it would be easier to sort what came up. Goldie held the helm steady as she watched her sun kissed grandfather's arm bunch under his rolled-up sleeves. He heaved and pulled until the net was up on deck. He went to the bottom of the net, where the shrimp basket was tied off and untied the series of half hitch knots quickly.

Goldie's eyes shined brightly as she watched their catch rush out onto the deck. Mack quickly climbed down her shoulder, expertly dodging the crabs that had come up with the shrimp to get to a small, flopping shad. Mack liked shrimping too and enjoyed eating the spoils of it.

Granda quickly threw stingrays back over and big trout. He didn't want to kill more than he had to, to survive. He looked up at Goldie and could see her about to come out of her skin. She wanted to be in the mix of things. He smiled at her and finally said, "Come on down here my Charm. Be careful still though. I could have missed something."

Goldie smiled and quickly moved from the helm to where she could sit and separate their catch. Granda constantly was on her to wear her rubber boots, but she never had them on. She would be barefoot as soon as his eyes were off of her. He worried about a stingray getting her, but the sea critters never seemed to bother her. She never was nervous around them. Goldie went and bent down and started sorting the shrimp into different baskets according to their size. Some they would keep alive in a live well for bait for their modest bait camp.

She was efficient, she got them sorted and on ice. She would even take the time to bag up shad and mullet if they caught them into nice size bait bags. All the while, Mack would be snacking. Granda would smile as he would watch Goldie hand the raccoon a single shrimp and Mack eat it and try to give her kisses. Goldie would smile and accept them.

Granda was proud of his lucky charm. Goldie really didn't have a woman in her life, only the old Irish man and a black woman who had taken a liking to her. He was doing the best he could with her and often worried about her being raised on a shrimp boat. He smiled watching her. Goldie had golden ringlets that framed her face with high cheek bones and a small upturned nose. Her light blue eyes always seem to be lit from within. Her smile was all her own too. She had a gap between her front teeth, but it didn't take away from her beauty. She was still a young las and he worried about her marrying and not being alone. All he ever wanted for her was to not be alone in the big world.

Granda was a tall man with a lean frame. He had a worker's hands and tan skin from the hours on the water. His hair was thick and dark with just a hint of gray at his sideburns. He had the same smile as his granddaughter, but with a strong jaw line. He had blue eyes too, but his weren't as light as hers.

His heart would ache sometimes as he looked at Goldie. Sometimes he felt guilty that her life was always on a boat. It had even started on a boat. She looked so much like her mother, his daughter, Enya. But his boat was named, Deirdre for his wife. The blonde hair had come from her. Granda thought about Goldie's beginning. They had left Ireland on a ship, shortly after Deirdre had died. Deirdre had just fallen sick and wasted away. They never really knew why. She had told him to take their girl to the land where dreams could come true and that it would be better for them there. He had agreed to her dying wish, never fully understanding why she wanted them to leave their home. He was a fisherman there and made a decent living.

Enya had become pregnant out of wedlock before Deirdre had died. He was furious with her. Her marriage prospects would be terrible. He assumed that was why his wife wanted her to be able to start fresh somewhere new. Enya talked about the child's father that he had never met, with nothing but adoration and love. She claimed to be in love with him. Granda was enraged when she couldn't find the boy who had tricked his daughter into falling for him. Heartbroken, she agreed to move with him after her mother died. Both he and his daughter boarded a ship, completely heartbroken.

By the time he had secured enough money to get them safe passage, Enya's belly was round. He was nervous about traveling with her in her condition, but she insisted they go. She wouldn't be ready to give birth in the twelve weeks it would take to get to America, so they should have enough time.

But as fate does, it played out in an unspeakable way. With only one week left of the journey, Enya's water broke unexpectedly on a night with a full blood moon. An older woman said it meant that blood would be lost that night. Granda sat by his writhing, crying daughter all through the night and prayed and prayed to whoever would listen to spare his child. When the moon was at its highest, Enya gave birth to a tiny little girl. Enya looked at her with glazed over eyes and cried as she looked at the baby girl. Her eyes had met her father's and she cried out when she realized the baby hadn't.

"No. No. Take me instead God. Please. Let my child live. Please!" Enya had cried out.

Granda cradled the tiny girl who was too small to live and went to be by his daughter. He placed the tiny bundle in her arms and said, "Hush now Las. Look upon your beautiful daughter. I love you Las." His voice had broken at her anguish. No parent should have to bear a dead child. His heart shattered with hers as she rocked the tiny girl.

Enya looked down at her and said, "Aren't you a beautiful golden baby. I had big dreams for you." And she kissed her head.

Granda assumed she just saw the bright moon's rays shining off the little bundle.

"Look Da she's a golden baby. She's so beautiful." Enya said as her eyelids grew heavy and her breaths came slower.

"Enya. Stay awake my love. Stay with me," Granda had pleaded as he saw the light going out in his daughter's eyes.

"Da, I'm just so tired. I'll sleep so that she can wake. I love you." Enya said as she closed her eyes for the last time.

"NO!" Granda screamed as he shook his daughter. As, he continued to shake her, the little bundle let out a tiny cry from his daughter's laxed arms.

Granda picked up the too small baby and cradled her softly. He kissed her forehead and somehow knew that Enya had taken her place. He was terrified. They still had a week on the boat and he had nothing to feed her and she was too small. She shouldn't be alive in all reality. As he pulled the bundle to him to give her his warmth, he looked down at her and noticed, she did look golden and not just in the moon's rays and the little fuzz on her head was blonde. He whispered, "Goldie."

Chapter 2

Goldie was a happy girl as she grew older. She loved her Granda fiercely. He was all the family she had. She learned how to cook. She had to, or they'd only eat fried bologna sandwiches and scrambled eggs forever.

Granda always said that her Granna, Dierdre, cooked the best food and he was sad that she wasn't here to teach her. Goldie made up for it though. She would ask for recipes from any woman that came into the small bait camp her Granda bought for them to sell their shrimp and other bait at.

The bait camp wasn't anything too special. It was a tiny white shack right on the saltwater where boats came and went. Granda could pull the shrimp boat right up to it, so they could easily unload any catch they got. The little bait shack he named Charm's Bait, for Goldie. He thought it was a little charm and lucky to still be standing after weathering a few hurricanes. The bait camp was only the size of a small kitchen at best. It had a single table with a pencil and receipt paper. Granda didn't believe in using anything but pencil and paper to keep the books. On the back wall it was nothing but pegboard with different types of hooks, lures, nets, and any type of fishing tackle fishermen may need.

The floor was old wooden planks that you could see the water underneath between the cracks. The little bait camp was a floating camp. It was on 10 empty drums that moved with the water. Outside the camp was two big round live bait tanks. They would keep shrimp in them when they got good bait shrimp. The live tanks just pumped water from the salty ocean outside the camp. There was no freezer or anything like that. Instead, there were three large chests that they kept ice in to keep shrimp cold.

Goldie was always good in the bait camp. Customers loved her and her manners. She had the slightest Irish accent, not from being in Ireland of course, but from being raised by her Granda. She was very smart and kept the books perfectly. When she wasn't on the shrimp boat or if the camp was already full before daylight, Goldie would work the camp alone.

Goldie didn't go to school. Her Granda taught her at home. She could read, write, and do arithmetic better than the kids in school. She learned history alongside her Granda. He would teach her of their homeland and then they would study together the history of America. Goldie did long to be around other kids her age sometimes. She would feel a sense of longing when she would see groups of kids hanging out together. The few times, Goldie did try to hang out with the kids, they weren't necessarily mean to her, but she didn't feel like she belonged.

"Hey tha Miss Goldie. How you doin chil?" Ms. Betsy, an older black lady said as she walked into the bait camp.

"Hi Ms. Betsy! I am doing mighty fine. How are you today?" Goldie replied cheerily.

"I am good. The good Lord woke me up this mornin'," said Ms. Betsy pulling out her cigarettes.

Goldie watched as Ms. Betsy tuned the cigarette carton over and opened them upside down, pulling the cigarette out from the end you light.

"Ms. Betsy, why do you open your cigarettes upside down?" Asked Goldie.

Ms. Betsy smiled and said, "Well chil, I don't wanna touch the part I put in my mouth with dirty hands, specially after I start fishing."

Goldie had heard people call her dumb for doing that, but Ms. Betsy was actually one of the smartest ladies around. Goldie smiled and said, "I think you are mighty smart for doing that. What can I get you today? Your usual?"

"Yes child. I'm going to go try to scare me up a croaker or two for supper," smiled Ms. Betsy.

Goldie nodded and headed to the fresh dead shrimp for her. Granda took care of his customers. Ms. Betsy didn't need a whole quart of shrimp. He would sell her just what she needed and not overcharge her. Goldie smiled as she grabbed a dozen shrimp and carefully put them in a bag.

"Good luck Ms. Betsy. I hope you get you a good one," said Goldie handing her the bag of bait.

"And bless you my chil. Oh an I wrote ya down another recipe to try. I'll bring it with me in a few days." She said smiling tenderly.

"I loved the last one you gave me. It was so good. I never knew greens could be good. And don't get me started on those ox tails." Goldie said rubbing her stomach.

"That's cause you are making you some good soul food. I'll bring you the cornbread recipe too. Nothing goes better with greens than some good cornbread. See you later chil," said Ms. Betsy turning around.

"Bye!" Goldie hollered happily.

Ms. Betsy was always true to her word and brought her the recipes. Goldie would ask her when she had questions that only a woman could answer. Ms. Betsy helped her navigate being a woman when her courses hit her at the tender age of 12. It had happened at the bait camp and luckily, Ms. Betsy was the first customer to walk in. Goldie was pale with Mack sitting on her feet as if protecting her. She thought she was dying. Granda was out on the boat and she was alone.

Ms. Betsy paused when she saw Goldie sitting in the corner all pale and her critter being protective. "Chil what's the matter?" She asked.

"Ms. Betsy, I think I'm dying. I'm bleeding badly," answered Goldie.

"Where from? Show me. Did you cut yourself?" Ms. Betsy asked frantically.

"I didn't cut myself. I'm bleeding from the inside. I don't know what I did to myself." Goldie softly cried.

Ms. Betsy looked at her with her head tilted and she noticed she was cradling her stomach and had her legs tightly closed. "Are you bleeding from between your legs chil?" She asked.

Goldie just nodded with the tears still streaming down her face.

Ms. Betsy let a gentle smile hit her lips. "It's ok chil. You're ok. You are a woman now. You've just gotten your courses. This is normal. It will happen every month now."

"You mean I'm not dying?" Asked Goldie shakily.

"No chil. You are not dying. You are a woman. It means that you will be able to have children now. Your body is changin into a woman's body. You will be fillin out now," explained Ms. Betsy.

"So I will do this every month? What am I supposed to do? I've ruined my clothes?" Goldie said.

Ms. Betsy nodded. "You will do this every month. You should write it down on a calendar to keep up with it. As far as the clothes, I can go get you some. I think I have something at the house that'll work fer ya. Now as far as keeping yourself clean, you will need rags to keep yourself clean. They make other products at the store now. You'll just look on the feminine aisle. I still just use my rags. They are already bought and they are comfortable to me. I'll be back in a bit. Let me go get you something else to wear and I'll get you a rag. Sit tight."

Goldie nodded. There was nothing else she could do. Ten minutes later she about died of embarrassment when a man in walked in to get bait. She looked horrified about the prospect of having to get up. She stiffened when the man looked to her and smiled. "I'm looking for some bait sweetheart." He said.

Goldie shifted uncomfortably and was about to cry again, when Ms. Betsy made it back. She looked quickly to Goldie and to the man and understood what was happening.

"Ah yessir. I'll be glad to help you get what you need sir." Ms. Betsy said with a nod and slid past him to hand Goldie the change of clothes with a rag underneath.

Goldie grabbed them with a grateful smile. But her smile again turned to horror when the man spoke. "I didn't know you had a nigga here. It's shameful to mingle with them girl. Your parents should know better." He said and walked out and never bought anything.

Goldie felt the tears stream down her face again.

"Chil it's ok. You have clothes here and you'll be fine. This is normal." Ms. Betsy said.

"I'm not crying about that. The way he talked about you. My heart hurts. He should of never been so ugly. You are one of the best people I know. You're nothing but kind and in my time of need, here you are. I'm so sorry. You didn't deserve that," whimpered Goldie rubbing her chest that ached.

Ms. Betsy's face softened even more. She cupped Goldie's cheek and said, "You are more than this world deserves Golden One. I understand why your grandfather named you Goldie. You are as bright as the sun from the inside out. You have a pure heart."

Goldie never understood why all the other bait camps would turn her away just because of the color of her skin. But, then again, her and Granda understood prejudices. Although their skin was white, they were looked down upon for being Irish immigrants. Granda was always very clear that they never turn anyone away and that all were welcome in their bait camp.

Ms. Betsy stayed with Goldie all day until her Granda made it back. Goldie softly told her Granda what happened and his face fell. He was only a man and he didn't know when he was supposed to have certain conversations. He thanked Ms. Betsy profusely and gave her two pounds of table shrimp to thank her.

Chapter 3

Goldie continued to grow up into a beautiful young lady. Her blue eyes only seemed to get lighter and her cheek bones more pronounced. On her eighteenth birthday she was out on the shrimp boat with Granda. She was tying off the shrimp basket for Granda and after she got it thrown in the water and the boat was dragging it's net, Granda called her to the helm with him.

When she got up to him, she smiled as he pulled a single cupcake out from under the console.

"It's not much my Charm, but it is your 18th birthday and you're stuck out here with me," said Granda holding a chocolate cupcake with chocolate icing.

Goldie reached for it. "Not yet Charm. I have to sing you happy birthday," said Granda smiling wide.

He belted out the song and Goldie laughed. He handed her the cupcake and she ate half of it before offering him the second half.

"No, that's yours. Enjoy it. I love you." He said with watery eyes.

Mack didn't seem to mind. He stole the rest of her cupcake and ran off to the back of the boat to sit on the edge. Granda and Goldie both laughed.

"And I love you Granda," said Goldie hugging him tightly.

It was a hot day. The sun was beating down on them and there were no clouds in sight. Their net caught on something on the bottom and tore a hole in it. There would be no more shrimping until they patched it up. Goldie decided that since they were already out, she might as well use the time for something fun on her birthday. She stripped down to her undershirt and shorts and dove off the side of the boat.

Granda laughed as she came back up to the surface. He watched Goldie in the water. It was like second nature to her. He never taught her to swim. She just was natural and took to it on her own. She would jump off the boat and swim for as long as he would let her from the time she was a very young child. He just always watched her amazed that she was his granddaughter. She swam like she was meant for the water, slicing through it and floating effortlessly.

Granda's heart jumped in his throat when the dark shadow came into view. He shouted when the fin broke the water. "Goldie! Shark! Swim to the boat now las!"

Goldie didn't feel fear as the huge animal swam towards her. She just turned and started to swim as fast as she could towards the boat. She was a very fast swimmer. Faster than anyone she knew, but she was not faster than a shark whose sleek body was made to project through the water. When she realized she couldn't make it. She turned in the water and faced the giant shark coming at her.

Granda screamed, "Las what are you doing? Move Now!"

Goldie didn't though. She treaded water firmly in place waiting to face down the shark. The shark didn't slow down. It came straight for her, until it bumped into her so hard that it pushed her body back several feet in the water. Goldie righted herself again to face down the creature. The shark came slowly this time. It seemed to stop right in front of her as if trying to figure out what she was. When the shark didn't make a move, Goldie slowly put her hand out and placed it on the sharks very sensitive nose. A shock ran through her from her hand to her heart. She stopped breathing at the sensation. The shark shook its head gently and swam off back towards the open sea. Goldie watched its form until she could no longer see it, still wondering what just happened, and then she made her way back to the boat.

Granda pulled her up quickly and wrapped her in a hug. "I don't know what just happened but I thank God he spared you again." He breathed into her hair.

"That shark didn't want to hurt me. It could have easily. I think it was just curious. It was a beautiful creature," said Goldie looking back out to the water and without fear.

"A beautiful creature that could have killed you," said Granda shakily.

Mack scampered over dragging her shirt across the boat getting it completely wet in the process. Goldie bent down and said, "Thank you Mack," and took her shirt from him.

"You and your critters." Granda said as he shook his head and went back to the helm so he could point them home.

Goldie stood at the front of the boat and let the wind whip through her hair as they made their way back to the bait camp. Mack was sitting on her shoulder enjoying the wind in his hair too. As they approached the camp she could see an old beat up Ford truck parked by the camp. She eyed the truck, wondering who would be waiting for them to return.

As Granda let off the throttle and let the boat glide in, Goldie got in place with the mooring rope and jumped on the pier to tie the big boat off. She secured it with the wide rope on a grapple close to the front of the boat and then, Granda threw her another mooring rope to tie the back off, to keep the boat in place and that way it wouldn't rock against the pier as other boats passed by.

Out of the corner of her eye, she saw someone get out of the old beat up truck and start walking towards them. When she looked up she saw a boy about her age and he smiled at her. As he got closer he said, "I didn't realize it was just you and your dad on the boat or I would have gotten over her sooner to help you tie the boat up."

Goldie was affronted. "That's my Granda and I can handle tying the boat up thank you very much."

The boy laughed. "I didn't mean it as if you couldn't. My mama taught me to be a gentleman and to always offer help to a lady."

She looked at the boy now and laughed awkwardly. "I'm sorry I took offense. Your mom raised a polite young man."

Goldie really looked at him now. He was tall and lean, even taller than Granda. He had dark hair that looked black and brown eyes that were the same color as dirt that had just gotten rained on. He had a long nose, almost too long and pointed for his face, but yet it was perfect on him. He had thin lips and a shy smile. He was cute. He studied her too. She felt her skin go hot under his stare.

"Who's your friend?" Granda asked as he jumped off the boat and headed their way.

"I'm Larry Quinn sir," said the boy extending his hand for a shake.

"Brian O'Connor," said Granda taking the boy's hand in a firm handshake.

"I've actually come to see if you're hiring. I'm looking for a summer job." Larry said looking into Granda's eyes.

Granda's eyes smiled and he asked, "Do you know anything about working on a shrimp boat lad?"

"No sir, but I'm a quick study and I'll do anything you ask," said Larry looking hopeful.

Granda nodded and said, "Well you can get started by helping me mend this net, so Goldie can take the evening off for her birthday."

"Granda you know you don't have to do that. I don't have anything to do anyway." Goldie said smiling sadly.

"Oh happy birthday Goldie," Larry said trying her name out on his tongue and then his eyes lit with amusement as Mack came running up to him to push him away with his little black hands and climb up Goldie to sit on her shoulder.

"And who is this?" Larry asked slowly reaching his hand out to let Mack smell him.

"This is my shrimp eating buddy, Mack," said Goldie scratching his chin. "Be nice Mack." She said to the raccoon on a whisper.

"Animals tend to like me. I'm sure we will be fast friends," Larry said as he gently reached his long fingers out to gently touch Mack's head. In the process, he skimmed Goldie's hand and a jolt went through her hand and to her gut. She looked up surprised to see the same look in Larry's eyes. He had felt it too. And if she wasn't crazy she could of sworn his eyes almost glowed.

Chapter 4

Larry watched Goldie walk away with the raccoon still on her shoulder. He studied her for a long moment before his thoughts were interrupted by Granda clearing his throat.

"Now lad, she is pretty, but you keep staring at her like that and I'll have to string you up in the nets," said Granda studying the boy.

"I'm sorry sir. She is pretty and that raccoon is not something you see on a girl's shoulder every day," answered Larry boldly looking Granda straight in the eyes.

Granda laughed and asked, "So Quinn? Irish dad lad?"

Larry replied," Something like that Mr. O'Connor."

"Nice manners. Ok let's go over here and I'll teach you how to patch this net," said Granda leading him towards the boat. They would fix it on the boat so they wouldn't have to move it off and back on.

Goldie stood in the shower washing the salt water from her hair. It felt heavy and a little crunchy. She scrubbed her scalp and let out a breath as she relaxed. The warm water always had a calming effect on her. She didn't mind working hard, but was glad to go ahead and get to come home. She finished scrubbing to find Mack asleep on the blue bath rug and gingerly stepped to the side of him not to disturb him.

She dried off and put on a pair of lounge pants and a tank top. She didn't bother with combing her hair and just left the towel on top her head and made her way to the kitchen to see what she could cook for dinner. As she was bent over in the fridge, she heard the front door open.

"In the kitchen Granda!" She hollered.

"I hope you haven't cooked anything yet las. I want to take you and Larry out for burgers and shakes," said Granda in the living room as he made his way into the kitchen.

Goldie turned around and to her horror saw Granda standing in the kitchen doorway with Larry right behind him! She was only in her pajamas and had a towel on her head.

"Granda you could of warned me you weren't alone! I'm not decent!" She shrieked.

"You're all covered up Charm. Go get dressed and we will get something to eat and celebrate you," said Granda with a twinkle of amusement in his eyes.

Goldie quickly shouldered past the two tall men and sped walked to her bedroom and shut the door forcefully. She put her hands over her face and took a deep steadying breath. She made her way to her dresser and pulled out a light green button up shirt and a pair of worn blue jean overalls. She then slipped her feet into white pull on loafers.

Goldie ran a comb through her still wet hair and decided to just put it up in a ballerina bun on the top of her head. She found herself studying her reflection in the mirror above her dresser, wondering if she should put a little rouge on her lips and cheeks. Ms. Betsy had given it to her for her birthday and told her less is more, but for special occasions, it was nice to have a little color. Today seemed like a special enough occasion. She dabbed the dark pink rouge on her lips and smacked them and looked at herself. She looked the same, but her bow shaped lips looked nice.

She shook her head and walked out of her bedroom to find two impatient guys waiting on her in the living room. Larry looked nervous almost. He smiled shyly when he saw her. Granda studied her face for a bit before saying, "You look nice Charm. Let's go eat. I owe this lad dinner. He wasn't lying when he said he was a quick study."

Larry followed Granda and Goldie to the Burger Place in his beat up truck. Granda's truck really didn't look much better. "Larry seems to be a good lad. He doesn't mind working and is smart. He ties good knots too. It'll be nice to have some extra help that way you can do more than be on the boat." Granda said looking at Goldie.

"Granda, can we afford to pay him and I love being on the boat. It doesn't bother me," said Goldie feeling defensive.

"I know you do and we can afford it. Last season was good to us. You are turning into a woman Goldie. You need to do more than just be on a boat with an old man. I want to you experience life and find a good man and settle down and have a family. I don't want you to be alone," said Granda feeling the ache in his heart.

"I don't need to find a good man. I have you and no one could live up to that for me. I'm not alone. I have you and.."

Granda cut her off, "The raccoon doesn't count and I'm not going to be around forever. You know as well as me how short life can be."

Goldie looked out the window. She didn't want to have this conversation. She longed for love too. The kind that Granda had for her Granma, but even when she had come across boys her age, she felt nothing. Not even interest.

"I only say these things cause I love you more than life my Charm," said Granda squeezing her shoulder.

"I know." She whispered.

When they pulled into the Burger Place, Larry parked right by them and quickly got out and opened Goldie's door for her. She looked up at him and said, "Thank you."

Something felt different inside her when she looked at this boy, like a piece that was missing was put back into place. He smiled and said, "You're welcome Goldie."

He seemed to like to say her name. "Alright you two, let's go get a burger." Granda said.

Again at the entrance of the Burger Place, Larry held the door. Goldie then again felt the shock of his of his touch when just her arm barely brushed his on the way in. She was almost scared to touch him. She never had that reaction with anyone or anything except the shark.

They all sat down in a small corner booth in the little diner and an older woman, with a red apron and hair back in a French twist came over to get their order.

"What can I get ya'll?" She asked overly cheery.

"Birthday girl goes first," said Granda winking.

Goldie moaned knowing he did that on purpose, so they would sing to her later.

"Oh we've got a birthday girl?" Asked the older woman looking happy.

"Yes ma'am. I've been blessed with the best Granda for eighteen years," said Goldie through a fake smile.

Larry's eyes shot up in surprise, but he stayed quiet.

"How sweet. What do you want to eat dear?" She asked.

Goldie answered, "I'll have the cheeseburger with everything, fries, and a chocolate shake with the whipped cream and cherry."

"I like a girl who know what she wants," replied the waitress with a smile.

Granda nodded his head to Larry who said, "I'll have the same please."

"And me too las," said Granda to the old waitress who blushed at him calling her las.

"Well didn't ya'll just make it easy on little ole' me," said the waitress grabbing their menus.

She went off to place their order. Goldie looked up to the back entrance to see Ms. Betsy making her way in. Excitedly, Goldie got up and all but ran to the back entrance that was for "coloreds only" and wrapped Ms. Betsy up in a hug.

"Hey chil. Be careful. You know how people be thinkin. And happy birthday my sweet chil!" Ms. Betsy said a little too loud.

"Thank you and I don't care what people think Ms. Betsy. You are good people and have always been so good to me and I'm happy to see you." Goldie said hugging her again, not caring who saw.

A man with a round belly and little white hat came out of the kitchen holding a small bag and flung it towards Ms. Betsy. "Careful now girl. Don't want people thinkin you love their kind. Might rub off on you," said the man to Goldie.

Goldie flinched as if he hit her. "I'd rather Ms. Betsy rub off on me than ugliness." The man acted insulted and then she turned and faced Ms. Betsy. "Thank you for my birthday rouge. I'm wearing it and I'm sorry not everyone sees how truly wonderful you are. I'll see you soon." And she walked back to the booth with her Granda and Larry.

"What was that about?" Granda asked.

"That man is just ugly and Ms. Betsy wished me a happy birthday. I wish people weren't so mean. Ms. Betsy is truly one of the best people alive," said Goldie looking back to the door where she had come in.

"I wish everyone had a heart as big as yours," said Granda squeezing her hand.

A group of kids about Goldie's age walked up and started making comments about her. One said, "Goldie you really could dress like a girl. I mean, overalls, again?"

Another said, "Is that shrimp I smell?"

The last girl said, "Good thing you don't come to school because you wouldn't make it there."

A boy spoke up and said, "I think I would like to see her there."

Larry stiffened and looked at him coldly.

"Nah she's a nigga lover. You see her hugging all over that nigga at the door. She's not meant to hang out with civilized people," said another boy who was large. He looked like a football player. Lineman.

Without a word, Larry slid out of the booth from beside Goldie where she was sandwiched between he and her Granda, and right hooked the guy who made the last comment. The huge guy fell to the floor knocked out cold. Larry looked at the other guy. The other guy put his hands up and said, "Hey man we are just poking fun."

"I didn't think it was fun and I'm sure Goldie didn't either. I don't appreciate the comments you girls said either. You just couldn't outshine her if she was in school with you. Stay away from Goldie," said Larry looking menacing with his hands still clenched in fists by his side.

"Look man, we really didn't mean anything by it. It was just words." The now scared guy said.

"Words have power and you'll do good to remember that." Larry said through clenched teeth, as if he was holding something back.

"What is she your girlfriend or something?" One of the rude girls asked.

"Or something," said Larry eyeing her and making her squirm.

Goldie looked up to him to meet his eyes and she saw the light again. Was she seeing things? His eyes softened when he looked at her.

"Hey what the hell is going on over here?" The man from the kitchen was coming over.

The boy on the floor stirred and his friend helped him to his feet. The boy spoke up, "Nothing Tony. We are just leaving."

Tony stalked over to their table. "Brian I like ya alright, but Goldie hugging niggas and now this boy punching customers…I can't have that in here."

Granda answered, "Is my money not as green as everyone else's? I was trying to bring my granddaughter out for her birthday and she has been nothing but verbally abused, not only by those kids but also you Tony. And this boy defended my granddaughter's honor. If anything, he deserves a pat on the back. I'd hate to lose your number and call someone else when I have good table shrimp."

Tony stiffened and said, "I'm sorry Brian. I just get carried away sometimes. Enjoy your meal."

Tony stepped out of the way for our waitress to return with a nervous smile on her face. She deposited all the food down and stepped away. The three of them ate in silence for a long while. Then Goldie broke the quiet. "Larry thank you for taking up for me. You didn't have to, but I certainly appreciate it. Let me see your hand. You must have swollen knuckles from that hard of a hit."

"No, I'm fine and I couldn't just sit back and listen to that. You are nothing but kind as far as I can tell and no one deserves to be ganged up on like that," replied Larry, clenching his jaw and looking off into the distance.

"Let me see your hand." Goldie said firmly with her hand out palm up.

Larry looked at her for a moment and then slowly placed his hand in hers knuckles up. They both jolted at the sensation. It was like an electric shock and a never ending tingle with their hands touching. Goldie shook the feeling as best as she could to look down at his hand. His perfectly fine hand. His unblemished, not swollen hand. Impossible. He had hit that guy hard enough to knock him out. His knuckles should be screaming.

"I've got strong hands. Not much bothers them," said Larry not taking his eyes off her.

"I s-see that," breathed Goldie.

"You two quit holding hands and eat your burgers before they get cold," said Granda gruffly. He didn't like how the lad was looking at his Charm or how she reacted to him.

They quickly dropped each other's hand and picked up their burgers and ate. Larry watched Goldie and made a confused face when she dipped a fry into her milkshake.

Goldie paused with the fry up to her mouth and said, "What?"

"You just dipped your fry in the chocolate." He answered as if that was enough.

"That's a weird way to put it, but yes. It's delicious try it," said Goldie moving the fry from her mouth to his.

He eyed the dipped fry and reluctantly opened his mouth and she popped the fry in. She didn't think of how it looked that she was feeding him, she just did it on impulse. Larry's eyes penetrated hers and that glow seemed to be there again. He chewed and swallowed and smiled. His whole face lit up.

"It's good huh? Sweet and salty. The perfect combination," said Goldie smiling at him.

"It is good. Yes, perfect combination," said Larry softly as if he may be talking about more than fries dipped in milkshake.

Granda studied them in a way father figures do. He liked Larry though. Something about him was familiar and put him at ease. But, he didn't like seeing any lad look at his granddaughter the way he was looking at her. The lad did stand up for her though. That counted for something.

Goldie giggled as she watched Larry dip his French fries in his milkshake. They finished up eating and got up to go. Larry again held the door for her. He told Goldie goodnight, thanked Granda for his food, and shook his hand before getting in his truck.

"Seems like a good lad," said Granda looking at Goldie to try to gauge her reaction.

Goldie watched as Larry pulled out and absent mindedly said, "Mmmhmm."

Granda chuckled. "So I take you took a liking to the lad then. He did punch that other boy in your honor."

Goldie flushed and said, "He is a nice lad Granda and I've never had anyone in my corner besides you, so it was very nice."

They rode home and Goldie replayed every minute of her eighteenth birthday from the chocolate cupcake, to the shark, to the punch thrown, and finally thinking about Larry's unblemished hand in hers. She still couldn't understand the sensation she got when they touched or understand how his knuckles were just fine. She could also swear his eyes glowed from the inside. Maybe she was just going crazy. All this time with a raccoon and with Granda had done her in.

Chapter 5

The next morning Goldie got up a little more excited than normal to be going to work. She dabbed the rouge on her lips again. Mack climbed from the top of her dresser to her shoulder as she made her way out of her room to the kitchen to start making coffee and breakfast. She decided to keep it simple, pan sausage and egg sandwich on toasted bread.

"Mmm. Smells good in here Charm." Granda said walking in in his old long sleeve shirt and stained jeans.

"Just keeping it simple with a breakfast sandwich. Coffee should be ready. Will you pour me a cup too please?" Goldie asked as she flipped a sausage patty over.

"You know it," said Granda as he made his way to the percolator.

Granda drank his black. Goldie liked two spoons of sugar and a splash of cream. He sat her cup by the small stove. Goldie smiled, nodded at him, saluted her cup at him, and took a sip. She groaned as it hit her tongue. Granda laughed and saluted her back with his cup. They always did silly little things like that.

Goldie finished up their sandwiches and made an extra for Larry. She wrapped them all up and poured the rest of the coffee in a big thermos before cleaning up the kitchen and leaving with Granda for the bait camp. They always ate their breakfast on the shrimp boat. She couldn't leave Larry out.

Larry was waiting in the parking lot for them when they got there. "I like that the lad is on time. That's a good quality," said Granda watching Goldie take the boy in.

"I think so too," answered Goldie getting out of the truck.

They walked over to Larry and Granda said, "Today Goldie will go out with us and she will show you the ropes. She knows what she's doing so follow her."

Larry replied, "Yes sir."

They all loaded up on the boat, double checked everything to make sure it all worked and they had everything they needed, and then Goldie untied the boat and pushed off from the dock. Granda smiled watching her work. Larry watched her too. Then she made her way to stand by Granda. Larry followed and stood on the other side of Granda as he expertly navigated the boat into the gulf.

Goldie dug around in her shoulder bag and pulled out the sandwiches and passed them out. "Here you go Larry, I made you a breakfast sandwich too. I've got coffee also," said Goldie as she pulled out little metal cups from her bag.

"Thanks a lot. You just keep feeding me don't you?" Larry asked looking quizzically at her.

The question struck Goldie as odd, so she shrugged her shoulders and just nodded.

Granda took a huge bite out of his sandwich and said, "Delicious as always."

Goldie smiled and took a bite from hers too. She looked over to see Larry was just watching them. He unwrapped his sandwich and took a bite. His eyes went wide and he took three more bites real fast.

"Lad that sandwich isn't going to go anywhere," said Granda chuckling.

Larry's eyebrows shot up and then he blushed. "I've never had one of these sandwiches before. It's very good."

Larry was so different. Who hadn't had a breakfast sandwich before? Goldie wondered what kind of family he must come from. He seemed intrigued by everything, but took it all in and was a really fast learner like he had said.

Larry watched Goldie as she walked up to the front of the boat with Mack on her shoulder. She leaned over and closed her eyes, letting the wind hit her face. She tilted her head up to the sun and smiled, feeling the warmth. When she opened her eyes they were alight and she studied the water for a beat and then she pointed her long finger out towards the left and hollered, "There Granda!"

"What is she doing?" Asked Larry full of wonder.

"My Charm is just that, my charm. She has this uncanny ability to just know where the shrimp will be. She's been pointing out which direction to drop nets since she was a wee las," explained Granda.

Larry nodded and went into deep thought.

Goldie watched Larry as he learned at her Granda's side. He worked in jeans, barefoot, and in a white wife beater shirt. He was slim, but all muscle. Goldie tried not to stare as she was at the helm and Granda showed him how to pull the nets over and dump them on the deck. His arms contracted and pulled and she could see his back muscles working under his shirt.

She looked away quickly when Larry looked over his shoulder and caught her looking. He gave her a small grin and she knew her face was red. After he and Granda got the nets emptied, Granda made his way back to the helm.

"Go teach him how to sort las," said Granda to Goldie.

"Yes sir." She said and made her way to Larry.

Mack had already beat her there and was munching on a flopping shad. Larry watched him smiling.

"Ok Larry, I'm going to teach you how to sort. If we hurry we can save some of these fish on deck. I don't like to kill more than we have to. Looks like all these are bait shrimp. We want to keep them alive. Bait shrimp bring in more money than fresh dead, so we pick those up first. Watch out for the stingrays. Their tails have barbs and can get you. Throw them out first," said Goldie expertly grabbing one and throwing it overboard.

They made quick work of getting the shrimp into the live well and then Goldie showed him how to bag up the shad and mullet for bait. Larry was great help. He worked fast. Goldie found it weird that he didn't wear rubber boots, especially his first time on the boat. She couldn't say much because she never wore shoes either. Honestly, if she had it her way she would never wear them at all. They made her feel confined. She would much rather feel the earth under her feet or the sturdy deck of the boat.

She couldn't help she had to ask him after their last drag of the day. "Why don't you have on rubber boots?"

"I don't like the way they feel on my feet. My feet like to be free. I really don't like shoes at all," said Larry wiggling his long toes. Everything on him was long and slender, including his feet.

Goldie laughed and said, "I actually understand that sentiment. I hate shoes honestly. It's so much more comfortable to be barefoot."

Larry looked at her and said, "I know you understand." His eyes penetrated her and seemed to glow again.

Goldie felt a little confused at his statement and her forehead creased in thought. "Why would you know I would understand?"

"Because las you're like me," said Larry letting an accent just brush the surface.

She looked up surprised and she saw something in his eyes, understanding, but she didn't know of what. She was so confused. "I don't know what you mean and your accent…Why haven't I heard it before?"

Larry was opening his mouth to answer, when Granda hollered over to them to, "Rake it down," meaning to sweep all the stuff they don't want off the boat.

Larry took the rake and cleaned the deck and Goldie got buckets of water and washed the deck down. It was really nice to have help. Then both of them went back to their places on either side of Granda at the helm. And as Goldie listened to her heavy accented Granda talk to Larry, she listened for his accent too. It was gone now. Earlier he had an Irish sounding accent, but it wasn't completely Irish. She had no clue what had happened. She felt a little angry at Larry. What was he hiding from her?

Chapter 6

The rest of the week went the same. Their nets were pulling up good shrimp and it was a great week to be in the shrimping business. Goldie kept her distance from Larry. She just wasn't sure about him. She had lost some trust in him with his accent slip and he just confused her. She did still make him breakfast each morning and he seemed pleasantly surprised each time. She talked to him when she needed to tell him how to do something, but she kept to herself, pointing out where to go and sorting with Mack.

One of the next days they were working, Goldie was standing beside Granda, while Larry worked on putting the door out to slide. Granda asked her, "Las has Larry done something wrong to ya? I'll get rid of him if need be."

"Oh no Granda. Don't do that. The extra help has been great. I'm just so busy, ya know." Goldie said shrugging her shoulders.

Granda studied her and just grunted.

The net was lowered and Goldie couldn't help but sing *Spirit of the Sea*. Goldie didn't realize she had closed her eyes as she sung until she heard Larry's voice melded perfectly with hers as she got to the third stanza;

"As I walk I can feel him,
Always watching over me...
His voice surrounds me,
My Spirit of the Sea.."

They finished singing the rest of the song together looking at each other very deeply. Again, Larry sounded almost Irish as he sang the old Irish song with her. Granda watched them closely. They shared a moment together and sounded like their voices were meant to be sung together. Granda was paying so much attention to them and their singing that he veered off course and their shrimp boat jerked violently. All three of them lurched forward. Granda cursed under his breath.

"Oh no Granda. You just rode over the old wreck," said Goldie feeling distraught. Their net would be tore up.

"I know las," whispered Granda hanging his head low.

"It'll be ok Granda. We will be able to fix it. We have extra help now. Let me shuck off my shirt and pants and I'll swim down and get us untangled," said Goldie.

"You will do no such thing. Larry is on the boat too!" Granda all but shouted.

Goldie blushed thinking about what she just said. She was going to strip into her bra and undies so she could swim better and not be worried about her clothes hanging up on the wreck too. She rolled it over in head for but a moment. There was no other option. She was the best swimmer and could hold her breath for a long time. She straightened her shoulders and looked her Granda in the eye.

"Granda, we don't have any other choice. You know it would be too dangerous for me to swim down in all my clothes. I can't take the chance. I'm not a big fan of Larry seeing me in my drawers either, but it's our only option," said Goldie.

Larry walked over and said, "I'm sure I can help. Let me swim down with you."

"No offense Larry but if you haven't untangled the net before, you might get in my way. I know this wreck too. I've swam it before," said Goldie.

"Where's your gear and I'll help you suit up," said Larry.

Goldie looked at him like he was crazy. "My gear?" She asked.

"Yeah like your oxygen tank?" Questioned Larry.

"My charm doesn't need it. She can hold her breath for a very long time and is a great free diver. I swear you would think her Ma was a mermaid," said Granda looking proud.

Larry's brown eyes went wide as Goldie pulled her shirt up over her head and flung it on the back of the captain's chair. She had on a light blue bra with little pink flowers on it. Her breasts were larger than her baggy shirts would lead you to believe. When she pulled her shorts off, he had to turn away. Her panties matched the top. Her legs were muscular. From all the time on the boat he was sure. She had larger calves than most girls would, but they suited her.

"Granda, give me your knife please," said Goldie holding her hand out.

Granda handed it to her and said, "I'm sorry las. It's all my fault. I have your modesty on display for Larry. I'm sorry."

"It's ok Granda. It's not any worse than any of the swimsuits girls are wearing these days," replied Goldie giving a small smile.

"Yeah but those girls aren't my las," said Granda with tears in his eyes.

Goldie reached up and put her hand on his cheek and nodded. Larry watched their interaction with fascination. He'd never seen a girl love her father the way Goldie loved her Granda.

Goldie walked over to the edge of the boat, took several deep breaths, put the knife between her teeth, and then did a perfect dive off the side. No water even splashed back up. Granda stayed at the helm, holding the shrimp boat steady.

"Go over to the side and watch for my Charm. Keep an eye out for her," hollered Granda to Larry.

Larry nodded and stood firm on the side where she had just jumped overboard. He could see the silhouette of an old wooden ship below and lots of fish life swimming around. He saw Goldie swimming down and could tell when she got to the net because she stopped and her hands were working. He saw her free a piece and cut some and she was working fast. Larry started to worry though. She was staying down for a very long time.

He almost panicked when she didn't come up, but just swam to a different section and began the same process all over again. He was about to jump in after her, when he did in fact panic. There was a shark coming out from the old wreckage and heading for Goldie.

He hollered, "Goldie, get out! There's a shark!"

"What did you say lad?" Granda hollered.

"There's a shark. I don't think she can hear me," said Larry panicked.

"No she can't not with the sound of the currents and the boat. Sweet Jesus take care of my las," prayed Granda.

Larry was unbuttoning his shirt and getting ready to jump in when he noticed Goldie look up to see the shark headed straight for her. Goldie never stopped working. She continued to free the net and just watched the shark. Larry gasped as it circled her. He noticed she didn't seem distraught at all.

"Goldie what are you doing?" He whispered.

Then he saw her get the last of the net untangled and just swim up for air. She breeched the top and hollered, as if she hadn't been under water for at least ten minutes, "Pull the net in Granda. It only got caught in two places."

The shark circled under her. "Goldie do you not care that a shark is circling you. Swim over here so I can help you out of the water," shouted Larry.

"The shark means me no harm. If he wanted to take a bite out of me he already would have," said Goldie seemingly fine as if she just hadn't free dove.

Larry shook his head and still watched the shark under her. He held his breath as he watched the shark circle closer. The shark swam right up to Goldie and just slowly swam past her. She put her hand out and let it slide down the shark as it passed by and swam out into the sea. Larry couldn't believe his eyes. Goldie laughed and it sounded musical. She was in her element in the water. Her skin almost glowed.

"Granda how bad was the net? I only cut it in two places," said Goldie looking up to her grandfather.

"Not nearly as bad as it should be las. Are you planning on staying out there a spell since you are already in the water?" He asked.

Goldie answered, "You know I am. Let me bring you your knife back. It's still in my hand."

Goldie slid through the water almost as easily as the shark had and made it to the side of the shrimp boat. "Watch out. I'm tossing the knife up." She said and then swam back out.

"She swims like she was made for the water doesn't she lad?" Asked Granda with a knowing smile.

Larry answered, "I've never seen anything quite like her. That shark almost seemed reverential to her. I thought I would need to jump in the longer she was under the water too."

Granda chuckled. "I was nervous the first time she stayed under so long, but she's been like that since she was a little girl. The shark is a new thing. It's almost like the animals respect her. She shows no fear and I think they sense that."

At that moment they heard splashing and turned to see Goldie laughing and swimming with a family pod of porpoises. They were blowing air out and breaching by her. She swam alongside them and laughed. She stopped to tread water and just watch them. It was like she was one with them. The baby of the pod swam up to her and put its head on her stomach. Goldie smiled widely letting her gapped teeth shine as she rubbed the baby.

"Aren't you just the most beautiful thing I've seen?" She asked rubbing the smallest of the family.

It squeaked at her and she laughed. "That solves it. I'll call you Squeaks." Goldie rubbed on the baby some more until one of the larger ones made a call and they all swam off.

Goldie watched them go and then she was finished. She made her way back to the shrimp boat all smiles. Larry helped pull her in from the water. He tried to ignore the water droplets sliding down her body. Goldie got her foot tangled in a piece of the torn net and fell forward into Larry. She gasped as her body meshed into his and his arms slid around her to catch her fall.

Her arms were awkwardly thrown around his neck and his around her waist and he was looking down at her. She knew for a fact his eyes were glowing now, but she saw her reflection in his eyes. Her eyes looked like they were glowing too. Her breath hitched as she stared into his eyes and he wasn't breathing. He stared back just as intently. Her hands slid from around his neck to his chest and then he took a breath and grabbed her hands and held them against himself and searched her eyes some more as if he were looking for something, but what?

"Uhhmmm." Granda cleared his throat.

Goldie quickly blinked and looked away and Larry shook his head.

"Not to break up a moment, but what is that about and Larry your holding my Charm while she is indecent. Kindly let her go and las put your clothes back on." Granda said sternly.

"I'm sorry. Yes Granda. I uh..I..I'll get my clothes," stuttered Goldie.

"It's true," Larry said under his breath.

"What lad?" Asked Granda.

"Nothing sir. I apologize for…whatever it is that just happened." Larry said, getting back to work and cleaning the deck.

When he peeked back over at Goldie he noticed her skin was no longer glowing, but he wouldn't have really noticed anyway. She was bending over to get her shorts pulled up. He swallowed hard and it took every fiber in him to turn back away.

When they pulled back into the bait camp, Goldie got all the bait they had managed to get before the mishap off the boat and put in its proper place in the bait camp. Larry and Granda stayed on the boat and worked on the net. When she was all done she went back over to the boat and asked if they needed any help. Granda said no and she was glad. She didn't really want to face Larry after whatever had just happened. She walked home with Mack on her shoulder.

On her way home Ms. Betsy spotted her. "Chil did you get any good table shrimp today?" She hollered towards the one lane road Goldie was making her way home on.

"No ma'am. Granda accidentally got the net snagged, so it wasn't the best day," replied Goldie.

"So I's guessing you didn't just swim for fun today," stated Ms. Betsy with her hands on her narrow hips.

"No ma'am, but I ended up having fun. A family of porpoises came and swam with me. It was so special," said Goldie smiling brightly.

"I bet that was really something. You'll have some good stories to tell your kids one day," said Ms. Betsy smiling.

"If I ever have children. I'd have to get married first and no one really wants the shrimper's granddaughter who loves the water more than land," replied Goldie frowning some.

"Nonsense that young man that's working for your granddaddy has an eye for you baby. I seen the way he looks at you. He couldn't take his eyes off you in Burger Place. I also heard he punched a certain football player in your honor. That sounds like someone interested and judging by the way you wear your rouge when he's around, I'd say you're interested too. It's ok chil. It's natural." Ms. Betsy said winking and wrapping an arm around her.

Goldie's face went hot with embarrassment. She didn't have anything to say to that, but she did let Ms. Betsy pull her to her front porch.

"Wait here chil. I made a big pot of chili and I have plenty for you and your granddaddy," said Ms. Betsy disappearing behind her old screen door in her one room, gray house.

"She came back out with an old white bowl full of chili. It smelled so good. Goldie's stomach growled and both ladies laughed. Ms. Betsy sent her on her way with some parting advice, "Don't be scared to live life baby. God puts people in our paths for a reason and he put that young man in yours. Be open to the possibilities, but be smart."

Goldie got home and showered. As she let the hot water wash the salt from her hair, she relived the day. Usually she would be consumed with thoughts of the animals she had encountered, but all she could think of was how it felt to be so close to Larry. Evey time she closed her eyes she saw his glowing ones and couldn't help but feel angry again. She liked the way it felt to be held, but she couldn't help but get mad. She knew he was keeping something from her. She'd never seen him before now and they never saw him out with his family. Who was Larry really?

Chapter 7

The next morning, Granda woke up not feeling well. His nose was running and he had a sore throat. Goldie tended to him and made him stay in bed. He tried to fight her and say he was well enough to go shrimping. She put silence to that real quick when she took his temperature and he had a fever.

"Granda there is no way I will let you get on that boat while you are sick. I can handle taking it out myself. You've taught me well. I want you take some aspirin and lay down and rest. I will get you some broth and water and leave them here by the bed. I will also tell Ms. Betsy so you don't get any wild ideas," said Goldie firmly.

"Fine las. I'll stay home. I really do feel wretched, but I don't want you to go out alone. Take Larry with you and only do a couple drags. If you don't have much luck, come on back in. " Granda said sneezing.

"I'll be fine by myself. I'll take Mack with me," said Goldie starting to feel nervous.

"How many times do I have to tell you Mack doesn't count. He can't help you if you get into trouble. I know Larry will. He seems to care and he likes the work. Take him with you so I can rest easier," said Granda pleadingly.

"Ok. I will. I love you and rest. For real," said Goldie sternly and kissing him on the cheek.

"Take the truck las. I won't be needing it today," hollered Granda from his room as Goldie made it to the front door.

"Thanks Granda! I'll be back later!" She hollered back grabbing his keys, as Mack climbed up to her shoulder.

Goldie didn't really drive often, but she was a good driver. Granda had taught her when she was really little, just in case something happened to him and they needed to make it to the hospital or something. She rolled both windows down to let the morning air in before the sun rose. She liked the way the morning smelled. Mack acted like a dog in the truck. He rode halfway hanging out the window.

When she pulled into the bait camp, Larry was already waiting. He eyed her warily as she slowly rolled the windows up and climbed out of the truck and walked towards him and the shrimp boat.

"Where's your Granda?" Larry asked as she got closer.

"He's sick, so I made him stay home. It'll just be us today. I told him I could manage on my own, but he insisted I take you," said Goldie shouldering past him.

She gasped as a shock ran up her arm when Larry grabbed it as she passed him. "Goldie, what have I done to make you so upset with me?" He asked and that hint of an accent crept back into his voice.

"That right there Larry!" She said a little too loud.

He looked confused. "I have not the slightest clue what you mean."

"Your accent Larry. You've let it come out a few times and I'm pretty sure on accident. And either I'm crazy or your eyes glow too. What are you hiding from me? I don't like liars." Goldie said straightening her shoulders getting ready for a fight.

Larry looked at her and let his eyes glow. Goldie gasped.

"I've never lied to you las. I just didn't tell you. And yes I'm not from here. Yes my eyes glow, but so do yours. You may call me many things but never a liar. I can't lie actually and neither can you. Have you ever noticed that?" Larry spat out.

Goldie took a step back looking up confused. His accent was a lot thicker. He had let it completely out. His eyes were so bright and when she looked into his brown glowing ones, she saw her blue ones shining too. She searched his eyes as if they held the answers she needed.

"You have no clue do you las?" He finally asked softly.

"Larry I know I'm different, but what are you talking about?" Goldie whispered. "And who are you?"

Larry answered, "You hold your breath for long amounts of time, you swim with sharks and porpoises, you love everyone, you sense where the shrimp are, and I know you feel the power that runs through your veins when we touch. You are so much more than you know."

"Who are you?" Goldie asked on a whisper.

He took a deep breath and said, "I'm not sure you're ready for all this. Let's get to work." He turned and walked away from her towards the boat.

"Did you just walk away from me?" Goldie said incredulously.

"I think that answer is obvious Goldie. Follow me and get on the boat. I'll tell you everything while we shrimp," answered Larry over his shoulder.

Goldie didn't say another word. She clenched her teeth and followed behind him. She got on the boat and fired up the motor and let it run to warm up before Larry untied it from the dock. She slowly navigated the shrimp boat away from the bait camp and out into the gulf. Goldie watched Larry as he readied the door and net. He worked efficiently as ever. Without her Granda onboard to watch her, she watched Larry more closely. It was as if is muscles were sculpted from stone and his body worked perfectly, only exerting the effort necessary for the task.

He must have felt her watching because he turned and looked at her. He let a half smile hit his mouth. She got mad knowing that he knew she was watching him. Mack was following Larry around and that made Goldie get even more mad. She didn't understand all the secrecy.

Finally she had enough. They were far enough out to drag nets, but she wasn't worried about that at the moment. She just wanted answers. She yelled at Larry, "I think we are far enough out in the ocean, neither one of us can escape the conversation. Tell me now."

Larry smiled at her and he let his eyes glow again and he looked into her eyes. Goldie jumped when she heard him in her head. He spoke directly into her head, "Goldie we share a bond. My eyes glow and so do you yours. You are not fully human. Your father has been looking for you for a long time. He sent me to find you."

Goldie quit breathing. How was it possible he was speaking to her in her mind? Her father? He didn't even know her mother had been pregnant. Her head swam and she felt dizzy. She blinked.

She blinked again and Larry was right in front of her. He shook her by the shoulders and said, "Breathe Goldie. Breathe."

She took in a deep breath and searched his face. "My father?" Tears filled her eyes.

Larry's eyes softened and he placed his hands on her face. "Your father Las. He's been searching for seventeen years. Our people need you to come home. He's had a broken heart since the day you were born and he didn't know where you were. He felt your birth, we all did. We know when one of ours is born and the paternal bond is set in ones' soul like a link in a chain."

"Who is he? He's been looking?" Goldie let the tears slide down her cheeks.

Larry brushed them away with his thumbs and nodded. "He's been looking. Your father is Oberon Fionn, King of Hollow Hill and all Fae. Your father is what legends are made of."

Goldie shook her head. "No. No. Fairies aren't real. I've never even heard of Oberon Fionn. There's no such person."

"Because he's not a person. He is a king in a realm humans only fantasize about. They have no clue it's real. You are real, so it is real. Goldie you are more Fae than human," said Larry still brushing his thumbs across her cheeks.

"Even if what you say is true, I'm only half. My mother was human. She died after giving birth to me. This can't be real," said Goldie shaking her head again.

"It is real las. My accent you can't place, it's the Irish Fae Realm. Your glowing eyes and ability to be one with the sea and its creatures is your Fae side. I'm guessing your Granna must've been water fairy. Las did you know your Granna?" Larry asked.

"No, she died before I was born. All I know is she fell ill and never got better," said Goldie sniffling.

"When fairies stay away from their home for too long that can happen. You have to re-tap the power of our people. You have to stay connected, or you become mortal. You know Fae were considered Gods at one time, because of our abilities. Did you ever wonder why your Granda had such a profitable fishing business in Ireland in a time everyone was struggling? Your Granna must've helped him." Larry said thoughtfully.

"None of this makes sense. Larry I'm just a normal girl." Goldie said trying to convince herself.

"You're not and you know it. It's rare that a fairy falls in love with a mortal. Play with them sure, but fall in love is something different. Your Granna chose to love your Granda over being immortal. She chose to stay away from the Fae realm so she could be with him. She could have gone back and regained her strength, but then her powers would have been too strong to go unnoticed. We are bound by our secret. She wouldn't have been able to tell anyone who or what she was, including your Granda. That was before my King's time though. Back then was dark times for the Fae. We fought with our own and had to hide from the humans. They humans killed off so many of us in the beginning. When your father took the throne, we went into hiding. It was the only way to save our people. The Hollow Hill is still our home and I have to get you back there, so you can realize your powers and your father wants you to rule by his side. He never had other children, because he truly loved your mom las. When we commit ourselves to someone it's forever," explained Larry.

"So my Granda doesn't know?" Goldie asked.

Larry shook his head. "He probably noticed different things about her, just like he does with you and your swimming, but she couldn't tell him. She would have been much like you, just a little more than normal ability and glowing eyes from time to time and the longer she stayed away from her people, the more human she would get."

"So she became human to love my Granda," said Goldie piecing it together. "And me?"

"You will stay human but we aren't sure how long you will live, unless you come home and take your place. Your father will have you home. I'm charged with that and I will not fail your father," said Larry.

"What about my Granda? I won't leave him. He deserves to know all of this. He deserves to know how much my Granna loved him," said Goldie with her eyes brimming with tears again.

"He can't know. The humans cannot deal with the knowledge of our people. It took hundreds of years to get them to believe that all the Fae stories were just stories and not truth," Larry said flatly.

"I will not leave without him. I'm all he has and he has been everything for me for my entire life. If he can't come or know the truth, I WILL NOT COME. You tell the king that," said Goldie firmly.

"I figured you would say that. You are strong. Your father will be proud. Let me talk to him," said Larry and he stepped away from her.

Goldie surveyed the water and she closed her eyes. She for once in her life thought about what she was doing. She opened her mind up to the sensations and thoughts. It had always just been second nature to point to the water and find the shrimp, but she never thought about how she did it. In that moment, she thought and felt it all. She could feel the tides and currents of the ocean under the boat. She felt the power running under her and through her. She felt the life of the ocean around her. She opened her eyes and knew they were glowing.

Larry was watching her and he smiled. She just looked at him and pointed out to the water. "We will drag over there. I'm going to get us there and then drop the door."

Larry nodded and let her have space to think. He worked and got everything done perfectly. Goldie had no critiques for him. In the first drag, their nets were full with shrimp. Goldie let out a breath and was glad. She didn't want to be on the boat any longer. She was done being around Larry for the day. She knew she shouldn't believe him. He had to be lying, but in her heart she knew that she was more and she knew he was too.

Chapter 8

Goldie got home and was happy to report to her Granda that she had gotten plenty of shrimp. She hugged him a little longer and made supper. He was so happy with her and Larry. She hadn't talked to Larry anymore and her mind was on her father the whole way home. She didn't know what to think. She was still angry at Larry for not telling her sooner. But he'd been so tender with her, wiping her tears and just being there. He said he would talk to her father. Her father. She didn't even know how that could be.

Goldie made up her mind as she sat at the dinner table with her Granda. She was going to tell him the truth. She didn't care what the consequences would be. He deserved to know and she loved him too much to keep him in the dark. After she washed dishes, she went to the living room to sit with him on their old brown couch with hideous orange floral print.

"Granda, I need to tell you something and it's going to sound crazy. Heck I'm still not sure I believe it myself," said Goldie shaking her head.

Granda looked at her and smiled. He nodded and said, "Go on."

"Larry told me something unbelievable today and against my better judgement, I believe him." Goldie turned to face her Granda and looked into his eyes. She prayed he could see without her having to tell him.

"My Charm, I know you are special. I knew it from the day I held you and it looked like you glowed. Your Granna was special too. Tell me what's on your heart and mine will be open," said Granda squeezing her hand.

"Granda did you know Granna was a fairy?" Goldie asked.

Granda laughed. "She was no fairy las. She had no wings that I know of. She was a Selkie. I of course wasn't supposed to know, but I did. I've always said it was like you were born of a mermaid, because las, your line kinda is. Your mother didn't have any abilities that we could ever tell. Your Granna didn't want her to be a Selkie. You know the legend. If someone takes their skins, they cannot leave them. That's not exactly true either, but there's something to every legend. I found your Granna injured while fishing and I pulled her on my boat and did my best to patch her up. She was stuck in between forms and would have terrified anyone else, but I would never let any creature suffer. I honestly thought I would just be there so the creature would not die alone. Little did I know your beautiful Granna was so strong. Her eyes were blue like yours, not as light though. That was the part of her I knew was human, or so I thought."

Granda continued, "Anyhow, I pulled her into my arms and brushed her blonde hair back from her half transformed face. I noted the wound to her stomach. It looked like she had been run through with a sword. Instead of shying away, I sang *Spirit of the Sea* to her and continued to brush her hair back. As I sang, her form morphed into the most beautiful thing I had ever laid eyes on. A glowing woman appeared before me, naked, and shivering. I had never seen a naked woman before and I know I turned my head away. I pulled my shirt off over my head and covered her. She grabbed my hand and said, "Thank you Laoch," in a such a soft broken voice it brought tears to my eyes.

"Laoch is hero right?" Goldie asked smiling softly.

"Or warrior or champion, but she meant it as hero. I've failed on teaching you our language las. I'm sorry for that." Granda said feeling sad.

"Oh Granda, it's ok. Finish your story," said Goldie, eyes lit with fascination.

Granda smiled and got a far off look in his eyes as if he were somewhere else with his memories. "I took her back home with me. Then, I lived in a small cottage in the hills by the sea. I didn't tell anyone she was with me. They'd thought I was crazy and for some reason I wanted to keep her to myself. I was surprised she was still alive, but then again she was more than human. I nursed her back to health over the weeks to come. She told me her name was Dierdre and that she was Fae. I had seen her partly in her other form, so she felt obligated to tell me. She made me swear secrecy. I asked her what happened and all she said was she escaped a bad man she didn't want to marry and that she could never return home. We grew fond of each other in those weeks. I would take her on walks by the sea and we would watch the stars together at night. I had given her my bed when I brought her home and had been sleeping on the couch. She told me she had never known a man more gentle than me."

Granda got a drink of water and grimaced. His throat was still hurting. He continued anyway; "I fell in love with her right away. I think she did with me too. She wasn't supposed to. The legends about men stealing their skin to keep them is not quite all the way true, but if they give you their heart they stay forever and this special necklace is what will keep them bound to you and not off in the water. The water is in their nature. It is said no one can tame that part of them and that the water will always call them back, unless you hold onto their necklace."

Granda pulled a necklace out from under his shirt. Goldie had seen it her whole life and knew it was special to Granda because it was Granna's, but she didn't know just how special.

"This necklace will keep a Selkie with you, because it houses part of their soul. It is cruel to steal one from someone, but if you are ever blessed enough for someone to give you that piece of them, you know the love is something beyond this world. I still feel you Granna here with me. She's the one who explained all this to me, but told me I must never tell anyone. Most humans couldn't handle the real truth of knowing there's more than us out there. Your Granna would fish with me and show me where the fish were like you point to where the shrimp are. She could swim like you wouldn't believe. I wish you could swim with her. You get that part from her. I'm glad I can share this with you now. You may even be a better swimmer, because you don't change forms. You swim in your natural state. It's beautiful." Granda said squeezing her hand again.

"Your Granna never left my side from that point on. She had nowhere to go and I didn't want her to leave. I asked her to marry me a year later and on our wedding day, she gave me her necklace and I knew she loved me as much as I loved her. I would have never bound her to me, but she wanted to be. She also had told me she would become mortal without being able to go back to her natural home, but she was ok with growing old and dying with me. We just never thought she would die so young. But she was actually much older than she looked. Fae age differently.

When your mom was born I was so happy. We watched her closely to see if she would get any Selkie traits. She had never shown any, so we never spoke of your Granna's stuff. We didn't want her to feel like she had something wrong with her, because she was perfect. We figured it was just because your Granna was more human than Selkie at that point. When your Granna died, a piece of me died with her. That was the darkest day of my life." Granda let the tears fall silently.

Goldie reached her hands over and dried his eyes. He continued, "I got lost in my work and trying to figure out how to get us to America, that I didn't keep a close enough eye on your mom. I loved her and I tried to be there for her, but she turned to some boy, whoever your father is. She got pregnant and I was so angry she got pregnant out of wedlock. I was embarrassed. I got us on the boat to America and you know the rest of the story there, but you were named Goldie, not just because you glowed from the moon's rays, but because my Charm you truly glowed."

"So, I figured you inherited something from your Granna but didn't think about it too much. I was terrified. I didn't know how to feed you or what to do and losing your mom was, I don't have the words for it. I knew you had Fae in you for sure when you took to the water like you did. Even as a baby, when I would put you in the bath, the water did something for you. You would go under the water even then and it scared me at first. I didn't send you to school because I was scared to. I didn't know if something else would happen. I had to keep you with me. I don't even know why Diedre wanted us to come to America so badly. I just know she seemed scared. She always said she shared with me everything she could, which meant she could only tell about herself. Fae are bound by loyalty to one another. They never tell anyone else's story unless they have special permission. I was in such a bad state then. You my Charm were my lifeline. You kept me alive all these years because I have a piece of the women I loved so dearly in you. I think you should hear whatever Larry has to say. I could tell he was a Fae kind. I just don't know what kind." Granda said scratching his chin.

Goldie smiled and said, "Now I know why we sing *Spirit of the Sea*. How lucky am I to have such an awesome Granda who saved a Selkie and loved her enough that she gave him a piece of her soul. There's more to Larry being here. I knew I had seen his eyes glow. When he got here something clicked into place with me. My eyes glow too and he can talk to me in my mind. It's weird. But Larry said my father sent him to find me. My father knows I exist and he said he's been looking for me for seventeen years."

Granda's eyebrows raised. "I didn't know he even knew. I don't know him. All I know is when your mom went to find him he was gone."

"I had no clue he knew I existed either. Larry said something about him being able to feel when I was born and that he has been looking for me. Larry also mentioned dark times and a bad king. I have no clue how it all works together. Granda what should I do?" Goldie asked with tears in her eyes.

"Las, my charm, it's time you meet your father. I would be able to die happy someday knowing you had family. You deserve to know who you are. I'd like to meet him too," said Granda straightening up some.

"Larry said I couldn't tell you, but I had to. They or I guess we aren't allowed to tell humans, but you sort of already knew. He said he would talk to the king about my wishes or maybe my ultimatum. I said I wouldn't come unless you could come with me and know the truth," said Goldie blushing.

Granda chuckled and said, "My fierce little one. I do love you, but even if I can't go, you should meet your father. I would like that for you."

"I will not go without you. I don't want to. Oh my gosh Granda. I gave the king an ultimatum!" Goldie shrieked.

"No las, you gave your Da an ultimatum," said Granda squeezing her hand.

A knock came at the door and Granda and Goldie both jumped. Goldie got up and opened the door. Larry stood on the other side with his hair disheveled and eyes glowing.

"Larry, what's wrong?" Goldie asked taking in his appearance.

"We don't have time Goldie. We need to go home. I need to take you home now," said Larry reaching for her.

"I am home Larry with Granda. I will not just be ripped from him. What's going on?" Goldie asked.

Larry looked over her and his eyes widened in horror when he realized Granda was sitting on the couch.

Granda gave him a small smile and said, "It's ok lad. I know all about the Fae. My wife was a Selkie and I knew that Goldie was more, but never knew I would have the need to tell her anything. She now knows the truth as I do and I know hers. Or what she knows at least."

Larry smiled at that. "I knew she would tell you. I just never knew you would have already known. So Selkie? That explains a lot."

Granda smiled and answered, "Yes, but my charm doesn't change forms. Diedre gave me a piece of her soul. I knew what she was when I asked her to marry me and she chose to give me that. Lad how I miss her."

"There's a lot going on back home in the Hollow Hill. I need to take Goldie home. She is needed. It won't be safe for you to come with us, at least not yet. King Oberon Fionn is working on that, but we need all our powerful bloodlines there to fix the problem." Larry said pushing his hair back.

For once Larry looked older than he seemed. He had shadows under his eyes and he looked pale.

"Larry what's going on? Are you ill?" Goldie asked.

"I've been away from home too long. We get weaker and start to turn mortal when we stay away from home for too long. You are special Goldie. It doesn't seem to affect you as much, but your father needs you now to help him. If we don't get home, war could break out." Larry said taking a shaky breath.

"Lad I don't want my charm to be in any danger. Will she be safe?" Granda asked as if he had made up his mind to let her go.

Goldie looked at him with her mouth agape. Granda gave her a small nod and Goldie swallowed and looked back at Larry.

"I can't promise she won't be in danger, but I can promise I will protect her with my life and I'm very good at my job and I never break my word. As Fae we can't lie or break our word," said Larry nodding at Granda.

Granda looked at Goldie, "My charm, you need to go. I don't know why, but my heart says so. I will come be with you as soon as Larry says it's safe. I don't want to be in the way and you need to meet your father. I think your Ma would have wanted that. Go and stay with Larry and write me letters as soon as you can. Find out who you are and stay true to yourself."

Goldie let the tears roll down her cheeks. Leaving Granda didn't feel right to her, but she heard him loud and clear. Part of her wanted to know what she was truly capable of and she did want to meet her father. She ran to her Granda and wrapped her arms around him tightly enough to make him gasp. He patted her back and smoothed her hair down.

"Don't cry my charm. This isn't goodbye. I've wanted to go back home to Ireland for a long time now and I'll get to do that, you'll just get to go before me. Larry will protect you. I have been around him long enough to know that he is a good man. Go pack your bags and I love you so much," said Granda letting a tear roll down his cheek.

Goldie went and packed her bags. As she did, Granda and Larry had a talk.

"Larry I don't know what's all going on, but it seems very serious. Goldie is my world lad and I expect you to be nothing but a gentleman and her protector. I may not be Fae, but my love for my charm will be enough to end you if you hurt her," said Granda with a hard look.

"That I don't doubt. I will protect her and never force anything on her romantic or otherwise. Her father would also ask for my head." Larry said shuddering slightly.

"You care about my las, don't you? I see something in the way you look at her," said Granda cocking his head to the side.

"Something pulls me to her. It's like nothing I've ever felt. I feel a connection to her, but I'm not sure if it's her and I or the bond I have with her father and my king," said Larry rubbing his head.

"What do you mean lad?" Granda asked him.

"We are all bonded to our king in a way, but I'm bonded to him like a son. He raised me from the time I was 6 years old. My mother was killed by the king who sat on the throne before him and left me alone. Oberon Fionn took me in as his own blood and eventually took out the tyrant king who ruled in a harsh way. He wouldn't let Fae marry for love. He was all about breeding strong bloodlines. Oberon had asked for permission to marry a human girl he loved and the king denied it, so he decided to take over so he could marry for love. But you know he never got that chance. His love was long gone before the battle even ended. It was said that the tyrant king's promised wife fled from him and stayed lost to the sea. But perhaps, she made her way to a human fisherman." Larry said looking at Granda.

Granda softly smiled and said, "Perhaps."

"Anyhow, after Oberon defeated the tyrant king, he had a Fae kingdom to rebuild and he raised me to take the thrown after him. He wasn't sure if we would ever find his heir, but now we have. So, Goldie is next in line to rule," said Larry.

"And that doesn't bother you lad?" Asked Granda with his eyebrows raised.

"Not really. I'm glad the man I respect more than anyone will have the chance to meet his blood daughter and I know my place will still be important to the kingdom. I almost feel bad that I got my childhood with him and she missed out. But, I can see you did a great job with her and the love you two share is pure. She is lucky to have you, just as I was lucky to have Oberon. I would dare not be angry to not sit on a throne I didn't earn, especially after all he's done for me," said Larry.

"So Lad what is your position then?" Granda asked.

"I am the king's best guard and right hand. I am of Earthen Fae and have specialized skills in weapons and Earth magic. I have other magic coursing through my veins, but I'm not completely sure what. I never knew my father and my mother did not speak of him. I protect my king at all costs and now am charged with protecting his daughter in the same way. I will protect her. My homeland needs her," said Larry looking into Granda's eyes.

Goldie cleared her throat as she walked back into the living room with one bag on her shoulder. "So you're my personal guard then?" She asked.

"That pretty much sums it up. I will also be your teacher until your father can show you the ways of your family," said Larry nodding.

"Don't you mean our family? Sounds like you are more of my father's child than I am," said Goldie giving him a soft, sad smile.

"Well I guess it could be said that way if you wish it," said Larry wrinkling his forehead.

"So you are basically my brother then?" Goldie asked.

"I would prefer you not think of me as your brother," said Larry quickly.

"Why not?" Goldie asked with a sly smile.

Larry just stared into her eyes and spoke into her mind, "Because, then I would feel like I've done something wrong. My feelings towards you are not those of a brother towards a sister."

Chapter 9

Goldie's heart thudded in her chest. She was pretty sure it was loud enough that it could be heard. She cleared her throat and pushed the strap of her bag further up her shoulder. Larry quickly stepped up and grabbed the bag from her.

"Are ya ok las?" Granda asked her, not aware of the words that were just spoken in her head.

"Um yes. It's just all so sudden. I love you," said Goldie as she hugged him once more.

"Ok Goldie, we should be going," said Larry putting his hand on her shoulder.

"Yes then be on your way," said Granda smiling sadly.

Larry shook his hand once more and then led Goldie out to his truck. Larry opened her door again for her and put her bag in the bag of the truck.

"Aren't you worried my bag will get wet back there?" Goldie asked.

"No because we won't be in the truck long. We will only be in here long enough to get out of town," said Larry backing out of the driveway.

"What? What do you mean? How else will we get to a boat to take us across the ocean to Ireland?" Goldie asked so confused.

"Las we are Fae. We can travel in much different ways," said Larry giving her a sly smile.

Goldie gulped. She wasn't sure what he meant. As she looked out the window, she hollered, "STOP!"

Larry slammed on the breaks and the truck slid to a stop. "What's wrong? Did you forget something?" Larry said quickly with his accent now super thick.

"No. I need to tell Ms. Betsy bye. I can't leave without seeing her one more time." Goldie said feeling her throat close up with sadness.

Larry nodded and let Goldie get out of the truck to walk up to the porch of a small modest home. Ms. Betsy was on her porch swing. She wore a soft smile on her face. "You comin' to tell me bye chil?" She asked with the smile still in place.

"How did you know that?" Goldie asked as she slid into the swing next to Ms. Betsy.

Ms. Betsy turned to face her and Goldie's breath caught in her chest as she saw glowing eyes looking deep within her own. Goldie let the tears fall and Ms. Betsy smiled and smiled again as she placed her hands on Goldie's face. She pressed her forehead to hers.

Goldie heard Ms. Betsy perfectly in her head, but now she sounded like more. Ms. Betsy had the same accent as Larry and sounded like royalty. "My dear child. I've known you were so much more from the beginning. I followed you here a long time ago from Ireland. I could never get back home though. I became a mortal being so far from home, but I knew I had to be here to protect you. Anytime you felt danger or scared I sensed it. That's why I was there each time you really needed something when your Granda wasn't. I'm empathic among other things. I can feel your feelings and sense your thoughts. My gift isn't strong at all now. I can't sense everyone around me. Only you. I know your Granna would have wanted me to look after you. I knew when your mother met Oberon and she got with child and that you would be so special. I love you as if you were my own. I'm sorry I couldn't share all of this before now."

Goldie cried hard. Ms. Betsy pulled her into her arms and shushed and rocked her. Goldie gulped air and said, "You knew my Granna?"

Ms. Betsy nodded, "And your Ma. She didn't know who I was though. She never got the chance to know about the Fae realm. Oberon wanted to tell her, but never got the chance. I followed your Ma after Deidre died. Your Granda has always felt like he's recognized me, but couldn't place from where. I look much different here than I do at home."

"So you've been like my guardian angel?" Goldie asked.

"More like an old guardian fairy, but without all the powers," laughed Ms. Betsy.

Larry was at the porch now, with wide eyes. "It was you that got the message to Oberon?"

Ms. Betsy nodded. "It took me so long to get it there being so mortal. I tried for years. Once I noticed how powerful Goldie would be, I knew it was more important now than ever."

"You served your king and fellow Fae with honor and we will always recognize your sacrifice Beatha Bringer of Life. You've been missed greatly at home, but now I understand your duty and sacrifice." Larry said bending down on one knee to prostrate himself.

"Beatha?" Goldie asked still holding onto Ms. Betsy.

"My given name. I only became Betsy here my child." Ms. Betsy explained.

"You gave up your immortality, power, and name to watch over me?" Goldie breathed out.

"And I would do it all over again. You are worth it all and I loved your Granna like a sister. Soon all the pieces will fall in place and you will understand everything," said Ms. Betsy or Beatha.

"Larry can she come with us? If she goes home will she get her power and immortality back?" Goldie asked in one breath.

Larry studied Beatha for a moment and he gave a slight nod. "I'm not sure how well it will all work. We've never brought Fae home that has been gone so long, but it's worth a try. Beatha Bringer of Life, needs to be back with her people to help life make its way back to where it should be."

Goldie squealed. "I'm so glad you get to come with me! Let's get you home and healthy again."

"My child I am healthy for human standards and a woman my age, but I would love to go home. Let's go." Ms. Betsy got up from the swing and looked to Larry. "Are you strong enough to get us both out of here? If you're not lad, it's ok. I made peace with dying here and mortal a long time ago."

"Alone no, I'm not strong enough. Goldie is with me though. Together her and I will get you home." Larry said.

Goldie was confused. She had no clue how she was to help get anyone anywhere. She had no real powers other than with water. Beatha smiled and said, "So lesson one then?"

Larry smiled and said, "Lesson one."

Chapter 10

Goldie was so confused. She kind of felt mad about being confused again. She was tired of feeling like she knew nothing. She looked between Beatha and Larry waiting for answers.

Larry smiled and spoke into her mind, "Getting impatient are we las?"

Goldie hit his arm and he laughed. Beatha clucked her tongue and said, "No need for violence my child. Larry will teach you what you need to know."

"Lesson one," Larry said, "You can fly."

Goldie's jaw dropped. "I can what?"

"You can fly but you have to learn how to call your wings out. We really don't have time for that here, so I will make a portal." Larry explained.

"Larry, you best move your truck and park it in the driveway or too many questions will be asked about a truck in the street." Beatha said looking at Larry.

Larry nodded and went back to the truck and pulled it into the drive way.

Before he got it all the way parked, Goldie looked at Beatha and said, "I have wings?"

Beatha smiled and said, "You are Oberon's daughter. You must have wings and I know you don't turn into a Selkie like your Granna, so it would make sense. Larry's way is faster though."

"Does Larry have wings?" Goldie asked Beatha.

Goldie's breath left her lungs as Larry stepped out of the truck glowing and took several steps away and whispered something. Huge translucent wings that were silver with hues of yellows, greens, and browns sprung from his back. He smiled at her and she saw a look in his eyes that looked like freedom. He felt free she realized. He tucked his wings back in from wherever they go and grabbed her bag out of the back of the truck.

He jumped suddenly and she asked quickly, "What's wrong?"

"Your bagged moved and I'm pretty sure it's not supposed to," said Larry eyeing the bag.

Goldie made it quickly to him and unzipped it to find Mack hiding in the bag! "What are you doing in there? You were supposed to stay home with Granda."

Mack chirped at her as if answering.

Larry said, "He doesn't want to leave your side. He feels bonded to you."

"You got that from his little sound?" Goldie asked teasingly.

Larry just looked at her and she said incredulously, "You understand him?"

"Well I am an Earthen Fae. We are one with the land and its creatures." Larry said with a twinkle in his eyes.

"So that's why Mack took a liking to you?" Goldie said.

"Just because I can understand him so to speak doesn't mean he has to like me. He decided that on his own," said Larry looking into her eyes.

Beatha cleared her throat and said, "As much fun as it is to get to know one another, it's time to go. We will be causing a scene before too much longer being all together."

"You're right. Let me get the portal drawn and you go in first Beatha and then I will follow with Goldie. You remember the first time can be unsettling," said Larry as he took a what looked like a stick from his pocket and he began to draw in the dirt.

Goldie didn't recognize the symbols he was drawing, but yet she felt them in her being. As Larry kept drawing, the stick lit up and so did the symbols. When he drew the fifth and final symbol and enclosed them in a circle.

"Goldie this is the part where I need your help." Larry said motioning her to come to stand behind him.

"How can I help you. I don't even know what kind of power I have or how to use it?" Questioned Goldie.

Larry gave her smile. "That zap you feel when we touch is our powers recognizing each other. Fae generally recognize Fae. I'm disappointed I didn't recognize Beatha at the diner. But she was far away and right now is more mortal than Fae."

"And you were more focused on Goldie. I know. I knew who you were when I saw you dear boy. You look so much like your mother," said Beatha with a sad smile.

Larry smiled softly at Goldie and continued, "You may not be able to use your power just yet. You will learn, but you can help me by lending me power. I'm weakened from being away from home for so long. Please place your hand on the back of my neck. Your power will embrace mine and we can open the portal."

Goldie tentatively walked over to him and slowly and gently placed her hand on Larry's neck. He let out a barely audible gasp and the sensation of her hand on him skin to skin. Goldie saw her hand slightly glow and felt warmth radiate from her to him.

"That's good child. Fae power has a lot to do with your will. Will him your strength and power. Think about what you want to happen and it will. Speak it into existence if you need to," said Beatha smiling softly like a proud mother.

"I wish to strengthen Larry. You may go to him," said Goldie willing her power through her hand and into him.

Larry shuddered and the ground slightly shook and a black sparkling hole appeared in the ground. Goldie felt slightly tired now and Lorcan reached his hand up and took it from his neck. He stood up still holding her hand and placed a gentle kiss on her palm and whispered, "Thank you."

Beatha smiled and breathed in deeply. "Time to go home. I'll see you on the other side Goldie. Lorcan thank you." She said and then stepped into the portal and was gone.

Chapter 10

Goldie's eyes went wide. Not only had she never seen anything like that but she turned her head and asked, "Lorcan?"

Larry's eyes glowed brightly when she said his name. He nodded and said, "Yes. I only recently have gone by Larry. Lorcan is my Fae name. Apparently humans recognize it as Laurence. I don't care for that one so I chose the nickname Larry instead."

"I feel like my head is going to explode. Ms. Betsy isn't really Betsy. You're not really Larry. I'm in a whirlwind," said Goldie not knowing what to think about anything.

"Our names may be a bit different, but we are still the same where it counts. We both still care about you and who you are. You can keep calling me Larry if you like. It makes not a difference to me as long as you are with me," said Lorcan.

"I think it does matter. Your eyes glowed brightly when I called you by your true name...Lorcan." She let the name slide across her tongue and found she liked the name alright, but it would be hard to just stop calling him Larry.

He smiled at her and said, " Now hold onto me. The first time going through a portal can be tough and if you don't know how to set your feet, you will fall on your face, but I will hold you through this first one at least."

Goldie stared at him for a moment before realizing he was holding his arms wide for her to step in. She looked at the bag in her hands with Mack in it. "Is it safe for Mack?" She asked.

"You're about to go through a portal and you're worried about Mack?" Larry or Lorcan laughed and then he said, "Yes it is safe for him. Put the bag over your shoulder and zip him back in and come here."

Goldie scratched Mack's head, zipped him in the bag, and slung it over her shoulder. She looked up to meet Lorcan's eyes and knew hers must be glowing too. She took two steps into his arms and this time wasn't surprised by the electricity that ran through her veins. She embraced it and as he wrapped his arms tight around her, she pressed her head into his chest and wrapped her arms just as tightly around him.

Lorcan didn't ask her if she was ready. He just gently picked her feet up off the ground like she was light as a feather and stepped into the portal with her. Goldie's stomach felt like it jumped up into her throat. She swallowed down her fear and opened her eyes.

An explosion of colors assaulted her senses. It was like going through a kaleidoscope. The colors were so vibrant and she felt like she could touch the colors as if they were their own entity. She loosened her grip on Lorcan and extended her arm out and ran her fingers through the pulsating colors. They seemed to dance with her fingers. She felt tingles in her hands and she let out a giggle. She felt eyes on her and looked up to see Lorcan watching her with a look of wonderment on his face.

 She smiled up at him and he smiled back at her. Goldie noticed the colors dancing around Lorcan's head and reached her hand up to touch the colors, but found her hand pressed to his cheek. She had no intention of doing that, but the colors seemed to have a mind of their own. She smiled and blushed, but didn't try to remove her hand. She felt Lorcan's grip around her tighten and pull her in closer. She went willingly closer to his body. He stared down at her as if he was trying to memorize her face.

Lorcan spoke into her mind, "Goldie you look so beautiful surrounded by the colors of our powers. What are you feeling right now?"

She blinked up at him and thought about projecting her thoughts into his mind. Beatha had told her that power had to do with her will. She made a conscious effort to speak back to him in the same way. She opened her mind up and replied, "The colors are alive. They are so pretty. I just wanted to touch them. You think I'm beautiful?"

Lorcan's eyebrows rose and a wide smile spread on his handsome face. He spoke back in her mind, "I've always thought you were beautiful, but to see you experience things for the first time and your eyes light up with wonder…You are beautiful."

Goldie smiled not worrying about her gapped teeth showing. She focused again and spoke back into his mind, "Thank you for letting me experience this and not have to do it alone. I think the colors wanted me to touch you like this." She moved her fingers that were still on his cheek.

He smiled and said out loud, "Perhaps."

Goldie knew she felt like she was being pushed further into his arms and she felt her body being pushed up higher, until she was eye level with Lorcan.

"Well that answered that," said Lorcan as he leaned in and gently pressed his lips to hers.

Goldie's breath was stolen away and she was consumed by Lorcan's touch and smell. He pulled his head back to look at her and she asked, "Answered what?"

Lorcan gave her a crooked grin, "Our colors as you called them, want us together."

"What are they Larry? I'm sorry I'm mean Lorcan," said Goldie sheepishly.

"Don't be sorry. I don't mind you calling me Larry. It's nice coming from your lips. These colors are more than colors. These colors represent the elemental powers that we both have. Some are just the colors of my powers and some are just yours, but it seems we share a couple because they pushing us together as if our powers are meant to be together," said Lorcan putting his forehead on hers.

Goldie couldn't help herself. She pressed her mouth back onto his and this time, it wasn't because colors had pushed them together; it was because she wanted to kiss him. Goldie didn't really know what she was doing. Lorcan was the only boy she ever wanted to even be around. Lorcan moved his hand gently up her back and placed it on her neck just under her head, like she had done to give him power earlier. His hand warmed on the back of her neck and she could feel his power dancing in her veins with her own. She didn't know how she knew but she did.

Lorcan deepened the kiss and Goldie let instinct take over. When she felt his tongue tentatively dip out to touch her lips, she opened her mouth and gave him access. She was shocked at first, but was consumed by his taste and feel. She relished in the closeness and as she found a rhythm with him, the colors exploded behind her eyelids and she felt as one with the powers coursing through, not only her veins but his.

Lorcan moved his hands to her face and caressed her as he left nothing unexplored in her mouth and she did the same with him. Lorcan kissed her as if he were starving and she was his favorite food and Goldie liked it. It felt like they had been kissing for hours, when they heard a throat clear.

Goldie quickly jumped back out of Lorcan's arms to find Beatha standing in a forest with her arms crossed across her chest. "Well I guess you two are getting to know each other. I mean I see why you kids would be drawn to one another. I take it the jump didn't faze you then child?" She asked looking at Goldie.

Goldie blushed to her roots and said, "I guess not."

Lorcan answered for her; "She opened her eyes and the colors caressed her. She lit up the whole portal. She is amazing."

Beatha's eyes widened. "I've always known you were special child. How many colors were there?"

"I saw blue, green, brown, red, orange, pink, silver, and white. I take it each color means something?" Goldie said curiosity brimming.

"Some of those colors were mine. Green, brown, red, and white are mine for sure, but we shared some," said Lorcan smiling at her.

"I've never heard of someone seeing pink. Blue is water. Green plants. Brown Earth. Red is mammals. Orange is fire. Silver is the moon. White is purity and life. I have never heard of anyone seeing pink. That's a new one. I've been around for hundreds of years too." Beatha said scratching her head.

"Wait. What? Hundreds of years?" Goldie asked.

Beatha smiled softly. "Yes child. Your Granna and I grew up in the old kingdom together. I will tell you all about it, but now we need to find somewhere for Lorcan to rest. Making a portal big enough for all of us to make it through took a lot from him after being away from home for so long."

Goldie looked over to Lorcan will concern etched on her face. "Are you ok?" She asked gently.

"I am definitely ok. That portal was worth my weariness," said Lorcan throwing her a shameless smile.

"Oh my gosh! Larry!!" Goldie shrieked.

He just laughed.

"I'm sorry Lorcan. Lorcan. I can't stop calling you Larry. It's seemed to have stuck in my head." Goldie said as she looked around.

"Where are we?" She asked.

"I wasn't strong enough to portal us into the Hollow Hill. Really only a few of us can even do that. It's a safety thing. But, I've been away from home far too long searching for you and then I somehow got a message from Oberon saying against all odds he had heard from Beatha Bringer of Life. She is a legend among our people and we've mourned her loss for seventeen years. Just think she was watching over our future queen. You are going to be so powerful as soon as we get you home and united with our power and people. Oh right you asked where we are. We are at what our people call Hazel Forest. The Hazel tree is so important to our people. It helped keep us alive during tough times. Beatha do you know that poem?" Lorcan looked at Beatha.

Beatha smiled and said:
"Two hazel nuts I threw into the flame,
And to each nut a gave a sweetheart's name.
This, with the loudest bounce me sore amazed,
That, with a flame of brightest colour blazed.
As blazed the nut, so may thy passion grow,
For 'twas thy nut that did so brightly glow."

"Thomas Grey wrote that in the seventeen hundreds. I always liked him. He was a romantic for sure. He was an English poet," explained Beatha.

Goldie smiled. "That was beautiful."

"Come on ladies. Let's find a place to camp. There should be a good spot about half mile from here," said Lorcan starting to walk.

Goldie followed with Beatha holding her arm. Goldie looked at Beatha concerned. She was old for human standards and she wondered if she could handle the journey. She thought about how Beatha had been in her life for so long. She thought of how sweet she always was to her and she thought about the lengths she went to, to keep an eye on her. She used a different name and used an accent. She was treated poorly because of her skin color. Lorcan had said she was a legend among their people, so apparently skin color didn't matter in the Fae realm. She went from that to being treated like she was less than the white folks.

"Child why are you feeling so bad right now? I can feel your sorrow," said Beatha looking at Goldie.

"I was just thinking of all you went through to watch over me. Not even that you ended up becoming mortal and aging, but how poorly you've been treated. Beatha I'm so sorry." Goldie said squeezing the old woman's hand who had filled a void in her life for as long as she could remember.

"I would do it all over again my dear. I lost my love a long time ago during the first king's reign. I don't know how much you know, but we only love once, so when he died before we got a chance to have children, I never had any. But, I have you." Beatha rested her head on Goldie's shoulder.

"Beatha will you tell me about my Granna?" Asked Goldie.

Beatha took a deep breath. "Normally we don't share other Fae's stories but she's not here to tell you, so I will share the stories how I remember them."

Beatha continued, "Your Granna, Deidre, and I were moon sisters."

Goldie cut in, "Moon sisters?"

Beatha laughed softly. "Be patient my child. I will explain it all. Moon sisters are girls born at the same time on the same night on a full moon. It says those who are moon sisters are destined to be best friends and have an unbreakable bond. It was true for your Granna and I. We grew up together in the Hollow Hill during dark times, but we made the best of it. All Fae are considered part of the same family so to say. She was a Selkie and I a powerful empath fairy with healing abilities. It didn't matter that she preferred water to the Earth. We would sneak out of the hill together to stare at the stars and go to the beach. I'd walk along in the sand while she swam her heart out. No one could swim like Deidre, not even the water fairies who could control the water. It was pretty clear that Deidre had more than Selkie blood running through her veins but we didn't know what else she was. She glowed like us. Most Selkies do not glow."

Beatha smiled, lost in her memories. "As we got older, mind you we age differently, when in the Hollow Hill, we are still considered children at 30 and most don't even marry or consider anything else until the human age of 50. It's just that way. Deidre always was so kind. It was clear as she got older that she was powerful and she was so beautiful. Men Fae noticed her everywhere. It was no surprise that the first king took notice. He had married three times and unsuccessfully reproduced. The women could not bear his children because he was too powerful. Most women died before ever birthing because their bodies could not handle the power forced into them. The first king only wanted strong bloodlines and his offspring to be the strongest. He would look for the strongest of the women and try to breed them. Breed is the only word I can use. It's harsh but it's the truth. He never had any offspring. He became so bitter that he decided if he couldn't have his own children that he would select only the strongest of his people to mate and bare him the strongest Fae for his army. He never let anyone marry for love. Many snuck off and married anyway, but so many were executed."

She shuddered and then continued, "When your Granna and I were 18 we stumbled across a young woman in labor hidden in a secret hollow of the hill. She hadn't followed the first king's rules and was pregnant with a love child. She was terrified for her life and that of her babe. She was laboring hard and the babe wasn't coming. She kept saying, "He will kill me. He will kill me." You Granna told her, "No one will kill you as long as I'm around. I will protect you and the babe. You are stronger than you know. Mother's must be." This was when I got my name, Beatha Bringer of Life. I didn't know I had healing powers, specifically as being a midwife. I opened my senses and I could see that the baby was stuck sideways in the small woman. I placed my hands on her and moved the babe with force and my power. The young woman screamed in agony when the baby shifted but she ended up being able to push him out. Lorcan was that baby."

"Her cries had gotten the attention of other Fae and in fear for retribution they called the king in. He came in a rush to see what happened and who had birthed. When he looked upon the young woman, he grew angry.

He hollered, "And why have you not told your king of this? I should have your head!"

Deidre stepped in without a care for her own life. That was her way. She stood in front of the king and stared him straight in the eye and said, "I will give my life for hers. Is her life not worth more after bringing life into the world?"

The king's eyes went wide and his face reddened at her boldness. "You would give your life so willingly for someone weaker than you?"

"I would give my life willingly for anyone who deserves to live." She had answered him.

The king studied her a moment longer and then he said, "You shall call me by my name, Balor, for you will be my bride and bear me strong sons. I sense your strength and see the fire in your eyes. Yes, you are worthy to carry my children."

Your Granna never faltered. She gave a slight nod. The young woman thanked us profusely. She kept her life because of your Granna's boldness. I was known as Beatha Bringer of Life from then on and I've delivered more babes than I could count, but I remember them each by name." She smiled looking over at Lorcan.

"Let me explain to you what your Granna agreed to. King Balor was a giant. He was no small Fae. That's part of the reason so many of the women couldn't birth the babies. They were just too big. Balor was the leader of the Formorians. Formorians are hostile creatures. They come from under the Earth and the sea and are almost impossible to beat. Balor was never challenged for the crown because everyone was terrified of him and his power. King Balor was a shadowed man and so powerful in strength and power. He had the blackest hair, black eyes, a strong jaw line, and long pointed nose. A lot of people believe he only had one eye, but the truth is he had three. You only saw the third one when he was ready to find the truth or deal a punishment out. His third eye could read the intentions of someone and burn someone from the inside out. A lot of artwork depicts him as the destructiveness of the sun. He was mean, but also handsome in a dark way. Many women thought they could change him, but no one ever could. He was just darkness." Beatha shook her head and continued on.

"Anyway my gifts were realized at the birth of Lorcan. I can see life inside the womb. I've been able to save many babes with this gift. Your Granna was a born leader. She took up for the people. She thought that maybe she could help change the kingdom by marrying the first king. She wasn't too thrilled to be married though. Every little girl whether Fae or human, dreams of her wedding day and wants to be married to her knight in shining armor. She wants to be loved more than anything else. Balor was no knight. He was a dark leader who loved himself and power over other Fae more than anything or anyone else. Balor decided that he didn't want to want to wait until Deidre was of proper marrying age. He was going to force her at 18. Her mother rejected the idea of it all, but she wouldn't have her mother get the rage of the king. She told her she would be fine." Beatha paused to catch her breath. The walking and talking was taking its toll on her.

"You can finish the story when we stop." Goldie said reaching out to touch her. She wondered if she could give Beatha some of her strength like she had done with Lorcan. She reached her hand to Beatha's neck and projected her youth and strength to her.

Beatha's body jolted and she looked up to Goldie with surprise in her eyes. Goldie watched as Beatha's face seemed to grow younger and the gray in her hair turned back to black. Goldie pulled her hand away when Beatha grabbed it and said, "Enough child. You've shared enough power today."

Lorcan had stopped to wait on the women and he watched in amazement. He then grew worried, when he saw Goldie slump down. He quickly made it to her and caught her before she could hit the forest ground. He picked her up and said, "Beatha are you ok to walk a little further now?"

Beatha said, "I am thanks to Goldie, but I fear she's given too much of herself before she's truly come into her power."

Lorcan pulled Goldie in closer to his chest and placed a soft kiss on her forehead. "Not much further las. We will stop to rest soon. I should have never asked you for help."

Goldie looked up to the hard lines of Lorcan's face and the firm set of his jaw. He was upset. She placed a hand over his heart and said into his mind, "It's not your fault. I would do it again and I had to help Beatha. I'm sorry to be more of a burden on you."

He looked down into her blue eyes, his softening and said, "You could never be a burden to me."

She shuddered slightly feeling yet another piece lock into place. She let her head fall on Lorcan's chest and dozed off. At one point, she woke up to hear Beatha and Lorcan speaking.

"You are sure you're ok to go further?" Lorcan asked.

"Yes. Goldie is way more powerful than we could ever imagine. There was so much more to her grandmother than we ever knew. She all but gave me my immortality back. We still don't know what her pink color represents." Beatha said thinking out loud.

"I've never seen anyone be strong enough to feel the colors of someone else like she did. She truly is amazing," said Lorcan.

"You know she is but a baby Lorcan," said Beatha sternly.

"I know but I can feel the bond. Our people haven't had them for so long that I never thought it was real. It is. I feel it with her. Our energies are like a current that is pulsing when we are together. Beatha, she fed me," said Lorcan with such emotion.

"Lorcan feeding someone is a very human thing. She had no way to know what it would mean to you. What it means to our people. Food is one of my favorite things about the humans. The food is so good and they love to share their food with one another." Beatha explained to Lorcan.

"I guess she wouldn't know that feeding someone is a sign of devotion to us. The food is quite delicious. You know I had never been out of the hill for a long time until now. The new experiences I had with her make me feel even more of a pull towards her," said Lorcan pulling her closer to his chest.

Goldie thought about the odd look he had given her the night she had fed him a fry dipped in chocolate shake and she thought about the times he was appreciative of breakfast. She hadn't known that feeding him meant so much more to him. But, honestly, she was ok with that. But what was he talking about a bond and Beatha called her a baby. Then she thought back to what Beatha said about Fae not marrying until 50. How old was Lorcan? She just always assumed he was just a couple years her senior, but now he could be what? Hundreds of years older than her? Her stomach clinched. It seemed like too much.

Chapter 11

Lorcan stopped eventually and made camp. He set up a fire and laid out blankets. He laid Goldie down on a blanket and brushed her hair from her face. She reached up and held his hand to her cheek and opened her eyes.

"Goldie your eyes are glowing las," whispered Lorcan.

"So are yours." Goldie whispered back.

Their breaths caught in their throats and they just looked deeply at one another as if they could see to what was at their souls. Goldie felt her body heat up and a light glow radiated from her entire body. She shown golden. Lorcan quit breathing and stared at her. His skin started to shine with hers, but his was more of a shiny silver.

Goldie smiled at him and said, "You're beautiful."

He shook his head and smiled. He said, "I'm supposed to say that to you. You are just so much more."

Goldie didn't know more of what, but she felt the weight of the word down to her toes.

Lorcan stepped away and went to gather fire wood. Goldie let her brow furrow when she noticed Mack following behind Lorcan. "That little Traitor," whispered Goldie with a small smile on her lips.

 Beatha chuckled to herself as he went.

"What's making you chuckle Ms. Betsy?" Asked Goldie who shook her head quickly and said, "Sorry Beatha."

"Child call me Ms. Betsy forever. I'm just so happy. What's funny is that Lorcan doesn't need to go collect fire wood. He could simply call the wood to him and make a fire with his power or magic as humans like to call it. He's giving you space and needs to think and I suppose is enjoying Mack. He let him out a while ago to stretch his legs. Mack is quite at home in the forest. He's giving us time to talk too. I'm sure you still have questions and I never finished telling you the story earlier." Beatha said sitting down on the blanket next to Goldie.

"Yes please finish the story. I love hearing about my Granna, but hate what she went through. I'm feeling much better now after resting in Lorcan's arms," said Goldie thoughtfully.

"You will feel stronger the closer we get to the Hollow Hill. You will feel the energy course through you. There's nothing quite like it," said Beatha smiling.

"Ok so where were we? Ah yes, your Granna agreed to marry Balor." Beatha said and the cleared her throat to continue.

"So Diedre agreed to marry Balor. With doing so she saved Lorcan's mother's life, possibly Lorcan's. Lorcan's mother became good friends with us. We loved the babe as if he were ours and took good care of his mom Tomar. She was an Earthen Fairy. Lorcan is very powerful too. He showed signs early. His father must have been powerful. Tomar never talked about his father and no Fae male ever showed up to claim Lorcan. It's really sad. Let me get back on track here. So your Granna told her mother not to worry that she would marry the king and figure out how to make it work. She said she may not love Balor but she loved the Fae and the hill and that she would do her best to make life better for everyone else. She wanted me to be able to marry for love and not just to find a male to make strong babies with."

Beatha smiled softly and looked off in the distance as if she were reliving something. "Diedre went to Balor's castle on her own. She waited at the gate and called for the king. Balor was so surprised at her show of strength he had her things moved to the castle that very day. He wanted to know what had caused her to come marching to his home instead of waiting for him to call her. She had told him that there was no need to wait. She knew he wanted to marry her soon. She only asked that in promising to marry him and give him strong children that he would let their people marry for love again and search for the sacred bond. He laughed in her face and asked her how they were supposed to take over the human realm too without strong Fae and plenty of them. Your Granna balked at that statement."

She continued, "Your Granma asked him why he would even want the human realm. She knew that we couldn't live in the realm that long without being back for our power. She asked why he would want to sacrifice people's sons and daughters. He was so hungry for complete power. He wanted to rule over the humans as if he were a god. Your Granna couldn't stand behind that. She pleaded with him to focus on making their kingdom a better place and their people happier before trying to get more. He was amused by her and her efforts to stand toe to toe with him, but when he grew tired of her, he slapped her across the face hard enough to blacken her eye and bust her lip. I was so angry when I saw her next. She again said not to worry, she would figure it out. It became clear though that Balor didn't want a queen, he wanted someone pretty to be on his arm and fulfill his every whim. Luckily for your Grannistigha, he didn't want to have her until their wedding night. He was so prideful over being the one to break her in that he told everyone in the castle they would hear her screams throughout the land on their wedding night. I'm sorry to share that part with you child, but you need to understand what type of man he is."

Goldie shuddered and felt her eyes fill with tears. She nodded and let out a breath.

Beatha rubbed her hand down Goldie's arm and kept telling the story. "Your Granna was terrified to marry him, but would never say anything to anyone. We kept tabs on Lorcan and she always was happiest holding him. She would tell him that she would do her best to make the Hollow a better place for him and that he was going to be a brave lad. Your Granna asked Balor to take her on a date. She said she wanted to get to know the man who was to be her husband. She wanted to try for a real relationship. She thought if she could get him to have real feelings for her, he would want to make her happy and nothing would make her happier than a happy, healthy kingdom. Balor was almost happy that she requested his undivided attention. He thought that she was trying to impress him and in a way she was. I helped her get ready for her date with him. He requested that she wear a black dress. You look much like her you know? She hated wearing black, but she did as the king requested. She wore her hair half up and half down. We painted her lips deep red and put black liner around her eyes. She wore no shoes. Fae never really wear shoes, unless we step out in the human realm."

Goldie smiled. That was one thing she understood. She hated shoes. It was then she realized that hers were gone. She looked at feet.

"Lorcan took them off. He knew you wouldn't want them on my child. He cares for you deeply. Anyways, your Granna looked so beautiful. We painted her nails the deep red to match her lips. Balor came to the door himself to get her. He didn't send a guard, which was surprising. He never took the time to do anything himself. His eyes had glowed a bright red when he saw her. It took us aback, but your Granna never said a word.

She bravely smiled up at him and said, "I'm excited to be on this date with you. Thank you for coming to get me on your own. It means a lot to me."

Balor's eyes had almost softened I thought and he replied, "I would have no other male look upon you and I adore you wanting my attention. An attentive wife will be a good wife. You look good enough to eat."

We both gulped when he said that. It had been said that Balor would feed from blood. Some even thought he was the first vampire. But there is such thing as blood Fae and Balor was quite possibly related to them somehow. So your Granna went on a date with the dark king. When she came back she was never the same. She said we could not let him reign forever and that he could never have an heir. She said that if he ever had a true heir, he would destroy both our realm and the human realm." Beatha let a tear slide down her cheek.

Goldie reached up and wiped the tear from her favorite woman's face. "Do you know what happened on their date?"

"All I know is she said all the rumors about him were true. She said he was the monster that everyone said he was and that he would do whatever it took to have absolute power and that she couldn't let it happen. She was scared. She said that he drank her blood without her permission, she didn't say how or from where. There were no bite marks on her neck or wrists. She said the king said her veins were rich with power and that their son would be the key to both kingdoms; meaning the human and Fae realms. Your Granna said she would stop him if it was the last thing she did."

"On her eighteenth birthday, Balor came and got her. He was so happy to see his bride to be that he forcefully kissed her in front of me and her mother. It was rough and dominating. He held her so tight she was turning red. He wasn't happy until she returned the kiss just as hard.

He grunted with approval and then told her mother, "Your daughter is much more than you led us to believe. She will bare me the strongest son and her line mixed with mine will bring about a new time of power for us."

Your Granna's mother screamed out, "No. No line will ever be blessed when it's not for love. Have you not learned that yet Balor?"

He was angry with her and stepped towards your great grandmother with rage in his eyes. Your Granna wouldn't allow him to hurt her so she grabbed Balor's hand and pulled him to her. He wasn't prepared and was shocked when she jumped up on him and wrapped her legs around his waist and planted her lips on his. We could see the white light radiate from her mouth to his as she devoured his mouth. He shuddered under her touch and when she let him free and slid down his body, he had a slight smile on his face.

She said, "My king there is no need to hurt her. The best way to hurt her is to prove her wrong and us bring our own children into the world. Take me home Balor."

When she said his name, something happened. He swept her up in his arms and carried her out of the house. Your Granna looked over his shoulder as they walked out of the door and gave her mother a slight nod. Your great grandmother crumpled to the floor and cried over and over, "I've lost my daughter. I'll never see her again. Watch over her Danu and Aonghus."

I knew I then I might not ever see her again either and that she would never be the same." Beatha had tears streaming freely then.

"Who is Danu and Aonghus?" Goldie asked while holding Beatha while she cried. Goldie had tears streaming too, but needed to know so much more.

Beatha's eyes softened. "Child you have lost so much of your own history. I will do my best to fill in the gaps. Danu is the Goddess of Nature. But, she was so much more than that. She is also the goddess of wisdom, prosperity, death, and regeneration. It is said she is the mother of the gods. Aonghus is the Youthful God of Love. He always had four birds chirping around his head wherever he went. He loves poetry and truly loved love. I think your great grandmother cried out to him in hopes Deidre could find love and of course she would want Danu to watch over and protect her. Your great grandmother always seemed to be more on the Celtic side than other Fae and she was considered a wise woman."

Goldie sighed heavily, "So I have a family full of amazing, strong women. What happened to my Granna after the king took her?"

"The women in your family are amazing and that includes you child. I don't really know what happened after he took her. Balor had the wedding planned he would marry her on the first full moon after she turned eighteen. We can only conceive on full moons. The night before the wedding, your Granna somehow managed to sneak out of the castle and come find me. I assumed she took her Selkie form to not be noticed. I don't know if Balor knew she was a Selkie or not. He drank her blood and seemed to know something more, but none of us knew what. I hugged her so tightly when I spotted my moon sister. She let out a shuddering breath. I cried when I truly looked at her. Her eyes were sad and she was pale. She had a bruise on her thigh and one on her arm. I couldn't ignore them. When I asked her what happened she said it was nothing I should worry about and that she would take care of it. She said she had a plan." Beatha rubbed her hands together.

"That night your Granna and I used our power to make sure that when she conceived, she would have only girls. She didn't want to give the king a son. She said it would end our people if he had a son. I asked her to just run away. She said it wasn't that simple. Your great grandmother and I went to the wedding. Your Granna was stunning. She was in a red dress that hugged her body and fanned out at the floor. They call them mermaid dresses now. It was perfect for my water loving friend. Her lips were red and all her hair was up. She didn't look scared. She looked resolved and held her shoulders up high. Balor of course being the self-important man he was had to speak. He said, "My Fae Realm today is a great day of joy and history. As I bind myself to this female, we will bring forth life like our people have never known. She is not only powerful but beautiful and I've found I've grown quite fond of her. She will make a good wife and one day maybe a good queen. I had not held much stock in..." He trailed off and looked at Diedre with his eyes wide." Beatha said remembering.

"Your Granna smiled sadly at him and put her hand up to his cheek. Balor placed his hand over hers and a single tear ran down his face. Your Granna stepped over to him and got up on her toes and softly kissed him. Balor softened for the first and only time ever. When he looked down at her, something clicked into place for him. He looked to the elder and said, "Marry us right now. She is mine. Only mine and she will grow heavy with my seed this night."

Your great grandmother cried silently next to me. None of us were sure what had happened. The elder nodded nervously and began the ceremony. We do a kiss the bride thing too, a little different, but we do it. When it was time for Balor to kiss his bride, your Granna did something we didn't know she could, she called the most beautiful blue and purple wings out and flew to hover over Balor. He was entranced and surprised as well. She slowly let herself come down to where she was just above his lips. It was significant to us, because she was showing us who was above who. When she placed her lips on his to seal the commitment, she pulled a blade free from her dress and stabbed Balor in the neck." Beatha shook violently at the memory.

"She was so strong Goldie. She did what everyone was afraid to do. She showed us that Balor could bleed. She understood our people would die with his greediness for power. Balor was shocked. He grabbed his neck, but still had one arm around Diedre. He pulled her in closer and kissed her harder. He tried to say something to her. If he did we couldn't hear it. He ran a sword through your Granna and said she was worthy of him after all. Your Granna never made a sound. I knew she had to be in red hot pain.

With her last strength, she used her wings to pull away from him. He was shocked yet again at her strength.

She said, "My body is not your body and I will not bear a son who will ruin our people. I love my people too much. I could have loved you Balor if only you'd let the light in."

She then with a ragged breath launched herself out of the courtyard and we heard the splash of her falling into the water outside. Everyone assumed she died with the major injury. Had she stayed, she could have been healed immediately. Her mother could have done it, but she didn't want to bring Balor's offspring into the world. It's so hard to talk about all this because there is so much we don't know. She heard and saw things we didn't. I think she thought either Balor would die or she would, but either way our kingdom wouldn't be taken down with them." Beatha explained.

"We all thought your Granna was dead. Balor really did mourn her being gone. We didn't know if it was because his dream of world dominance died with her or if actually cared for her in a twisted way. He had everyone scour the water and every part of Hollow Hill looking for her. We never found her. But you know about our bonds. Your great grandmother never truly lost her bond, so she knew she was alive but barely. She knew she could never come back and slowly the bond lessened over time. It wasn't until two years later, on a full moon, I heard her in my head.

She said, "Sister I am alive and well. I am in deed a mother to a beautiful daughter. Do not worry for me. A king cannot rule for an eternity. Love will be his ruin."

"I told only your great grandmother. Anytime I could sneak out from the Hill I would look for her. I never found her. I knew she had to be by the water somewhere because it would call to her. I figured she used what last of her powers she had to conceal herself. But many years later, a young girl so beautiful showed up. She was wondering through the forest and stumbled upon a cave. The cave is an entrance into Hollow Hill. Only those of us with Fae blood can enter. I stayed in the shadows and watched her. She entered in the cave and nothing happened. I knew then she was Diedre's daughter. I wanted to run out and hug her, but I didn't. I feared if I brought attention to her, the king would notice. I was so fixated on watching her that I didn't see Oberon coming back in from a scouting mission. He stopped dead in his tracks and his eyes locked with your sweet Ma's. I saw the bond latch in place on them. They were like moths to the flame and just came together. I turned away not to intrude on their moment. They were meant for one another. Our bonds when they happen are for life and they click into place and there's nothing you can do to stop them. It's as if a piece of you that was missing finds its way home. They snuck away for any moments together they could after that. I followed your Ma home one day. I needed to see Diedre one more time." Beatha paused to catch her breath.

"I saw a mortal man smiling at his daughter as she came home with a basket full of hazel nuts and I saw Diedre holding onto his arm and kiss his cheek before embracing her daughter. She was full of love and happy, but I could see that she was sick. I went to her in the night when I could sneak in unseen. She cried when she saw me. I cried at her frail state. I told her to let me sneak her home to heal her and she said she couldn't be in the way of fate. That it was her time and that she hoped I would be lucky enough to love and be loved like she had been. She said that being mortal wasn't as bad as the Fae made it out to be, it just made you make sure each day counts because they don't go on forever. I told her about her daughter who I learned was named Enya. She was named after your great grandmother. I told her about her sneaking to see Oberon. I told her they had a true bond. She had smiled and was happy about that. She told me that love would end the dark king's reign, but it wouldn't be her daughter who did it. I think she knew that you would be coming. Some Fae can see pieces of the future." Beatha said looking off again.

"I snuck to see my dear friend as much as possible. I died with her when she did. When a moon sister loses her sister, it takes a piece of you and leaves a mark." Beatha showed her her palm. In the center of her palm was a scar in the shape of a crescent moon.

Goldie's breath hitched in her throat. She looked down at her palm. There in the middle of her hand was the faintest line of a crescent moon. She had been born with it. She held her hand up to Beatha.

Beatha smiled. "It seems you have a moon sister somewhere. You will find her in the hill and your life will be richer for it. Anyway, I went to check on Enya. I vowed to watch over her. When I got to the house on the hill by the water, she and your Granda were gone. When I made it back to the Hollow Hill, war had broken out. Oberon was trying to overthrow Balor. Balor wouldn't let him marry his bonded mate. He wanted to mate him with a fire fairy so they would make strong babies for his army. Oberon had asked politely. He had told him she had to be Fae because she had made it into the cave. Balor had asked him to describe his bonded mate and Balor became convinced that it was Diedre he spoke of. He had told Oberon to bring him this girl. Oberon asked his king why and he said, "Because she is my wife." Oberon flew into a rage and struck out at the king. In the end Oberon knew that Enya couldn't have been Balor's wife but he assumed that your Granna had something to do with it. He had cried out when the war was over and your mother was gone. He knew the moment she died because around his wrist golden waves appeared. See child when we lose someone we love deeply, we don't lose them completely, a mark is always left. But he also felt the bond of his child. He knew then he had to find you. He would find his and Enya's baby if it was the last thing he did. I saw his anguish and I left to find you. I flew out over the seas and found a boat and I found you and your Granda alone and scared. I've watched over you since, but I lost my power. I used so much power flying to you, I couldn't mind communicate back to our people. I was too weak to go back so I stayed. I watched over you and I think when you came into some of your power, it lent me some power somehow and I was able to get a message to Oberon and he sent Lorcan to find us. I want you to understand child, I would have stayed with you even if I could get back. Your life is more precious than mine. You are my moon grandniece and I'd do anything to protect you."

A twig snapped underfoot and both women turned to see Lorcan standing there with his arms full of sticks. Goldie smiled at him and he had an odd look on his face. His eyes warmed and he smiled back. He said, "You are my light."

Chapter 12

Goldie wasn't sure by what he meant by saying she was his light, but it filled her with warmth. Larry quickly made a fire and sat by Goldie. She laid her head on his shoulder and she swore he sighed. He laid his head on hers and they sat there just watching the fire together. Beatha rummaged through her bag and pulled out a plastic bag full of snacks. Goldie smiled at her. Leave it to Beatha to feed them.

"I made brownies just yesterday and I've got some grapes and ham. It's not much, but it'll tide us over until tomorrow," said Beatha opening the bag and passing it to Goldie.

Goldie grabbed it and said, "Thank you. You are still taking care of me."

Beatha put a warm hand on her cheek and said, "Child, today it was you who took care of me. I don't feel like such an old woman and I feel my strength coming back."

"Beatha it's always meant the world to me when you shared recipes or food with me. Is it because I'm Fae?" Goldie asked.

Lorcan shifted next to Goldie. "So I take it you heard part of our conversation then?" He asked.

"I did." Goldie simply answered looking now at Lorcan, trying to judge what he was feeling.

"I thought you were asleep las. I'm sorry. I hope I didn't make you feel uncomfortable," said Lorcan searching her eyes.

"I don't think I feel uncomfortable. To be honest, I'm not sure what I'm feeling. I know I feel so much more than I have ever before. I think I would feed you again even now knowing that it means more to you. I don't know

Lorcan. Everything has happened so fast. I don't understand the bond and I've heard it said that Fae only love once. Is that what this is? Am I falling in love with you or was I destined to? What's the bond? I have a million questions and a fluttering heart," said Goldie speaking fast and throwing her hands in the air.

Lorcan didn't say anything back. Instead, he grabbed Goldie's face gently with his hands and pulled her lips to his own and planted a soft kiss. As he did he started to lightly glow and projected his feelings to her. Goldie started to shudder as she felt the intensity of him. She felt warmth, devotion, protectiveness, pride, and she felt; she felt love.

She looked up to him after a moment and kissed him gently back and pictured every moment she had had with him so far. He saw in his mind what she saw when she looked at him. Lorcan saw the first time she had seen him walking towards her from his beat up truck at the bait camp and he saw the shy smile he had given her. She showed him how she looked when he didn't always notice. He saw how she studied him. He saw himself punching the guy in the diner that had been so rude. He saw what he looked like from under the water. He saw what he looked like the first time he had held her wet body next to his after helping her up on the shrimp boat. Lorcan saw himself in the portal as he held Goldie and he saw how she saw the kiss. He didn't know how he knew, but he knew it was her first kiss. He saw how she saw him and he felt; he felt love.

Lorcan looked down at Goldie with more emotion than he had ever felt in his life. No one had ever shared memories with him in such a way. He was in awe of the young woman sitting next to him. He pulled her into his lap and wrapped his arms tightly around her and just held her for a long moment. She held on tight as if her were her life line. Neither one could quite understand what was happening, but they knew their lives were tied completely to one another.

The moment broke as Beatha spoke into their minds, "Children we are not alone. As sweet as your realization is that you are heart mates, it's time to be serious now. I know none of us is full power."

Lorcan quickly set Goldie to the side and looked around. He was embarrassed. He was the king's right hand man and best guard and he let them get surrounded. He surveyed the woods around them looking for power signatures. He could make out the shapes of what looked like warriors. He looked closer and he felt the power of his people.

"Beatha it's ok. It's our people," said Lorcan.

"Come out brothers and sisters. We are here and safe," shouted Lorcan towards the trees.

Hundreds of Fae came from the trees' shadows. They all looked differently but carried the same shields, but in different colors. They circled Goldie, Lorcan, and Beatha. Lorcan looked around at everyone. The soldiers stood firm and surveyed their group.

 Goldie looked around nervously. She lost her breath when the circle parted and a man larger than life walked through. He was wearing a golden yellow robe that went down to his ankles and no shoes on very large feet that had long toes. He had a very long sword that laid across his broad chest and he was so tall. His golden blonde hair shown in the sun and went in waves down to his shoulders and on top of his head he wore a gold crown and around his neck he wore a necklace made of leaves and flowers.

Goldie looked to the man's face and when his pale blue eyes met hers, something inside her clinched and clicked into place. She fell to her knees and tears fell freely.

A deep, musical voice came out of the giant of man's mouth as he simply said, "Daughter."

The bond tightened in Goldie and she felt the pull towards her father. It was real. She could feel her tie to him. She didn't have time to even stand when her father was kneeling before her, looking at her searchingly. The tears didn't stop flowing from her eyes as she gazed upon his angelic but hard face. The lines of his jaw were straight and strong. The lift in his brow hard. He had a single scar going through his left blonde eyebrow and his eyes held pain and kindness. When he gave her a small smile, Goldie saw the slight gap between his front teeth.

She didn't flinch away when he brought his hand up to her cheek and brushed her tears away with a calloused thumb. She closed her eyes and felt him. She could feel what he was feeling. She didn't know if he was allowing her that or if she was taking it. She didn't care. He was feeling sorrow, joy, and love all at once while he stared at her.

After a long moment he finally spoke, "My daughter, it is you. You look much like your mother, but I see me in you too. I've been searching for a long time. I could feel that you were close." He smiled again.

Goldie looked into the pale blue eyes that were so much like her own and softly smiled back. "I didn't know you knew about me. I can feel you, Da."

Oberon's eyes filled with tears as he swooped his daughter into his arms for the first time and hugged her fiercely. She hugged him back just as tightly and they sat like that for a long time, the guards never moving around them.

Goldie realized that Lorcan hadn't said a word since her father had arrived. She looked over to him to see him kneeling with his head bowed and then she looked to find Beatha the same. She looked up to her father then and he looked back down at her. He smiled again and before squeezing her one more time.

"Lorcan rise." He commanded.

Lorcan did as he was asked. He still didn't utter a word.

"I asked you to find my daughter and you did. I however, do not appreciate finding her in a compromised state. Lorcan, we could have been someone else that meant you harm and you did not notice us." The king stated, face turning red with anger.

Goldie broke in. "It's not his fault. I did something. We had a very intense moment. I mean Beatha said he's my heart mate. I don't even know if…"

Oberon cut her off, "Beatha?" He questioned eyebrows raised.

"Yes sire. I am here. I was the one that got you the message. I've been looking after Goldie all these years and was not strong enough to make it home. Just recently Goldie has come into some of her power and I think her power lent me strength to reach out to you," said Beatha looking up from where she knelt.

"Beatha, Bringer of Life you're alive!" Oberon exclaimed as he pulled her into a hug.

"Yes my child. I am. I've missed home," said Beatha hugging him back.

"You look different. The human realm was tough on you?" Oberon asked.

"If you think I look different now, you should have seen me earlier. I was an old woman. I aged in the human realm. Goldie lent me power to make the journey and she did more than just give me power," said Beatha sending a hidden message to Oberon as she spoke.

His eyebrows shot up in surprise. "Oh. Oh yes." He said and then turned back to Goldie. "Your name is Goldie. I like it. It fits you and our family line. All of us have golden hair and the most powerful of us glow golden too. But, you know about glowing don't you?"

Goldie nodded nervously.

Oberon said, "I know you have a lot of questions and I will be happy to sit down at dinner with you and answer them all. I've missed so much of your life. Let's go home."

Goldie took the hand he held out towards her, smiled, and said, "Ok Da. Home."

Chapter 13

Goldie walked alongside her father's left side hand in his and Lorcan took the right side. They walked in silence for a long time. Finally the silence was driving Goldie mad, so she reached out in her mind for Lorcan.

"Lorcan are you in trouble? I hope not. You've done nothing but help me this whole time. I mean you carried me a lot of this journey. Sure, it was because I shared too much power but I'm fine and it was all worth it. I want to kiss you again. Oh my gosh I would never say that out loud. Forget I said that. Or thought that? Oh my gosh! Shut up brain! What's a heart mate? Beatha said we just realized we were heart mates before my father showed up."

Goldie noticed her father stand taller and then she heard Lorcan's voice in her head. "Goldie, you are holding hands with your father and you share a parental link. While you are touching him, whatever you are thinking, he can hear."

Goldie blushed to her roots and before she could cut off her thoughts, she projected, "Oh my goodness. What a way for my Da to get to know me!"

Lorcan made a choking noise under his breath and Oberon looked at him side eyed. Goldie put her head down and kept going. She felt her father's gaze on her so she looked up. He spoke into her mind. "My daughter there's nothing you could say or do that would diminish my joy for having you in my life. It was a shock to see you with Lorcan like that, but I shouldn't be surprised. He is a good man and you are special. It would be my daughter to have the first heart mate after so many years and to reestablish the true bond. Would you like to fly with me?"

Goldie's eyes grew wide and she said out loud, "Yes. Please."

Oberon laughed then and pulled her to a stop. He said in a booming voice, "My brothers and sisters I wish to take my daughter to touch the sky. Please get Lorcan and Beatha home and we will meet you shortly after. My daughter and I have much to see together."

The king whispered, "Speir," and his wings shot out from his back. They were grand. They were translucent with golden veins and hung almost to his ankles and stood well over his head.

Goldie looked at him wide eyed. She reached her hand up tentatively and ran a fingertip along the edge of his wing. The king smiled at her. He wrapped her in his arms and slowly carried up out of the trees with the gentle flapping of his wings. Goldie let out a giggle of complete happiness as they broke the canopy of the trees. She looked down and locked eyes with Lorcan, who smiled at her happiness.

She saw Beatha pull on Lorcan's arm to keep moving. He was reluctant to take his eyes off Goldie but he began to walk again. Goldie looked up to see her father studying her again.

"You look much like your mother. She was the most beautiful creature I had ever laid eyes on. You are the only creature I've ever seen to even compare to her beauty. But you would, wouldn't you las. You are part her and I still can't believe part me." Oberon said smiling with pride and so much emotion in his eyes.

Goldie reached her hand up and placed it on her father's face. She gasped when she felt what he was feeling. He was feeling so much joy and a deep sorrow that seemed consuming. She projected her feelings to him. His face showed his shock and then he covered it up quickly as he felt her feelings. She shared joy, wonder, curiosity, love, and feeling of completeness. Oberon smiled at his daughter and placed a kiss to her forehead. When he took his lips from her head and warmth spread from her head to her toes and she looked at her father with wonder in her eyes.

She saw a glow starting to radiate from her and she felt like herself again, except stronger. Her father began to glow too. He smiled at her and asked, "Feeling a bit better now? I can share my power with a single kiss. It should hold you until we get home. Our people will rejoice at your coming home."

"Larry, I mean Lorcan," Goldie started before her Da laughed and said, "Larry is what he decided on?"

Goldie nodded and laughed a little too, but she much liked Larry. "Anyway Da. Lorcan said I can fly too. Will you teach me?"

Oberon's eyes glowed brightly as he smiled wide. "There is nothing more I'd find joy in my las. Soon I will teach you. First, I need to get you home so you can replenish your power and realize them. You would not have had your full potential in the human realm. Beatha says you're very powerful. That means a lot coming from her. I'm so happy to see her alive after all these years. We thought she was lost to us."

"She went by Ms. Betsy where I grew up. She always was there to take care of me. She was like a mother figure to me. I love her like that too. I don't know what you know about our world, but the color of your skin matters. She wasn't treated fairly in my realm, but the color of her skin never mattered to me," said Goldie.

"As it shouldn't. What creatures are on the inside is what matters, not what we see. But, I will admit that I do admire beauty. Look las, down there is a waterfall and over there are the ruins of some of the first people." Oberon spoke as he flew towards a hill and pointed significant things out along the way.

He landed in front of what looked like an empty cave. Goldie could feel the hum of energy. Her veins felt like they were tingling. She looked around. Oberon set her gently on her feet. "I met your mother out here. She had wandered up here. She loved exploring the woods. She felt drawn here and never knew why. I could tell she was Fae, but didn't know how much. She could have perhaps realized her powers if I could have brought her in the hill, but I never got the chance. I'm sure you want to know all about her. I will tell you in time my daughter. Come on, let's go home."

Oberon's wings went back into his back and he gently took Goldie's hand. He could feel her nervousness. "Don't be nervous las. You were loved when no one even knew who you were, but now that you're here and in person, they will more than love you; they will serve you."

Goldie gulped in air. "Serve me?"

"You're my daughter. That makes you princess and these will be your people. They will all but worship you. You being home, means our realm will continue to live on. We must find strength to continue to live and keep our people alive. There is much you do not know. For now just come meet your people." Oberon said with a soft smile and a tug on Goldie's hand.

Goldie followed her father into what looked like an empty cave. She gasped when they walked through an invisible veil. Her eyes burst with color. It was like the colors she saw when she teleported with Lorcan. Everything shined like polished gem stones. As her father pulled her further in, she felt her body start to hum. Her hair lifted up on end around her body. Her clothes changed literally on her body into a robe that matched her father's but was more feminine. On the bottom of her robe, little sea creatures seemed to be alive and shimmering. She felt her eyes light and knew she was glowing. She looked at her father to see him smiling as he watched his daughter's transformation. Gently, his hand raised as he placed a small gold crown on top of her head.

Goldie was speechless. She didn't understand what she was walking through. It felt magical. She didn't know if it was her father's doing or if it just was. She continued to put one foot in front of the other as Oberon led her deeper into the cave. She felt like they were spiraling down, deep into the Earth. A soft cry left her lips as she felt a tearing at her back. She turned her head to see wings!

Tears filled her eyes at the pain and the beauty. Unlike her father's, her wings were a translucent blue with golden veins. Hers only went to mid-calf and up to the top of her head. She didn't know what caused them to come out, but she let out a giggle as they flapped on their own. Her father laughed with her. He ran a fingertip along the edge of her wings, much like she had done to him. It tickled her and she laughed and her wings shuddered.

"Well las, you're going to have to learn how to control them. They can have a mind of their own. They are absolutely beautiful. To put them away all you must do is say, istigh." Oberon explained to her.

Goldie didn't want to put them away. She felt the pieces of herself coming together. "Do I have to tell them yet?" She asked.

Oberon smiled and said, "Las, you're home. You can keep them out for as long as you wish. You will not be judged here. You will see there are many different types of Fae. Some may seem frightening to you, but I assure you, they are all our people and will not harm you. We put our wings up to protect them. It's easier to maneuver in small places with them up, but enjoy them for right now."

Goldie clapped her hands in delight and fluttered her wings. After the initial shock of pain of them popping out, they felt amazing. It was like being able to stretch out after being in the hallway for an hour in school for a tornado drill. Her steps started to feel more sure. She felt the connection with her father next to her, but she could also feel another connection, a connection in her heart. She knew Lorcan was close. She smiled as she kept in step with her father.

Finally, they stepped out of the long, winding colorful hall into a magical world lit from within. Goldie gasped at the sight before her.

Hundreds of Fae were on bended knee with their heads down in what looked like an open park. In the middle was what Goldie would call a water fountain, but it shimmered with the colors of the rainbow as it bubbled. The grass was the most vibrant green and seemed to glow. Everything glowed. Goldie realized they were deep in the Earth where there was no sun. It seemed as if life itself was the light. She looked around in wonder.

Her father's booming voice commanded the very air. He said, "Rise my brothers and sisters and greet your Princess. This is Goldie, my one and only daughter and heir."

In unison the whole crowd stood and erupted into cheers. Goldie saw all kinds of emotion. Some of the older looking Fae were even crying. She looked from face to face and creature to creature and was astonished by the many types of Fae in the crowd. She put on a brave smile and awkwardly waved. She felt her heart pull and looked into the direction it was pulling. Down in the center in the very front row was Lorcan looking up intently at her. He wore no expression on his face.

He was in a black robe down to his feet. His robe had an x crossed across his chest on either side of hips were two swords. They gleamed silver. Around his writs were black bands and on the underside were small knives. Then, around his head was a single black braided leather, that set somewhat like a crown. She wasn't sure what it all meant. She saw a few other men dressed similar to Lorcan, but they had no braid around their heads.

Goldie felt her wings flutter and without commanding them they fluttered up and away from her father. She got nervous. They were taking her down to Lorcan. His expressionless face quickly turned into one of confusion but then softened as he realized she was being carried to him. A word escaped his lips that Goldie couldn't hear and then wings as big as her father's maybe bigger sprang from his back. She loved his silver wings with the hues of yellow, green, and brown.

His feet gently lifted up from the ground and he met her in the air above the crowd. He wrapped his arms around her waist to steady her wavering flight. She wrapped her arms around his neck and rested her forehead on his. The crowd gasped as they hovered in unison and glowed brightly. Lorcan's lips gently brushed hers and when Goldie opened her eyes, their colors intertwined around them.

Goldie heard the whispers from below; "The bond is real." "It's true." "Heartmates are real." "They are powerful." "Of course she's powerful. Oberon is her father."

Lorcan helped them get to the ground. Beatha waited with a look of shock on her face. When Goldie's feet hit the ground, she felt a jolt come up through her body as if the ground itself was sending its power to her. Then from nowhere, Mack ran through the crowd to climb up Goldie's robe and sit on her shoulder. The crowd looked at her with curiosity and then they stepped back as their King ascended from where he had just stood with his daughter.

He landed in front of Goldie. Beatha and Lorcan immediately went down to a knee. Goldie looked to each side at them and then up at her father. She wasn't sure if she was supposed to kneel too. She reached out in her mind to her father, "Da I don't know what I'm supposed to do."

Oberon smiled at her and spoke back in her mind to her. "Las do what feels natural to you. You are my daughter."

With that, Goldie leapt at her father and wrapped her arms around him and hugged him tightly. The grass at their feet, glowed brightly and something deep within in the hill settled into place. The hill gently shook and the people collectively gasped and cried and clapped. Then Goldie's mind broke open wide and she could hear everyone's thoughts all at once. "We are saved!" "She's home!" "Our king smiles again!" "She can't have him..." Goldie clapped her hands over her ears, as her father still held her.

Oberon looked down at his daughter and saw her distress. He spoke in her mind, "Las, you have to shut them out. Think of only my voice and who you want to be connected to. You can do it. You are learning everything the hard way, but you can do it. Focus just on me."

She did and the voices quieted. She opened her eyes and looked up at her father and for the first time could see a father's pride in his eyes. Still looking into her eyes, he said, "Rise family. Meet your princess. The bond has been solidified between her and I. You must realize that she was not raised here. She is not aware of all our customs and is just coming into her power and learning. She will help deliver us, but not alone. It would appear her fate is woven with Lorcan, my right hand and chosen son. I could not be more proud."

Lorcan stood and Oberon took a big hand and wrapped it around the back of Lorcan's neck to bring him into an embrace, with Goldie still clung to his side. The crowd clapped. Lorcan embraced Oberon back and let a hand wrap around to find Goldie. Mack chattered and Oberon let go.

"And who is this?" He asked scratching Mack on the ears.

Goldie was about to reply when he said, "Nice to meet you Mack. Our home is your home. You will find some of your kin in the back tree."

Goldie's mouth dropped open. And Mack put a little black hand on her chin and pushed up and then climbed down her to run through the crowd as if he was going somewhere.

Oberon laughed from his belly. "There is much for you to learn las. He's headed to the back tree. Many of us can communicate with the animals. You probably can too now that you have realized your power. You felt it didn't you. When your feet hit this ground it zapped through you and your power through our home. You returning home revived our home. And Beatha Bringer of Life helped too. We will be healthy and prosperous again."

The crowd clapped again and closed in. People brought gifts for Goldie. One wrapped a flower necklace around her neck. Another put a gold bracelet on her wrist. Another kissed her cheek and warmth spread through her body. Goldie met so many Fae. Some were the most beautiful fairies you could imagine. Some looked like elves. Some had horns. Some had scales. Some looked dark. Some were green. She met creatures she couldn't have imagined in her wildest dreams.

Finally Goldie decided to call her wings in. She didn't want to. She enjoyed the feel of them, but she understood why they didn't just keep them out all the time. It was hard not to bump them on the crowd or maneuver in tight spaces. "Istigh," whispered Goldie and her wings just tingled and went back into place.

Then there was hush over the crowd as giants made their way forward. Goldie's eyes met with a huge woman. Her hair was jet black and her eyes glowed red. "Formorians," whispered Goldie.

The woman's head cocked to the side and she simply said. "Yes."

Goldie studied her. She remembered they were ruthless from Beatha's story. Goldie didn't feel threatened though. Her eyes locked with the Formorian woman that stood a good foot and a half taller than her. Someone from the crowd shouted, "Kneel before your princess."

The girl spoke with authority, "But she's not really my princess is she?"

Goldie looked at her and when their eyes met this time, the Formorian's eyes went wide. Goldie was glowing brightly again and light radiated from her hand. She looked down to see the crescent moon on her palm glowing red and she looked to the tall woman to see her looking down at a golden glowing moon in her palm.

Beatha said, "It can't be."

Goldie had been thrown into this world, but she understood prejudice. She had lived though it in her realm. She knew that the Formorian's had been seen as bad, but they had bad leadership. Surely, not all of them were bad. Sometimes there was a reason behind why people did what they did. Goldie spoke slowly and clearly, "No, I'm not your princess. I'm your moon sister."

The Formorian's eyes went wide at the statement. She said, "And you would claim me as such?"

"Why wouldn't I? Neither of us can deny what just happened and everyone saw. Let me see your hand." Goldie said.

The huge woman tentatively put her hand out palm up. Her hand was enormous compared to Goldie's. Goldie traced the crescent moon with a finger and smiled. Goldie had a feeling that this woman could hurt her if she chose to, but she knew this was a defining moment and she needed to set a precedent. She had looked forward to having a moon sister after what Beatha had told her about them. Goldie placed her hand out palm up with her crescent moon showing. She let the large woman look at her palm.

Goldie held her hand up in front of her with her palm facing the giant woman. The giant mirrored her movement. Goldie placed her palm on the larger palm and clasped her fingers around the woman's hand. The woman gasped in surprise and then her large fingers swallowed her hand. Their hands heated and began to glow and power burst from them. Goldie spoke aloud, "From this point on you are my sister."

The Formorian woman let a tear escape down her cheek before she said, "Princess Goldie, I am Angrbora, leader of the Formorians."

"Nice to meet you my sister, Angrbora. I wasn't raised here, but you will come to learn that I do not hold prejudices and will love everyone if they want to be loved." Goldie said still clasping the woman's hand.

Angrbora, squeezed slightly and said, "I will hold no past hurts on you either and hopefully together we can forge a new future of prosperity for all Fae including my people."

Goldie smiled and said, "I hope so too and you're people are my people. Fate has brought us together as moon sisters and we will break the mold."

Angrbora let go of her hand and took a step back. She bent to a knee and bowed her head in front of Goldie. The ground shook as the dozen giants behind her did the same. Goldie felt an emotion sweep through her and her power build inside until she too stood as tall as the Formorians had when they were not on bent knee. Everyone gasped around her as her body glowed brightly.

Angrbora looked up and with a shaky breath and whispered, "Goddess."

Chapter 14

Goldie looked down at the giants on bended knee and her moon sister who was completely in awe. "Please rise." She said looking at her radiating skin as she made the motion.

The Formorians stood reverently. Goldie turned to see everyone in hushed silence and back on bended knee. They all looked much smaller. Goldie didn't really know what to do and when she saw her father on his knee with his hand across his chest, she startled. "Please. Please. Everyone stand. I'm no one special." She said in a rush, hearing her voice had a different ring now. It sounded richer.

"My child, but you are special," said Beatha standing slowly. "You are more than Fae. You thought that you had so much human in you, but the truth is, you are part of all of us. Child you are part Goddess. We haven't had contact with any of the Gods of old for so long. We thought they had forgotten us."

"But I'm no goddess. I'm just Goldie. I just found out that I'm more than human. I can't be a goddess. I don't even know our history yet." Goldie said with tears coming to her eyes.

Her father stood and made his way to her. He was a large man, but now she was taller than he as well. He reached his hand up and cupped her cheek. "My daughter, you don't need to know our history to be a good leader or a goddess. Fate has a way of choosing for us. I couldn't be more proud of you than in this moment. You handled a situation that you had no grasp on with such humility and poise. You gave a race of Fae a chance to be part of us again. We could learn a lot from you my daughter."

Goldie let the tears slide down her cheeks. She had dreamt of her parents and to hear her father say he was proud of her made her feelings spill out of her eyes. She had the desire to hug him tightly. That desire manifested itself in her going back to what she viewed as her normal size and wrapping her arms around her father. He wrapped her in his arms tightly and whispered into her hair, "My Goldie we will figure it all out together. All that matters is you're here now. I love you."

Goldie looked up to her father's tear filled eyes and said, "I love you too Da." When the tears spilled from his eyes, she wiped them from his face and said, "Together."

He nodded and the crowd collectively sighed and then cheered. They were so happy to have their heir home and couldn't believe they had witnessed something divine. But when great power returns home, so does great fear. Goldie felt those feelings and decided she would do her best to be the best whatever she was.

Goldie turned again to her moon sister and smiled. "I'm glad to know Angrbora. I would like to see where you live tomorrow if that's ok with you. I'd like to get to know you and the rest of your family."

"It would be an honor. I'll come to get you at noon tomorrow. We will prepare lunch for you," said Angrbora with a slight nod.

She was taken aback when Goldie walked up to her and hugged her tightly. She stiffened but then returned the hug. Then, the giants left to return to their homes within the hill.

As Goldie turned around, someone said, "Princess Goddess you shouldn't go to their dwelling place. It may not be safe. Surely you know the stories of them."

Goldie didn't try to find out who said it. Instead she addressed the whole crowd, "I do know that today I found my moon sister. That is so special to me. It's true I don't know much about our history, but I choose to believe there is good in everyone. I believe in moving forward in unity and peace.

I do know that my grandmother gave up a lot to see our people find happiness and peace and my father did as well. My father fought for it. I will fight for it too, but in my way."

The crowd didn't say anymore. They bowed their heads and let her make her decision. She wasn't mad at them. They just wanted to keep her safe. She searched the crowd for Lorcan. She didn't see him and her heart sank.

She called out in her mind to him. "Lorcan."

"I'm just here las. I wouldn't leave you," replied Lorcan in head.

She turned to find him in the shadow of a dark evergreen tree. She realized then, when she noticed his hands on his swords and his stance, that he was ready to jump into action at any moment. She also realized in that second that he was ready to fight for her, to protect her. She noted that he blended so well into the shadows that she didn't even see him.

"I'm ok Lorcan. Will you please come walk with me?" She asked in their mental link.

He gave her a sad smile and said, "If that's what you want Goddess, but I'm not good enough to walk on the same ground as you."

Goldie's brow furrowed. "I don't understand that. You are good enough for me. Come here please. I need your strength."

Lorcan's eyes went soft. "It's not you who needs my strength, but I who needs yours. I will never be good enough for you, but I will never deny you what you want."

Goldie got tired of the waiting and back and forth in their minds, so she just walked to him. Lorcan's smile grew wide as she closed the distance to him. When she made it to him. She softly took his hands off the hilts of his swords and held them in her hands. Her hands glowed and his did in return.

"You are my light Goldie," said Lorcan, kissing each of her hands still in his.

"You are my strength," said Goldie staring into his glowing eyes with hers. Goldie thought she saw a flicker of something in his eyes.

Lorcan bent his head and kissed her softly. Goldie melted into it and rested her body against his and just let him hold her up. He wrapped his arms around her and she rested her head on his shoulder and they stood like that for a long time.

Oberon watched his daughter with Lorcan. His heart ached for the love he had once had, but he was happy his daughter had found her heart mate and in a man he had raised and loved. It was hard for him to have to share her so quickly after just getting her home, but he knew Lorcan would protect her. He had been ready to battle when the Formorians came up. He would die for his daughter, his goddess. The king shook his head and continued to stare in amazement. How could she be his daughter? There was so much he didn't know. He always just thought Enya was half human and half Fae, but clearly there was more to her bloodline.

Goldie, Lorcan, Beatha, and Oberon all walked together. Beatha's smile never left her face. She thought she would never return home. Goldie took everything in with racked attention. The hill was amazing and the different kinds of Fae lived in different types of dwellings. The Earthen Fae lived in mud huts with grass roofs, but were very homey. They didn't lack for any necessities. Sky Fae lived in giant tree houses in the most beautiful yellow leafed trees. All the houses were connected with ziplines and intricate walkways. Some Fae lived in literal carved out caves within the shimmering rock of the hill. The colors of all the plants were so vibrant that Goldie couldn't believe her eyes.

There was no electricity. It wasn't necessary with the magic. Water Fae had dwellings along the river and some lived actually under the water. Goldie couldn't wait to see their homes. The creatures were different too, but the same. There were cats and dogs, but their eyes were different and they literally were in every color imaginable. She spotted blue bunnies hopping along in a meadow.

"This way las. I want to show you this particular tree," said Oberon stopping in front of what Goldie would call a large oak. But, it's leaves were silver. Oberon knocked on the tree and four raccoons popped out of nowhere. Goldie laughed in delight. These raccoons looked the same as any other raccoons, except their fur had shades of purple. Goldie all but danced with happiness when Mack came out last.

"There you are Mack! Are you making new friends baby?" She said scratching his ears and kissing his nose.

His nose twitched and Goldie heard him plain as day, though his little mouth never moved. "I am Momma. They like me. They let me play and the girl thinks I smell good."

Goldie's eyes went wide and she said, "I just heard him."

Oberon laughed and said, "You are connecting with your powers here. You can understand the animals, though it's not always perfectly clear, but you raised this one so I imagine you understand him just like you would me."

Goldie smiled brightly letting her gap show. "Mack I'm so happy that you like them and you do smell good. See all those baths were for your own good."

"No Momma. She likes the way I smell. Can I sleep here tonight? I think she wants me to stay," Mack communicated to her.

Goldie's eyes glistened and she replied, "Yes my baby. You are growing up. Just remember to come visit me."

"Oh Momma, I'll never leave you for long," said Mack in his way.

"Yes you will and that's ok. You have to live a good raccoon life and she will be more important than me I have a feeling. Enjoy your freedom my Mack," said Goldie kissing his nose once more.

Mack licked her cheek and ran off after the purple hued girl raccoon who thought he smelled good. Goldie watched them run and chase each other and then smiled as she watched her boy give the girl a hazelnut he must have been hoarding. The girl took it and nuzzled him. Goldie sighed and leaned into Lorcan.

Lorcan chuckled and said, "Ahh yes. Young love."

Everyone laughed and Oberon said, "Are you ready to go home Goldie?"

Goldie looked at her father with excitement and nodded. He took her hand and led her along a hand placed stone pathway. As they walked he said, "Beatha you will come live with us at the castle."

"Oh I couldn't impose like that," replied Beatha.

"You're not imposing. You have nowhere else to go anyway and you're family. You've watched over Goldie all these years and I think having you close will be good for her." The king said in a final tone that brokered no argument.

"Beatha I would love that. It'll be good for Granda too to know you are close to me," said Goldie feeling happy about this turn of events.

"Lorcan where do you live?" Goldie asked him.

He smiled at her and said, "In the castle with your father. I have a room next to his and a room in the training camp for our soldiers. I expect I'll be staying in the training camp for now?" He asked with an eyebrow raised to Oberon.

"You expect right son. I trust you, but the bond can be a lot and there are some things a father will never be ready for," said Oberon.

"Wait. What?" Asked Goldie.

Beatha cleared her throat and said, "Um child, you and Lorcan won't be able to help yourselves, ya know? The bond pulls at you in mysterious ways and as I told you, you are still considered a baby here at just 18. Marriage isn't really a thing until about 30."

Goldie blushed to her roots. "Wow. I uh, wasn't expecting this conversation right off the bat. I've lived in the human realm for a long time. Many girls get married at 18. I don't have any intention on waiting until I'm 30. We only love once right? So why wait if Lorcan is my ever after?"

Lorcan squeezed her hand.

Her father spoke again, "It's more so you have time to mature and you're ready for all things. In the Fae realm everything is a life time commitment."

"Da, marriage is a life time commitment in the human realm too. My Granna was going to wed at 18 to save our Fae. Why would it be so bad for me to marry at 18 for love?" Goldie asked.

Oberon was quiet for a while and then said, "I guess you're right, but he still sleeps in the camp. And las, he hasn't even asked you to marry him yet."

Goldie blushed again and looked up to Lorcan with an apologetic smile. He kissed her forehead.

"I'm not good enough for her, but if she will have me, I'd be honored to be her husband. I will respect your wishes to sleep in the camp." Lorcan said.

"I don't understand why he can't sleep in his normal room," said Goldie.

"Because Las, it's next to your room. Your bond will pull you together and I just can't handle that tonight," said Oberon.

Goldie still looked confused so Beatha stepped in, "Baby we can see you are still pure by your aura and Fae, your father in particular has very good hearing. Like in the human realm some things should wait until marriage, like living under the same roof. Then again, you wouldn't be here had your father and mother not.."

"Beatha. She doesn't need to know everything. I understand the heart mate pull. It'll leave you mindless to realize your love in the flesh las. I would just rather you wait until you're married and out of my earshot." Oberon finally just said.

Lorcan choked on air and Goldie sucked in a breath. Goldie just nodded and looked up at Lorcan who looked like he could die at any moment.

"We will respect your wishes." Lorcan said to Oberon.

Goldie looked up to see a shining castle on a the top of a hill that was covered in blue flowers. Her breath hitched in her throat and she said, "It's beautiful."

"Those were your mother's favorite flower. That was the first thing I did when I became king. I covered the castle hill in her favorite flower." Oberon said watching his daughter's reaction.

Goldie let a tear slide down. The castle seemed to sparkle. Just like everything else it was vibrant. She didn't know what it was made out of. She had never seen anything like it before. It was sleek and sharp. It looked as if it were carved from the clearest crystal. Twinkling lights shown everywhere. There was a large gate at the entrance. It had an O and an E intertwined in the shiny metal. Goldie's breath hitched again. Fae love was truly forever.

Her father whispered something and the gate opened. He took his daughter's hand in his and said, "Welcome home Princess."

Chapter 15

When they walked through the gate, Goldie's body tingled. Her grip tightened on her father's hand. He squeezed back reassuringly. He stopped to pick one of the blue flowers. He reached to Goldie and placed it in her hair and the most radiant smile lit his face. "I never thought I could be this happy again. Losing your mom broke me and then not even knowing about you and losing you…It's been a very hard 18 years."

"Well Da, let's make the next 18 years happy together." Goldie said touching the flower in her hair with just her fingertips.

Goldie noticed little cottages along the outside gate towards the left side of the castle grounds. Lorcan came to a stop, so Goldie did too.

"I will take my leave until dinner and head to the camp. I need to see what's been going on since my absence," said Lorcan looking at his king.

Oberon nodded.

Lorcan looked down at Goldie and smiled. She smiled back at him and warmth filled his body. He leaned his head down to place his lips on hers. She reached up to meet him. The kiss was meant to be brief, but when their lips touched their magics mingled again and it was as if they needed that kiss to breathe.

Lorcan spoke in her mind, "Goldie I'm not strong enough to pull away from you. We are putting on a show for your father and this is why he doesn't want us in the same hallway. I love you and I'll have you without a second thought and that isn't fair to you. Pull away from me las."

She spoke back in his mind, "I don't want to pull away. I want you Lorcan. I need you to be mine."

"I've been yours since the day I laid eyes on you las. Pull away for me before I'm not even allowed in camp," said Lorcan in her mind.

Goldie screamed out in her mind and it physically took every ounce of strength she had to fight the magics' urge for them to be united. When she finally put some space between them, she was panting hard and had to clinch her fists not jump right back into his arms. He wasn't looking at her.

"Las you have to come walk with me. He can't walk away from you. I understand the bond. Come inside, clean up, and get to know your home." Oberon said.

Goldie let out a broken sigh and shuffled her feet away from Lorcan. She whispered in her mind to him, "This is the only time you're ever allowed to ask me to pull away. I won't walk away from you again."

Lorcan whispered back, "Don't be angry with me for doing what's best for your da today and for you. I'll be stronger next time."

Goldie didn't understand what he meant by the best thing for her and she was pretty upset at the whole situation. She was upset that he asked her to walk away. She was upset she barely controlled herself. She was upset because she felt ignorant in all things Fae. Clearly the bond was much stronger and deeper than she knew.

Goldie followed her father up the stone pathway and up to the castle. It was even more beautiful up close. It had so many facets of color, but there was no door. She looked puzzled at her father. He smiled down at her. "All you must do is walk through. Anyone welcome is welcome to enter." He said to her and walked literally through what seemed to be a rock wall.

Beatha took Goldie's hand. "We will walk in together. I can imagine how strange this is to you. Let's go together." Beatha reassuringly squeezed her hand and they stepped through.

King Oberon was waiting on the other side and smiled as the two ladies came through. "I never knew if this day would come. My baby girl walking into her home," said Oberon searching his daughter's face.
"You look sad las. I feel your sorrow. What is it?" He asked.

"I don't want to hurt your feelings Da, but I miss my Granda so much. It has just been him and me all this time. I feel like I just left him, you know? And I'm just wishing I would have met my Ma and Granna. I'm sorry to be so sad," said Goldie looking at her father with tears in her eyes.

Oberon took a deep breath and said, "There's nothing for you to be sorry for. I missed Lorcan terribly while he was gone. We will get your Granda here after you're settled in. I promise that. I wish you would have met your Ma and Granna too. They were both amazing women. I was very young when your Granna stood up to the first king. Come with me. Let me show you something."

Oberon put a hand out for Goldie and she took it and let her father lead her. Goldie looked around. She was so fixated on her father that she hadn't noticed the vines growing up the walls. It was as if the plants themselves were art, hung about everywhere. Butterflies floated freely through the corridor. In the middle of the room was a huge tree. It looked like a weeping willow, except with glowing golden leaves reaching to the ground. Around the tree there was almost a small river and it was the deepest of teal colors.

Goldie gasped at the beauty. She couldn't believe that this was in an actual castle. "Da it's so beautiful." She said.

He smiled at her. "Come with me." She followed behind him with her hand still in his. He walked up to the tree and as he went to step out on the water a small bridge appeared. They walked across. He parted the willow branches and held them open for her to walk under. When she made her way through, her breath hitched in her throat. Surrounding the trunk of the tree were the same blue flowers that grew on the hill. There was a bench at the base of the tree. It looked like it was carved from emeralds.

"This is my favorite place. I know your mother would have loved it. This is where I come to remember her. Come sit with me." Oberon said to Goldie.

She did and to her surprise the bench wasn't hard like it looked, but in fact formed to her body. She sighed as she sank into it. Oberon smiled watching her. "I only saw your mother in you, but now I can see me too. Look at the trunk behind us las."

She did. And in the trunk a woman was carved out. The woman was smiling and she had eyes that smiled too. She had a crown of flowers around her head. Goldie touched the face gently, recognizing herself in the woman carved. "It's Ma," said Goldie with a shaky voice.

"I carved her myself. I never wanted to forget. This is where I come when I want to feel close to her. You can too. She loved these flowers so much and water too. I would call her my water bug. I never realized who her mother was though, but now it all makes sense. Your Ma just stumbled into my life one day and it was like she had been there all along. I selfishly couldn't let her go and I didn't have the power to. Her and I were the first heartmates to come about after the first king took over. That bond is so strong. I would like to say we are better than animals, but our magics will push us together, especially on a full moon. Your instinct to reproduce and bodies will take over, much with the overwhelming love you have for that being. Goldie, tonight is a full moon. I would have chosen Lorcan for you if I had the choice. I'm glad he's your heart mate, but I would like you to do better than your Ma and I. Get to know each other more and be married. Beatha was right in saying you're so young, but your Ma was around the same age." Oberon said looking at the carving of his love.

"I do not know for sure how you will age, but I'm guessing it'll be much like us now that you're home. These are things we will figure out. Eighteen is so young. Lorcan is actually pretty young too. He's only 37. I've had him with me since he was six. His mother died during the first king's reign. I actually was caring for him when I met your mother. When lost your mother and you, taking care of Lorcan is what kept me going. I ended up being king because I defeated the first. I never really wanted to be king, but I'm here. I had my people to worry about. I felt it when you were born. It was my joy and my heartbreak all at once. I felt our bond get weaker and weaker as you went further away. I knew you were still alive though, because I would literally feel your death if it had happened. I clung to that hope all these years," said Oberon reaching out to squeeze her hand.

"I'm here now Da, but I'm afraid I don't know much. I have no clue how to be a princess much less a goddess." Goldie said taking a deep breath.

"You will learn and by what you've already done, you are a born leader. You single handedly took on the Formorians. I even handle them with great care. They are ticking time bombs. They get angered easily, but the first king came from their race and her ruled them relentlessly and they did all his dirty work without question. They hold little compassion. They are just fighters, but I guess you believe that they are fighters because they had to be." Oberon said thoughtfully.

"Well my moon sister is a Formorian, so I have to believe it's all for a reason. My goddess side didn't come out until they showed up. So much is happening so quickly," said Goldie shaking her head.

"Well it's believed that Formorians are the result of the gods sleeping with humans. So they are half god and half human and full warrior. They were considered an abomination, so they were cast out of the human realm and not good enough for the Gods' realm. They were stuck here and never truly fit in." Oberon explained.

"Well no wonder they feel the way they do," said Goldie.

Goldie looked around again and sighed with contentment. It really was a beautiful place. She got up from the bench and knelt by the water. She ran her fingers in it and the sound of the water racing past her fingers made a musical sound. She giggled. Little fish swam up curiously. She could only describe them as something similar to Beta Fish. Their tails were long and full. She marveled for not the first time that day of the colors they were. A purple one seemed to dance with her fingers. She smiled and said, "Hello there."

The fish seemed to acknowledge her. Her father walked up behind her and knelt beside her. "You love the water too?"

"I prefer to be in the water over land. I love to swim. My Granda is shrimper in Texas. I'm good on a boat and I can always seem to find the shrimp. The water feels free to me and like home. It makes sense. My Granda just told me before we left that my Granna was a Selkie. But after talking with Beatha, she was more than that because she had wings too. I guess we are just a bunch of mismatched genetics." Goldie said with her brow furrowed.

"I suppose so, but that makes it exciting. Come now Goldie, let me show you the rest of your home." King Oberon said.

Oberon showed Goldie through the entire castle. It struck Goldie odd that there were no servants. In all the fairy tale stories, there were servants. There was also no kitchen. There were more rooms than she cared to count; A big hall, A court for seeing people of the realm, A water room, literally made out of water, and A flower room, you guessed it, made of flowers. There was a huge dining room with a 16 seat octagon shaped table and high winged back chairs. There was a chandelier of sorts. It was an upside down tree, yes alive, hanging from the ceiling with little pink and white flowers all over it that glowed, lighting up the table.

Goldie noticed there were no lightbulbs in the entire castle. Things emitted their own light. They went down a long hall and on it were paintings. Goldie stopped to look at them. Her father stopped with her. "When I moved into the castle, everything was black. The castle reacts to your magic. The first king was dark. I love life and have a lot of Earthen magic along with many others in my blood. The castle has its own magic and builds around what magic I throw off. I was so sad at first and missed your mother terribly. The blue flowers bloomed first in the center of the entry room. You may start to notice minor changes throughout the castle. It'll just be reacting to your magic now too. Did you see how the water room reacted to you. The walls actually danced when you entered."

Goldie thought about it. She smiled remembering how the water walls danced when she ran her fingers through it. "I think the water room is my favorite. But I really love the whole place. My Granda will be in shock when he sees this place. Da, I am concerned though."

Oberon raised his eyebrows and said, "About?"

"Where's the kitchen? Where's the food? How do I cook here?" Goldie asked.

"Oh yes. The kitchen is where humans make food. I remember you mother speaking of a kitchen. We don't need them here. I am powerful enough that my magic fills the table with food. But if a kitchen is something you really want, I'm sure I can work with the castle to make you one," said Oberon smiling.

Goldie nodded. "Ok Da, so where's my room. I'm tired. I'd like to rest and shower before dinner."

Oberon nodded and took Goldie's hand. In an instant he teleported them to a room. Goldie didn't feel fuzzy. She looked up at her father in awe. "Will you teach me how to do that? And when Lorcan teleported us from Texas he drew symbols on the ground."

"I will teach you anything you want to learn," smiled her dad. "And when we teleport over long distances we have to put more magic into it. Here you can create a portal with just your thoughts."

Goldie looked around. They were in a completely empty room. She looked to Oberon confused.

He smiled at her. "Close your eyes and feel your magic flowing through your veins. Picture in your mind what you want your room to be. Anything you want in here and your magic and the castle will work together."

Goldie did as he said. She closed her eyes and listened to her heart beat. She felt the hum of her magic inside her. She didn't have to open her eyes to know she was glowing. She smiled as she thought about exactly what she wanted. Some of the things she wanted were memories and things she couldn't have possibly seen, but she knew she wanted them. She wanted a huge bathtub in her own bathroom with the softest rug imaginable. She wanted a waterbed that felt like it moved with the current of the gulf she loved so much but was still soft and welcoming. She wanted a vase with her mother's favorite flowers. She wanted a tree that Mack could play in if he came to visit.

"My girl, your room is beautiful," Oberon said in wonder.

Goldie thought she heard a hitch in his voice. She opened her eyes and saw him standing in front of a miniature version of his golden weeping willow. The castle had taken her wants and turned them into a masterpiece. On several of the branches at eyelevel were pictures. There was one with Mack on her shoulder and one of her and Granda on the shrimp boat. Another picture was of her swimming with the dolphins and one of Granda holding her birthday cupcake. There was a picture of her and Beatha when she was still Ms. Betsy to her cooking together. She smiled when saw the picture of her and Lorcan in the portal he had made. She couldn't have seen that but the house took what she imagined and made it real. There was a picture of Lorcan the first day she saw him standing by the beat up truck. There was a picture of her and her Da flying together and one of them sitting together on the emerald bench in his favorite spot. She walked over to her father to see the picture he was staring at. It was a family photo of her, him, and her mother. She could have never gotten one, but the house provided. She let a tear slide down her cheek as she laid her head on her Da's arm.

"This my daughter is beautiful. This is your innermost wants and it proves you have a beautiful heart just like your ma." He said with a crack in his voice.

Her Da looked around the room smiling. It was an intimate way to get to know his daughter by seeing what kind of space she wanted to be her own. He smiled seeing her large water bed with silk blue sheets and his heart skipped a beat when he saw the white vase with blue flowers on a small night stand next to the bed. She only had a single dresser in there. She had a large window with a seat to look outside. She had soft grass growing all over her floor. Across her ceiling was a blanket of ivy with little yellow and blue flowers lighting the room. He heard running water and walked into the bathroom she had imagined. It was her own water room. The walls were all water and had tiny fish swimming throughout them. Her bathtub took up most of the room and it had assorted bubble baths and shampoos. She had a single sink with an old looking mirror. Seashells adorned the counter. She had the softest bath rug that looked like it could be seaweed. Her towels were a coral color and plush, but she only had two. His daughter wasn't greedy.

"This is better than anything I could have imagined. You've got the best of all your worlds. I'm so proud to call you blood of my blood. I will take my leave to let you rest. So you know anything you want all you must do is feel you magic and ask for it. Clothes, food, just anything. If you need to find something just ask and the castle will light the way. If you need me, just call for me and I will be here. I love you." Oberon said.

Goldie smiled and said, "I love you too King Da."

They both laughed and the king left her to enjoy her new creation of a room.

"Thank you castle. This is more perfect than I could have ever done on my own. I hope you enjoy me being here," whispered Goldie feeling silly to talk to a house.

Her room seemed to shimmer in answer and seemed to sigh in place. Goldie smiled and said, "I'm glad to be home too."

Goldie decided to bathe before she got in her luxurious water bed that she could see gently moving as if it had the tides running through it. She stripped off her dirty clothes and let them fall to the floor. Before she could blink the clothes disappeared. She just shook her head and slid into the warm, bubbly water that appeared with just her thought of wanting a bath. She would have to get used to things happening because she willed them. She understood now why there were no servants.

She sighed as she sank in the water. She watched the fish swimming in her walls with amazement that this was her life. She closed her eyes to relax and saw Lorcan's brown eyes when she did. She was missing him. She sighed inwardly and thought, "Lorcan I miss you."

"Miss you too love." She heard in her head. It startled her and she sloshed water.

"Are you ok Goldie? I heard you shriek in your thoughts," said Lorcan sounding ready to do something.

Goldie giggled. She projected her thoughts back to him. "I'm fine. I was just thinking about you and didn't realize you could hear me while we are not close."

"Not everyone can do this. Only bonded ones. You probably could with you da since you share a parental bond. So you're thinking about me? What are you doing?" Lorcan asked sounding curious.

Goldie inwardly cringed.

"Goldie are you mind ignoring me?" Lorcan asked.

"No. I just wasn't going to answer. In short yes I'm thinking about you. I feel crazy because I can't stop. I feel like something is missing with you not here," said Goldie being honest.

"I never quit thinking of you either. So why won't you tell me what you are doing? Is it bad or are you supposed to be listening to your da or something right now?" Lorcan asked seeming amused.

"Fine if you must know, I'm in the bath," said Goldie in her mind a little huffy.

There was silence.

"Lorcan?" She searched.

"I'm here love. Just trying not to think of you in the bath with where I'm at," answered Lorcan.

Goldie's interest was piqued. "Where are you?"

"I'm in a meeting with the head soldiers." Lorcan said smoothly.

"So you're the one not paying attention to something you probably should be," teased Goldie.

"Hey love, you called for me in your thoughts as you are in the bath that I need to quit picturing before something embarrassing happens over here." Lorcan said sounding a little flustered.

"I'm sorry I bothered you while you're working. Glad to know I can call you like this whenever I want. Go pay attention. I love you. See you at dinner." Goldie said in her mind smiling.

"See you later love. I love you too," said Lorcan back.

Goldie laid her head back smiling to herself. She couldn't believe she had just thought about a man in the bath. What had she turned into? She thought about her life up until recently. Before Lorcan, she never even cared about the opposite sex, other than her Granda and Mack. She didn't have the desire to touch or be touched by any of the boys that were ever around. None of them were particularly nice to her either. Now, all she did was crave Lorcan. She wanted him to be with her in every way imaginable and the thought made her nervous. She didn't know how to be with him. She was ignorant to those type of things. Granda would have a heart attack if he knew how she was thinking of him before marriage.

Goldie shook her head. Beatha and her da kept talking about the bond and how it takes over. Was she just to be ravenous creature out to reproduce. She wasn't particularly ready for children. The full moon was also mentioned. Full moons seemed to be so important to her world with moon sisters and all. She thought about her moon sister and what it all meant. She replayed every part of the day and tried to piece it all together of where she fit into this puzzle.

She bathed and got out. She sighed when her feet landed on the softest bath rug ever. When she went to grab her towel, it opened up and wrapped itself around her on its own. Instead of freaking out like she kind of wanted to, she simply said, "Thank you."

A robe was waiting on her bed. It looked plush. She hurried over to it and ran her hand down it and smiled. "Guess you got me figured out castle. I like soft things. Do you have a name?" She asked out loud.

The room shimmered again. She took that as a sign the castle was pleased with her. Somewhere deep within her mind she heard, "Bhaile."

The voice was neither masculine or feminine. It just was. She smiled and tried the name out, "Bhaile. I like it."

Her room shimmered again. She smiled and put the robe on. She pulled back the blue silk sheets and laid down on her waterbed. She sighed when she settled. She could feel the rhythm she knew so well from home rock her to sleep.

Chapter 16

Goldie was running. Her feet were bare and they were bleeding and hurting from stepping on thorned vines that ran along a dark forest. Everything was black and she felt like she was choking. Something was chasing her. It was a monster and she knew she had to get away. It was closing in. She wouldn't make it. She didn't want to die, not like this and not without him. She screamed out, "LORCAN! I NEED YOU! HELP!" But there was no answer.

Goldie shot up with a jolt as her bedroom door busted open. Lorcan ran into her and ran his hands over her body checking for injuries. "Goldie are you ok? I heard you cry out to me for help. Are you ok?" He asked sounding panicked.

Goldie shook her head feeling groggy. "I was dreaming. It was a bad dream. I didn't want to die. I wanted you." Tears fell down her cheeks as the helpless feeling in heart shook her. It was just a dream but it had felt real.

Lorcan wrapped her up in his arms and shushed her. "Shh. Shh. I'm right here. I've got you now."

Goldie clung to him. She had been so distraught that she didn't notice her father and Beatha standing in the doorway. She looked up to see worried eyes. She didn't know why they would be so worried over a dream. She looked up to Lorcan to see his face worried too. "I'm ok everyone. It was a bad dream." She said stilling herself.

Lorcan wiped her face with long fingers. He looked into her eyes and kissed her forehead. Goldie looked down and to her dismay, she was still in the robe. It was slightly open now and you could see the top of one of her breasts and she knew if she hadn't been under the blanket, everyone would be getting a show. She blushed.

Lorcan noticed her red cheeks and he in turn blushed when he looked down the top of her robe. He didn't hesitate to pull her blue silk blanket up to protect her modesty. Beatha came to the bedside and crouched down to her knees. It was funny because just two days ago, she would have never thought Beatha would be so youthful.

"Goldie I need you to tell me everything in your dream ok?" Beatha asked in a soothing tone.

"I'm ok it was just a dream." Goldie said shuddering in Lorcan's arms. He squeezed her tighter.

"Child, I've been visiting with your Da and getting caught up on everything. I'm sure Lorcan mentioned you are to keep peace and there could be a possible war?" Beatha said searching for what Goldie knew.

Goldie scrunched her forehead. "He mentioned something to Granda and me about war and needing our power to be replenished. I don't understand what this has to do with my nightmare," said Goldie confused.

Beatha grabbed her hands. "Child in our realm, we don't have bad dreams. We create our own or sometimes people we trust can influence them. Lorcan heard you cry out in your dream. Your da and I didn't know you were dreaming. Lorcan was frantic. If you had a bad dream, something or someone caused it. I need to know what you saw."

Goldie's stomach sank and she swallowed hard. She nodded her head and closed her eyes to remember what she had dreamt. "I was running through a dark forest. I don't mean just dark as in light, it felt dark, like bad. There were vines covered in thorns all along the ground and my feet hurt so bad. They were bleeding and each step hurt worse. I'm not sure what I was running from. I just knew I had to get away. It was a monster I think. I never saw it, just knew it was coming for me. I couldn't breathe and I didn't want to die. I wanted Lorcan. I cried out for him, but he didn't come." Goldie had tears streaming down her cheeks.

Beatha wiped Goldie's cheeks with her hands. "But he did come. He is right here." Beatha said giving a look to the king who was now standing next to the bed.

Lorcan pulled her in closer to him. He spoke softly then, "My heart aches when yours does and I will always come when you call me if I can possibly get there. I promised your Granda I would keep you safe. I guess that means from dreams too."

King Oberon Fionn stiffened. "Lad I love you like a son, but you will not be sleeping in the same room as my daughter."

Lorcan looked up at him and said, "Then what will you have me do. You cannot step into her dreams and fight for her. I won't leave her unprotected."

Oberon nodded and said, "Fine. But.."

Lorcan interrupted, "I know."

Oberon looked down at Goldie and grabbed her hand in his large one. "I'm so sorry las. I'm sorry that you have to come home for more than just to meet me. When bloodlines are together and strong, it makes our power strong. Just like this castle works with our magic, so does the world around us. A darkness has been creeping into our hollow. The forest you spoke of from your dream is real. It's slowly spreading from the north towards our home. We have to stop it. Dark magic is very real and it's dangerous. When I dispatched the first king, we hoped all his darkness left too. But slowly it's seeped back in. The Formorians are restless seeing the dark magic return. They do not know who they will be following. If the darkness is back, that means someone who is dark and powerful must be alive."

Goldie shuddered again. How could the terrible place from her dream be real? Lorcan rubbed her shoulders. She rested her head on his chest and took a deep breath. She closed her eyes. He always smelled so good. When she opened her eyes they were glowing.

"So what do I need to do Da to save our realm?" Goldie asked.

Oberon smiled at her. "First we need to find out what you can do and teach you how to use your magic. With you being my daughter and now part Goddess, our magic together should shine a light through the darkness and take over. I'm going to go down to the dining room and get food in place. Get dressed and come down and eat."

Beatha said, "I'll help you. Goldie your room is breathtaking. I love it child."

Oberon and Beatha walked out leaving Goldie still wrapped in Lorcan's arms. She loosened her grip on him and she felt him relax some. She looked up to him to see him with a distant look as he looked out her window towards something. "What are you thinking?" She asked him.

"I'm thinking that I could never let anyone or anything hurt you. I'm thinking it's going to be so hard to control myself sleeping in the same room with you." He answered honestly.

"Wait. What?" Goldie asked sitting straight up.

"It's the only way I can protect your dreams. I'll have to sleep in here with you," said Lorcan with a half-smile.

Goldie felt a breeze across her chest and quickly pulled her robe together, but it was a little too late. Lorcan's face had grown hot and his eyes glowed.

"I'm sorry Goldie. I can't help but to look at you. I know you will be mine. I still can't quite believe I even have a heart mate. I want to possess you." Lorcan said.

"Possess?" Goldie asked feeling nervous.

"I want every inch of you mind, body, and soul to be only mine. Call me a bastard, but I want it all," said Lorcan not wavering.

"I will call you no such thing, but just remember that works both ways. I'll be yours if you are mine," said Goldie searching his face.

Lorcan smiled at her and bent his head to place his lips on hers. Goldie turned her head away. Lorcan stiffened. "What's wrong?" He asked and turned her face to face him.

"The last time we did this, you made me walk away. We almost couldn't stop. I didn't want to stop Lorcan. I don't know who I've turned into." Goldie said looking in his eyes.

His face softened. "You've turned into a princess goddess who is my heart mate. We won't be able to stop. Our magic and our bond will push us together. I will do my best to refrain from kissing you until you ask me to. I want to really bad though, just so you know."

Goldie giggled and said, "I feel wanting. I've never experienced even noticing a man and then you show up. I've never wanted anything or anyone so much and I'm a little scared."

"I feel the same way about you. I don't want to disappoint you. You are smart to be a little scared," said Larry with a distant look again.

Goldie searched his face and then leaned up and kissed his cheek. Lorcan smiled and said, "You do like to push it. Now get up and show me your room. It seems like it came together nicely. I know this bed is amazing."

Goldie slowly climbed out of his arms. She wanted to just stay there. She fastened her robe again and pulled him up to his feet. He stood so tall over her and she looked up at him and her breath caught at the sight of his glowing eyes. She knew hers must have been too, because his breath caught in his throat. She reached her hand up and placed it on his cheek. She felt stubble on his jaw line and watched him as he took her in. He pulled her flush against his body and she gasped as she felt herself warm up from the inside out and she felt heat coming from Lorcan.

He looked down at Goldie, his long nose so prominent. He spoke into her mind, "Mine. You are mine and I love you. Show me your room before we do something we can't take back."

Goldie slowly nodded and pried herself off of him. She immediately missed the warmth from him. The first place she took him was to her golden tree with pictures. Lorcan gently reached his hand out and ran a finger down the picture of them in the portal. He smiled softly. "Our first kiss was in that portal."

"Mmhmm. That was a special night. It seems like so long ago, but it was just last night. Lorcan, is the way I feel about you normal? I feel like I literally can't live without you. I feel like I've known you my whole life and this is just how it's supposed to be." Goldie said looking at the man she couldn't sum all her feelings for.

Lorcan turned and looked at her and grabbed her hands. He said, "Goldie this is a first for me too. Our people haven't experienced a true heart mate bond in a very long time. Sure, there's love. Our people love deeply and we have marriages out of love, but the last Fae to have a heart mate was your da. He's really the only one that would have the answers. All I know is that it's forever and you can't stop it. I don't want to stop it. I'm in awe of you and I know I need you like I need my next breath. You are my light."

"So we learn together," said Goldie grabbing his hands.

"Together," said Lorcan planting a kiss on her forehead.

Chapter 17

 Lorcan studied Goldie's room and learned so much about her. She truly loved the whole Earth; water and land and animals. Her bed was nothing he would have ever imagined and now he found himself wanting to hold Goldie in that bed. Her picture tree was beautiful. To see what she wanted materialized and he to be included in it made his heart beat even more for her. He looked down at Goldie as she smiled showing him her own "water room." She ran her fingers through the wall smiling as the little fish swam with her movements. The water really did run in her veins.

Both of them looked up quickly when they heard Oberon's voice in their minds saying, "The table is set and dinner is ready."

Goldie looked down at her robe and up to Lorcan. "I can't go to dinner in a robe!"

Lorcan laughed softly. "You're still not used to our life here. Remember just use your magic and ask for it."

Goldie looked at what Lorcan was wearing. He was wearing black. He had on black leather pants and a tight black shirt that showed off his impressive long, torso. Of course no shoes. Goldie closed her eyes and imagined what she would feel comfortable in. When she opened her eyes she was in a blue jean dress, no shoes, but her toenails were painted white, and her hair was up in braids on her head.

Lorcan smiled at her. "You're so human to not be much human at all."

"I can't help it." Goldie said smiling.

"Thank you Bhaile." Goldie said in her head as a lighted path showed up.

Lorcan smiled wide. "Who is Bhaile?"

Goldie looked up surprised that he didn't know the castle's name. She answered, "Bhaile is the castle."

Lorcan's eyebrows went up in surprise. "You can hear it." He didn't ask, just stated. "You make friends everywhere you go my light."

They walked hand in hand down the corridors. They passed many of the rooms her da had shown her. They made it back to the octagon table and Beatha and Oberon were waiting. They smiled as the two heartmates walked into the room. Goldie's eyes went wide as she looked at the feast laid out before her.

King Oberon smiled and said, "Beatha helped me with the food. She made sure your favorites were on the table. I have to say I'm extremely excited to try some of these things. Apparently our food is very different."

"Where would you like me to sit Da?" Goldie asked.

Oberon looked conflicted for the first time and Goldie could tell he didn't want to answer. Lorcan cleared his throat and answered for him. "You sit at your Da's right hand because you are his heir."

Understanding dawned on Goldie and she looked up to Lorcan with even more love in her heart for him. "Is that where you've sat all these years Lorcan?"

He gave a simple nod. Goldie squeezed his hand.

"Da is that the way it has to be?" Goldie asked.

Oberon looked at her confused.

"I'd like to let Lorcan keep the spot he's been sitting in for all these years. He truly has been and is your right hand. I don't think it's fair for me to push him out. Why don't I sit on your other side and that way you have someone who cares about you on each side?" Goldie asked.

The king smiled brightly. "I think that is a fine idea. Tradition sometimes gets in the way of things. You are the princess and I am the king. We can sit where we want."

Beatha clapped her hands. "Child you are so smart and wonderful. Now everyone sit down and eat. It's going to be fun to introduce King Oberon to your food."

There was chili, cheese burgers, Caesar salad, fried shrimp, French fries, milk shakes, and everything else Goldie loved. Goldie groaned as she took a bite out of the cheeseburger. King Oberon laughed and said, "It's that good is it?"

Goldie nodded with her mouth full. King Oberon took a bite out of a cheeseburger and his eyes went wide and he quickly took another bite. Beatha laughed. "Human food is quite tasty. I see you like it."

By the end of dinner Goldie had everyone dipping French fries in milkshake and laughing. Beatha told stories of learning to cook and how she had burnt cornbread the first time she had made it. She talked about learning to cook so she could give Goldie recipes. Goldie felt the tears prick her eyes.

"I love you Beatha." Goldie said looking deep into her eyes.

Beatha's eyes softened and she smiled and said, "And I love you as if you were my own."

The king cleared his throat and said, "I think it's time to retire for the night. I'm actually pretty worn out today. This is the most eventful day I've had in a very long time. Lorcan I expect you to be a gentleman. You two figure out how to make it work. You understand she has to fall asleep first for you to be able to get in her dreams and stay in there to keep her safe."

Lorcan nodded and said, "I understand completely."

King Oberon got up and took Beatha's hand and kissed it, patted Lorcan on the shoulder, and then bent down and kissed Goldie on the forehead before he just disappeared from the dining room.

"I'll never get used to that," said Goldie.

"I'm going to bed too in my very own room," said Beatha smiling.

Goldie looked at her confused.

Beatha smiled and explained, "While I had what you would consider my own home, I never really thought of it as mine. Someone else had built it and I didn't truly pick those things. Here my room is all mine and what I truly want and what my magic can make. It's mine."

Goldie nodded her understanding and then thought how hard it must have been for Beatha again. After having her room the way it was and her truest desires, she could imagine Beatha never really feeling at home.

Goldie rose from her chair and walked over the other woman and hugged her tightly. She didn't say a word to her. She didn't need to. Beatha knew what she was feeling because Goldie let what she was feeling flow to Beatha.

Beatha squeezed her tightly and sent back feelings of warmth, love, security, and pride. When they let go, they still didn't utter a word. Beatha just put a hand on Goldie's cheek and simply vanished from the room.

Goldie turned and faced Lorcan who was studying her. He spoke into her mind, "You are too good for me."

Goldie shook her head at him almost angrily, because he was everything she wanted and her body craved him. She spoke back into his mind, "I'm ready for bed. Are you coming?"

Lorcan smiled at her. He spoke into her mind, "Are you asking me to portal you there or am I to follow you. I'm really ok with either one."

Goldie stuck her tongue out at him and he made his way to her. He wrapped his arms around her waist and in a blink they were in her room.

"You're really going to have to teach me how to do that," said Goldie still holding onto to Lorcan.

He smiled down at her and said, "And miss a chance getting to hold you...I think I'll wait to teach you for a bit." Lorcan kissed her nose and let go, backing away.

Goldie looked at him confused.

"Goldie, this is going to be really hard." Lorcan said looking her over.

Goldie still wasn't quite sure what he meant.

He sighed. "I'm not sure how well either of us will manage sleeping together without getting too crazy. There's no way your da would let me in here, had it not been for the attack on you earlier."

Goldie went rigid. "Attack?"

Lorcan nodded slowly. "The dream you had wasn't just a fluke. It was done on purpose. You were being tested most likely to see how strong you are. For someone to be able to get into your dream and not be close, well that takes a lot of power and dark power at that. I can help protect you in your dreams because of our bond. Together we will keep you safe. When you're sleeping your guard is down and someone could access your memories or find out plans. It's a sneaky warfare, but wars have been won with sneaky information."

Goldie felt light headed and invaded. She swayed and Lorcan caught her. "Hey it'll be ok. I'm here." He said rubbing her back.

Goldie shook her head and whispered, "I'm not sure I can do this."

Lorcan kissed the top of her head. "You are the daughter of King Oberon and part goddess. You can do anything."

Goldie sank into him stealing some of his strength. She knew she would need it.

After a moment, Goldie picked her head up and looked up at Lorcan. His dark eyes gazed down at her. "Can I see your room?" She asked suddenly wanting to see that part of him.

He studied her a moment and then gave a short nod.

"It may disappoint you Goldie. I've never really wanted much." He said as took her hand and led her out of her room and down the hall to the left.

They stopped in front of what looked look like a heavy wooden door with iron hinges. A simple, L, was carved in the middle of it. Goldie traced the L with her finger and her hand glowed. She looked up at Lorcan to see he was studying her again.

"I carved that when I was a wee lad with my first knife. I didn't have anything of my own and this was the first thing I did when your da gave me a room. I wanted a big door to feel safe and I wanted it to be known it was mine. Silly young boy thoughts I suppose." He said looking at the roughly carved L.

"May I?" Goldie asked putting her hand down where there should have been a handle.

Lorcan smiled. "No need for a handle in here. Anyone who is welcome can just walk through. I promise you're welcome."

Goldie was still not used to that. Her door had a knob, but that is how she had envisioned it. She took a deep breath and walked through.

Chapter 18

Goldie's senses tingled on the other side. It was dark in Lorcan's room. His ceiling looked like the midnight sky dotted with stars. His walls were all dark. He wasn't lying when he said he didn't want much. There was a bed in the middle of the room on an iron frame with iron head and foot boards that had dark green vines with red flowers growing on it. His sheets were red satin. He had a single black table by the bed with a picture of a woman on it. Goldie walked over and picked the frame up. She immediately knew it was his mother. She had the same eyes and lips. She looked so kind. Goldie traced her fingers across the picture.

Goldie let her fingers trail to his bed. She gently touched a red flower on a vine and it glowed. She smiled down. She heard Lorcan whisper under his breath, "My light."

She walked the small room. In the corner of his room was a set of armor with two swords. She recognized them from earlier. When she looked back over to the little table by the bed, there was a picture of her. She looked up to Lorcan.

"I decided I needed something else," said Lorcan shrugging his shoulders and smiling sheepishly.

Goldie walked over to an opening to the side of his room. It was his bathroom. She smiled as her feet hit grass. There was no mirror in his bathroom. He did have a giant shower that looked more like a waterfall with cascading water and smooth rocks. He had a single bar of green soap. He had a tree in his bathroom that two towels hung off of. It was simple and efficient. She felt kind of sad for him in that moment. She wondered why he didn't have more.

She walked over to Lorcan and wrapped her arms around his waist. She heard a hum of approval in his chest as she laid her head against him. She thought about how she had felt when she called her room to existence with her thoughts. She thought about how she had felt. She was so happy and curious. Her heart felt whole for the first time. She wondered if Lorcan had ever felt that way. Sure, her father had taken him in and raised him, but he had lost his mother in a violent way. She wondered if he felt that he was just passing through and scared to really set up roots.

Goldie took a deep breath and said, "Lorcan I want you to kiss me."

"Goldie." He warned with a pained groan.

"Lorcan you said you wouldn't kiss me again until I asked. Lorcan will you please kiss me? I need you to kiss me right here. Right now in your room." Goldie said stepping closer to him.

A torn look flashed in Lorcan's eyes. "Goldie I can't promise I'll do right by you if…"

Goldie cut him off with a raised hand. She stepped right in front of him and put her hand up to his face and looked into his eyes. She tried to push her feelings to him. She felt love, adoration, and hope. His eyes softened and he pulled her flush against him. Goldie sighed into the contact. Her hand was still on his face and Lorcan turned his head to kiss her palm. Her hand glowed at the contact.

She smiled up at him and he smiled back. Goldie got tired of him being a gentleman and without prompting, her wings popped out from her back. A surprised gasp shot from her and her feet were off the ground and her face hoovered just above Lorcan's. She smiled down at him. She wasn't going to wait on him, because he wanted to do the right the thing. In this moment she just wanted him to be hers. She smashed her lips on his and his surprised groan made her body melt into him. She felt her wings fold back in and Lorcan's arms wrap around her to hold her steady.

Goldie parted her lips on Lorcan's and he took the hint. He opened his mouth to her and they left no part of the other unexplored. They kissed for what seemed like a lifetime, before Goldie decided to begrudgingly come up for air. When she opened her eyes she let out a shocked gasp.

Lorcan's room was lit up. The walls shown silver and plants sprouted from the floor and walls. On one wall there were pictures of Goldie and Lorcan together. His magic had reacted to his room and now wasn't so dark. Lorcan looked around and smiled and said, "See you are my light."

Goldie smiled at him and made a dissatisfied grunt when he set her back down.

"Goldie as much as I want to let that kiss turn into so much more, we can't. Not here." Lorcan said.

Goldie could see he was pained and she blushed when she looked down at his pants to see the bulge.

Lorcan smiled and said, "Yes you see what you do to me. Your father is just right down the hall. I imagine if we get married he'll move or have us moved."

"If?" Goldie questioned.

Lorcan shook his head and said, "Goldie listen. Really listen. Quiet your mind."

Goldie closed her eyes and shut down what she could of her senses and focused on her hearing. Her eyes popped open wide when she realized she could hear everything. She heard the water in her room and a breeze rustle through the tree. She drew in a gasp when she realized she could hear her father and Beatha down the hall.

"See what I mean? Your father would hear us and that wouldn't be good for him and really not for me. Our first time together should just be for us. I don't know how we will manage it tonight, because the pull for me to have you is almost too much to bare. But I have to try." Lorcan said still keeping distance between he and Goldie.

Goldie nodded. She really didn't want anyone to hear her and then she went pale. Had her father heard her ask Lorcan to kiss her? She had already accidentally let him hear her thoughts before she knew he could hear her. They understood that the bond had pulled them together, but that didn't mean he should hear those things.

Goldie titled her head to the side when she heard her name from somewhere down the hall. Beatha and her da were talking about her in a hushed tone. Lorcan took note and seemed to be concentrating too.

"Goldie doesn't know how much power she has. You would need years to train her properly," said Beatha quietly.

"I know, but we don't have that time. You heard her dream. He's come back I'm afraid," said Oberon.

"But you killed him King Oberon." Beatha said sounding nervous.

"But did I kill his magic or just his body? I have to protect my daughter, but she's all that can save us," said Oberon on a shaky breath.

"And Lorcan. What about him? He loves her and she loves him. Fighting isn't going to be on the top of their list. They won't be able to fight the pull much longer. You can't have Goldie fight for us if she's with child. I won't allow it." Beatha said firmly.

Goldie took in a deep breath and walked over to Lorcan's bed and sat down on the edge. Lorcan moved to sit by her and put a reassuring arm around her.

"What am I to do Beatha Bringer of Life? I'm her father but I am also king. I have the whole Fae realm to think of." King Oberon said on a shallow breath.

"I don't know my son. I do know that we can't take her love from her or she'll resent us. That resentment can turn anyone's magic dark. Lorcan will strengthen her and give her something to fight for, but you have to figure out what we are up against. Her grandmother took a stand a long time ago. Her bloodline will end this darkness." Beatha said sounding soothing.

"I just got her back. I'm not ready to lose her Beatha. She's all I have left of my love." Oberon said sounding pained.

"She is strong enough to be here. Goldie will find a way. Let your daughter be your daughter and find her own way. She handled the Formorians beautifully and I think her time in the human realm prepared her for things that she couldn't have known if she had been raised here. Teach her what you know, but don't try to tie her down." Beatha said sounding sure.

Oberon sighed. "I just love her so much Beatha. The chain that links us together really did click into place the moment our eyes met. It's more powerful than I thought it would be. I have the overwhelming desire to just protect her, but our roles are reversed this time and she doesn't even know it. She will be ruling our kingdom soon."

Goldie shut her eyes tight. She didn't want to hear anymore. She wished she hadn't eavesdropped, but if she hadn't she wouldn't have realized how serious the situation was. And Beatha saying she could be with child. Was that really how it would be? She would just be pregnant as soon as she gave that part to Lorcan? She could think of worse things than carrying his child, but she wanted to have time with him first, but the pull to be with him was so strong. She wasn't sure how to manage this new life.

Lorcan spoke softly, "I don't think they realized you would figure out that you could hear like that. There's so much going on here and you are most likely the salvation. If I have you tonight, on a full moon, you will almost surely become pregnant with our child. You understand how important full moons are. My whole body is aching for you, but you have to be sure before we take that step. You need to know what's coming before we bring life into our world. The only thing I can promise you, is I love you more than my own life. I will always do what I have to do to keep you safe. I love you."

Goldie fell into him and said, "I love you and to be by your side is the only thing I can see in my future."

The two just held each other for a long while. Lorcan broke the silence. "We have to get some rest. Would you like to sleep in my bed or yours?"

"Here is fine," said Goldie sleepily into his chest.

"Ok I'm going to get up and go to the washroom and change into something more appropriate for sleeping," said Lorcan getting up.

Goldie looked around his room. He still had no dresser. It was weird to her still that the house could just provide what you needed. Lorcan disappeared into the washroom. When he came out, he was in cotton pajama pants and no shirt and his hair look tousled. Goldie bit her lip.

"Don't do that. I won't be able to stand it," said Lorcan looking at the lip in between her teeth.

Goldie took in a deep breath and got up to go to the bathroom to do the same. She walked into his washroom and eyed the waterfall shower again. She would love to use that one day soon. There was still no mirror. It kind of bothered her. She wanted to be able to see her reflection. A hand mirror popped into the air in front of her. "Thank you Bhaile." She said in her head.

"You're welcome Goldie Divine."

Chapter 19

Goldie startled at the title but managed not to drop the mirror. She noted that her body seemed more golden than before. She guessed she really was divine, but it was so much to take in. Lorcan had set out an extra toothbrush for her. She smiled and brushed her teeth. She giggled when it disappeared when she was finished. Without asking, her clothes changed. Then she was in a light yellow nightgown with blue flowers on it. It was a spaghetti strap and had a little bow in between her breasts. It went down just above her knees. Goldie laughed. She still looked innocent. She wondered if that would change after she gave herself to Lorcan. It was only a matter of time. She knew that she couldn't fight the pull much longer.

She stepped out of the bathroom to see Lorcan lying on his bed. He was so long and lean. His skinny feet sticking out from his pajamas even looked strong. Goldie shook her head. Lorcan looked up at her and a small smile caressed his lips.

"Shall we sleep?" He asked gesturing to place next to him.

"We can try," said Goldie slowly walking over to the bed to crawl in beside him.

Lorcan let out a snort. "I guess you're right. I'm not likely to sleep very well with you beside me and the full moon."

Goldie climbed into bed beside Lorcan as he held the satin red sheet up. She faced him. His breath smelled minty. She looked up at him. She longed to have her lips touch his again. He looked down at her.

"Your thoughts are very loud," said Lorcan looking down at her.

"What?" Goldie said.

"I guess I should say your feelings? I'm not sure, but while we are touching like this," said Lorcan taking her hand palm to palm and raising it above them and then running his hand down her arm. "I can feel what your feeling and I'm pretty sure I know what you're thinking."

"Oh." Goldie said shivering. Then she focused on Lorcan instead of her own feelings. She felt love and a deep need. She also felt a hidden fear. The fear barely registered because the need was red hot. "Oh," said Goldie again blushing.

Lorcan raised an eyebrow at her and smirked. Goldie hid her face under his chin. Goldie smelled the hollow in between Lorcan's collar bones and all but moaned. He smelled so good. Not thinking she placed a soft kiss there. Lorcan shuddered and closed his eyes. He wrapped his arms tightly around her.

"Goldie I need to keep you with me so I can be part in your dreams, but I can't handle brushed kisses in places only meant for my heartmate. Don't you feel the pull?" He asked.

Goldie did feel the pull. Her body was heating up as if it were preparing. She went to look out of Lorcan's window, but there was no moon to see.

"Lorcan there's no sky down here in the hollow. Why is the moon so important then?" She asked.

"The moon still is full outside the hill. We still need the moon's gravity for the tides and to hold our Earth steady. Although we can't see it. We can feel it. You are a magical being. All the Earth's tiny things will affect you. The moon just happens to be the most significant. We used to venture out of the hill more and would go see the moon. Now we only do that once a year on a full moon." Lorcan explained.

"I love how your ceiling looks like the night sky. It feels like home. I take it you love the sky," said Goldie looking up at his ceiling.

"I love the night sky. The stars are my favorite part. I also like the dark. I have been lucky enough to be one of the Fae that gets to venture out and see the night sky from time to time. I'm the only Fae that has traveled far off on purpose for a mission. I will treasure my time out and with you," said Lorcan squeezing her again.

Goldie's body grew hotter and she felt her insides pulse. She tensed and Lorcan did too. She didn't have to speak for her hammering heart's question to be answered.

Through gritted teeth, Lorcan said, "The moon is at its peak. Our bodies feel it."

Goldie nodded. She began to ache. She whimpered. Lorcan rubbed her back in circles. She could feel his hardness against her. It felt like it was pulsing. She didn't dare look to see. Lorcan let out a groan of discomfort.

"Lorcan?" She whispered.

"I've never experienced this either Las. All I know is our need for each other will become more and more unbearable until the sun rises on the outside world." Lorcan explained.

Goldie tried not to focus on her own feelings. She focused on Lorcan's. He was so uncomfortable. She wiggled against him and felt the sweat starting to bead on her. She threw the sheet off. She felt like a rabid animal and all she knew was her body craved the handsome, tall man next to her. She got out of the bed and paced around the floor.

Lorcan watched her through half lidded eyes and a clenched jaw. "You need to try to rest. I'll get up and watch over you." He said trying not to clutch himself.

"Let's be honest Lorcan. Neither of us is going to sleep while feeling this. I don't know if I can handle it. I don't want to handle it with you right there. I just want to feel you. I want you to make this burning ache stop. Make it stop Lorcan," pleaded Goldie.

Lorcan looked so torn. The words seemed to literally hurt him. "Goldie there will be no turning back. I want to make the ache stop for you. I want to be the one for you," said Lorcan.

"Then be him," said Goldie through clenched teeth and a shaking body.

"Your da...." Lorcan trailed off looking to the side.

Goldie spoke with authority now. "Bhaile can you make this room sound proof?"

Lorcan's eyebrows shot up in surprise. "Goldie what are you doing?"

"My da won't hear us if the room is sound proof. Only we will hear the other and we won't hear the outside world either. Bhaile will take care of us." Goldie said inching back towards Lorcan.

"You sound proofed my room?" Asked Lorcan feeling surprised.

"I didn't, Bhaile did," said Goldie making her way back to him.

Lorcan let out a pained laugh. "Goldie I still have to refuse you. It's not right for me to do this to you."

"What's not right is this ache I'm feeling. It hurts. You can fix it," said Goldie now back at the bed.

"Goldie, once we start I won't be able to stop. What if we make a baby tonight?" Lorcan asked trying to be the responsible one.

"Then we will have a baby and we will figure it out together. We are heartmates and will be with each other forever. Let's start forever now," said Goldie tracing a trembling finger down his arm.

Lorcan looked up her now with glowing eyes. "There's much you don't know Goldie. I will try to be gentle. Forever starts now then. We will be truly bound together from this point on."

Goldie felt her eyes glow too. She gasped when she saw a fleck of red in Lorcan's eyes. Before she could register it, Lorcan was up and in front of her. She hadn't even seen him move. Her body pulsed and his nostrils flared. He reached his head down just under her ear and ran his nose along her neck to her collar bone. A tremble racked her body and Lorcan picked her up and laid her in bed.

"Lorcan I need…"

"Shhh. I know what you need," whispered Lorcan as he placed his mouth over hers.

He kissed her deeply and passionately. The ache only got worse. Goldie tried to pull him closer to her. It wasn't helping. Lorcan ran a shaking hand across her breast and Goldie arched up into his hand. The ache didn't go away but this helped. He caressed her through her night gown. Goldie moaned as he pinched lightly. He then gave the other attention. Goldie started to pant.

Lorcan slid his hand under the night gown and Goldie cried out at the sensation of his hand on her breast skin to skin. Lorcan kissed her deeply and then replaced his hand with his mouth. He kissed, licked, and sucked until Goldie was breathless.

Goldie wanted to touch him too, but she didn't know how. Tentatively she rubbed down his chest and stopped at the top of his night pants. She looked up at him and saw he was breathing heavily. She placed her hand down the top of them and gasped at the firmness that met her. She wasn't sure what to do so she just gently rubbed, until Lorcan took her hand and helped her to grasp him and then he moved her hand slowly up and down.

Goldie gasped as he grew even larger in her hand. She wondered if he would fit. Lorcan closed his eyes and placed his forehead on hers. He spoke into her mind, "Say no now and I will portal away."

Goldie didn't respond instead she made her nightgown disappear. Lorcan took the hint and his pants were gone. Goldie looked down and was shocked at what she saw. They were both glowing. She felt another ache deep inside and she cried out. Lorcan slid his hand down her body and looked into her eyes as his hand reached the only place he didn't know. Goldie let out a sigh when his finger rubbed her little bundle of nerves she didn't know existed.

The ache dulled as he touched her gently. Goldie wanted, no she needed more. Her body pulsed again and Lorcan's nostrils flared again. She arched off the bed. "Lorcan, I need you." She whimpered.

"You're not ready las. I need to get you ready," said Lorcan breathing hard.

Goldie assumed it was taking a lot for him to just not take her. She let out a silent cry as one long finger entered her. It didn't hurt but it was a foreign feeling. He started to slowly move it in and out of her and she writhed. She continued to stroke him. He watched her so intensely. He kept careful watch on her face as he added a second finger. This time it hurt a little, but the horrible ache was even less now. He pumped his fingers inside her and Goldie felt something building. Her eyes went wide. Lorcan still studying her added his thumb in circles over that sensitive nub and Goldie cried out.

Goldie felt weightless as the sensation washed over her. She looked at Lorcan in wonder. He kissed her gently and thoroughly. When Lorcan pulled his fingers out and tasted them, Goldie shook with need yet again. The ache came back even worse and even Lorcan doubled over as her hand slipped from his hardness.

Goldie knew the only way to make the pain stop was to have Lorcan completely. She wasn't nervous until he poised himself over her and she felt him at her entrance. She knew how large he was and was scared it would hurt badly. She had never been touched until just moments before. Lorcan kissed her and entered slowly and stopped. It did hurt. He let her adjust to him and then pushed in some more. Goldie was panting. The ache was completely gone, but now she felt the stretching and tearing of herself as he tried to get into her most secretive place. Lorcan looked down at Goldie with so much love in his eyes that she would take whatever pain that came with being his.

She spoke into his mind, "I'm ok. I'll be better after you are where you need to be."

With that Lorcan pushed the rest of the way in and Goldie cried out as she felt something tear inside and a gush come out. Lorcan stilled deep within her. Their magics mixed and their colors lit up Lorcan's room. He looked like a God hovering over her deeply looking into her eyes. Goldie no longer ached. The pain of his intrusion slowly died down some too. She gasped when he started to move within her and their colors danced with them. He went slowly and moved deliberately. He got more bold as Goldie started to meet his thrusts. She started to pant.

The pain went away completely and all that was left was Lorcan, Goldie, their breathing, and their magic swirling around about them. Every part of Goldie's body felt kissed and touched, as if his magic was making love to her too. Lorcan started to move faster and Goldie arched off the bed. The same feeling from before was building inside her but stronger this time.

"Lorcan," whimpered Goldie, with a voice that sounded to sultry to be hers.

"Yes," said Lorcan in her ear.

He angled his hips so his pelvis hit her just right and he went deeper. Goldie moaned and he let out a groan. Goldie's body started to shake and the feeling was almost at its peak. This was the point of no return. She started to unravel around him and cried out his name. She felt him start to surge inside her and her eyes went wide when she looked up at Lorcan. Fangs protruded from his mouth and he was bearing down on her. He thrust in one last hard time to her core and bit her.

Chapter 20

Goldie woke sometime later. She must have passed out. She felt groggy. Lorcan's arm was protectively wrapped around her chest. They were both still naked. Lorcan must have passed out too. Goldie quickly reached her hand up to her neck. She felt no puncture marks but it was sore. Almost as sore as she was in between her legs. She wasn't sure what had happened. She reached her hand up and carefully pulled Lorcan's arm off of her and slide out of bed.

The painful ache from earlier in the night was gone. There was so much Goldie didn't know. She assumed that them becoming one flesh, made it stop. She looked over to Lorcan again, confused. Why had he bitten her. He didn't tell her he would. It scared her some, but she didn't remember it hurting. All she knew was the heartmate bond was still there and all she could feel was love for him.

When she picked up her hand to brush her hair out of her face, she noticed her crescent moon was glowing. She wasn't sure what that meant either but wanted to find out and needed some air. Lorcan wouldn't need to save her from her dreams if she wasn't asleep.

Goldie wasn't sure how to get out of the castle without waking everyone, so she spoke to Bhaile in her mind. "Bhaile can you hear me?"

Bhaile responded, "I always can Goldie Divine. What is your desire?"

"I want to go out without waking anyone. I know you sound proofed this room. Can I get out from here?" She asked.

"Yes Goldie Divine. You must only walk through the wall, but you must have your wings out to fly or you will fall. Perhaps young Lorcan should accompany you?" Bhaile questioned.

"I'd rather go alone this time Bhaile," said Goldie.

"As you wish. Wings out before you go and you might want to add some knickers and a blouse." The castle reminded before Goldie felt a magical push towards the wall facing outside.

Goldie looked down and blushed at her naked body. She took Bhaile's advice and put on pants and t-shirt. Goldie had an inner talk with her wings, "Ok you've just kind of been popping out when you feel like it. Will you come out now when I want you to?"

Nothing happened. Goldie threw her head back in frustration and then went still, as Lorcan grumbled something in his sleep.

Goldie scrunched her forehead and thought. What had her father said? Then Goldie parted her feet and whispered, "Speir."

Goldie held in the gasp as her wings sprung out from her back. It still hurt at first. She was finding that everything hurt at first. She looked down at her hand to see the moon still glowed. She took a deep breath and gathered her courage and walked through the wall.

At first she was free falling and then her wings took over. It was like instinct. They went to work when she needed them. She realized they were driven by her need. She felt the need to be with Lorcan the first time they had come out. She smiled as she flew out into the dark with only small flickering lights. She felt free. Her heart still pulled back towards the castle, but she knew she needed to step out on her own for a bit. She looked down at the glowing moon on her hand again.

She had the urge to see her moon sister. Goldie rubbed the moon and said, "Angrbora."

Her wings took off without warning and pulled Goldie to the left and headed towards a dark patch of forest. Her wings flew faster and Goldie let out a laugh as wind blew through her hair. On the top of a small hill she saw a form sitting. As she got closer, she could tell the form was a woman and she was looking at her hand. Her hand was glowing with a golden crescent moon.

Goldie's wings slowed and she came to a stop on the hill in front of a giant woman. The woman stood up with a knife in hand. "Angrbora, it's just me." Goldie said raising her hands.

Angrbora quickly put the knife away. "How did you find me?" She asked sounding wary.

"My moon was glowing red and I felt the urge to be with you. I simply said your name and my wings or our bond brought me to you. Are you ok?" Goldie asked.

Angrbora looked at her troubled. "We will be able to find each other then? I am in turmoil yes."

Goldie tilted her head to the side. "Can I help?"

The giant looked at her and studied her for a moment. She then said, "For as long as we have existed, Formorians are taught to trust no one. We have been rejected by our own parents and by any other kind we encounter. We tried to make it on Earth, but were quickly brought down. We don't always choose wisely who to follow. I'm sure you know the story of Goliath. Nowhere in our history has anyone of us every been openly accepted or had a moon sister. Change scares creatures and it scares me."

Goldie nodded in understanding. "Angrbora, I won't pretend I understand completely what you've gone through, but I too lived in a world among people who never truly accepted me either. I guess they can sense I was different. Heck I didn't even really know. I'm scared I'm not cut out for here either. I know literally nothing. I spent my first full moon with my heartmate and it was very intense. But I fear I may have made the wrong choice. The only reason we were spending the night together is because I had a nightmare. He was to protect me from my dreams, but...." She trailed off.

"The moon pulled you together and you couldn't help it. I've heard the stories of the ache that only your mate can quench. A lot of us have never seen heartmates. The first King, our King, didn't believe in heart mates. He wanted to make a strong realm with breeding. That's why he embraced our race so well. There's not much tougher than a Formorian going to war. And we can handle the human realm very well." She explained.

"So my father isn't your king then?" Goldie asked.

"No is the short answer. We do not hate him. He could have had us all killed but he didn't. He spared all the young Formorians and one elder who didn't fight for his own reasons. Formorians don't marry. We don't want to create more cursed babies, so we are raised by older Formorians. But, you see sparing all of us was not just kind, it was cruel. We had no real parents to speak of so taking out all but one of the older Formorians left us without older ones to look after us. Fae were tasked with caring for us, but we had no real relationships after that. The Fae never trusted us and treated us like outsiders. Your father did what he thought was best. He couldn't have the Formorians rise up against him and they might have. I don't know, but my people have a deep heartache. We are still judged by what our elders did and have no real chance to ever rise up in the ranks of anything. Many of us would be in the army if we were allowed." Angrbora told Goldie.

"So you would fight in an army who follows the king?" Goldie asked.

"I know it seems weird. Really all my people need is a chance. There are bad kinds in every type of creature. I would like to think most of us are good though. Some remember how it was with the first king. We had more power and were free to roam anywhere. Some wish for freedom." Angrbora stated full of emotion.

Goldie asked, "And what is it that you wish for Angrbora?"

Her eyes filled with tears. "No one has ever asked me what I wanted before." She thought for a moment. "I wish to serve a good leader I can trust and be a great general for the army of all of Fae realm."

Goldie's eyes glistened too. "I would trust my moon sister as head of my army if I had one."

Angrbora smiled softly, "But you do have an army. As goddess we are your army. We are your children. For hundreds of years, we've lived as forgotten mistakes that the gods created with their lust for humans. We live to serve gods who don't care we exist."

Goldie's hand glowed brighter and so did the giant's. She grasped Angrbora's hand in hers and they glowed together and something else clicked into place. Goldie felt Angrbora's feelings. She felt pride, fear, determination, and hope. Goldie projected her feelings to her moon sister. She gave her love, confidence, respect, and hope back. Angrbora squeezed her hand.

Goldie leaned in and placed a soft kiss on Angrbora's lips. The giant stiffened in surprise. Then she softened under the onslaught and closed mouthed kissed back softly.

Goldie pulled back and said, "From this point on we are one in the same. I promise to do my best for our people, but I will need your help. I will need someone's guidance I can trust. Are you that leader for me Angrbora, moon sister?"

Angrbora let the tear slide down her cheek and nodded. "I promise for you my goddess, my sister."

Goldie kissed her tear away and cupped her cheek. This feeling was foreign to her, but she loved Angrbora deeply. More deeply than a sister or lover. Best friend, confidant? Goldie shook her head to clear it. This moment would forever be on her heart.

"So I assume you came out because you feel troubled?" Questioned Angrbora after she regained her composure.

Goldie let out a nervous laugh. "I'm that easy to read huh? I will have to work on that."

"I'm not sure of all the moon sister rules but while the moon is full I can feel you and I feel your turmoil. I can't read your thoughts or anything like that." She reassured her.

Goldie took a ragged breath. She never shared intimate stuff with anyone besides Beatha, but she didn't want to share this with her. She looked up at her moon sister and nodded. "Ok so tonight I gave myself to Lorcan. It was my first time obviously. The ache the full moon causes is so bad it pushes you to let go. I feel like I am weak because I didn't fight it. But I didn't want to. I wanted him so badly. He was gentle and loving with me.."

Goldie trailed off looking away.

"So what's the problem?" Angrbora ushered.

"When we, you know were at the end, he grew fangs and bit me as he…well you know. And I guess I blacked out?" Goldie's statement rose up into a question.

Angrbora's face went blank. She stiffened.

"What is it Angrbora?" Goldie asked feeling concerned.

"I'm not sure. Are you sure that's what happened and you didn't imagine it from all the fun?" Angrbora asked.

Goldie's forehead scrunched up. "I'm sure. I was shocked. It didn't hurt I don't think."

"Well it wouldn't hurt you. You are his heartmate. The blood Fae were killed off during the war. It was thought no more were alive. Your father must have not known and I'm sure Lorcan is only a small part blood Fae. No one knows who is father is. We just know the first king killed his mother during the war and that your father took him in. Just ask him. He is your mate. He will tell you." The giant reassured her.

Goldie smiled and nodded and said, "You are right. I feel better already after talking to you. I guess it doesn't say much about me that I ran out on him while he was sleeping after our first time together."

Angrbora snorted. "He'll just think that you thought he wasn't very good in bed and he will be out to prove you wrong."

Goldie put her head in her hands and said, "Oh geeze. That's not the case at all. My hand started glowing and I felt the need to get out and then the pull to you. I was called here to you. I guess our magic pulled us together."

"The moon pulled us together. We were both in inner turmoil and we are supposed to be there for one another. I do love you goddess. As weird as it is, I do. I'm not used to this," said Angrbora gesturing between the both of them.

"Me either. I went from only having two people in my life to a whole realm and three new people that I'm bound to by blood, heart, magic, and moon." Goldie replied. "Hey where are we anyway?" Goldie asked.

"We are on the edge of the dark forest," answered Angrbora.

Goldie shivered. Angrbora put her arm around her. "What is it?"

"In my nightmare I was running through this forest barefoot while a monster chased me. I knew I was going to die. I called out for Lorcan but he wasn't there. He came in real life of course, because apparently heart bonds make it to where he can hear my thoughts and my distress in dreams." Goldie said shivering again.

Angrbora rubbed a big hand up and down her arm. "You can always call for me too and I will come. Maybe not in a dream but in real life. The dark forest isn't too scary if you know where you're going. Most Fae are scared of it because it comes from dark magic, but I think the world needs both light and dark."

Goldie thought about that for a moment and said, "You may be right. Day needs night. The sun needs the moon. It's balance. So our realm is out of balance then?"

Angrbora just shrugged. "I don't know about all that. I do know that heroes arise from hardships. I think it takes it all to make the world go round."

Goldie and her moon sister sat on the hill and watched the darkness slowly turn into light. Goldie stared at the black thorned vines in the forest in front of her and at some point her and Angrbora fell asleep leaning on each other on that hill.

Goldie awoke to hear rustling coming up the hill and voices shouting her name. She opened her eyes to see her father and Lorcan topping the hill. Her eyes met Lorcan's and his glowed. Immediately Angrbora jumped up with her knife ready to defend Goldie. Lorcan pulled his swords.

"How did you get your princess out of the castle Formorian?" Shouted the king.

"She is not my princess. She is my goddess and sister," spat Angrbora.

"You better have not harmed a hair on her head," said Lorcan through clenched teeth.

Angrbora looked straight at him and didn't say a word. Lorcan blanched and swallowed hard. Angrbora just nodded.

Goldie started to shake with fury. How could the people she loved act so ignorantly. She felt her body heat and she began to glow. "ENOUGH!!" She boomed and light shot out from her causing everyone to drop their weapons and shield their eyes.

"Forgive me goddess," said Angrbora going down on one knee.

Goldie grew in height and cut her eyes at everyone. Her voice took on another dimension as she spoke with authority. "I can't believe what I have witnessed this morning. The three people I am supposed to be closest to going at one another like school children. I've heard prejudice, insinuation, and coldness. I left the castle last night. I needed air and to think. Did not one of you just think to call for me? It was a full moon, my first full moon here with a heart mate and a moon sister. I was called to both. Did no one think this would be a lot for me? Angrbora is not the problem here. She was a true sister to me last night and she will be my head council."

The king started to say something but Goldie held her hand up. "Da I love you but there is much you don't understand that I do. The Formorians need a chance. Angrbora has pled her allegiance to me and her and I are one in the same. How you treat her is how you treat me. She was here for me last night in a way that neither one of you could be."

Lorcan spoke now, "You couldn't have discussed it with Beatha? She's been by your side your entire life."

Goldie narrowed her eyes. "Some things you don't talk about with your mother figure."

Lorcan looked down and the king looked at him now. "I thought you were going to respect her. I thought I could trust you. I didn't hear anything…You took her innocence the first full moon?"

Goldie threw her hands up and more light shot to the men. "Ugghh! Da I sound proofed the room. You of all people should have done a better job of warning us about what would happen. I ached so badly it hurt. Lorcan could fix that. I all but made him. I gave him my innocence because I wanted to. Who says I didn't take his?"

Lorcan looked at the ground again and Goldie huffed. "Of course I didn't take your innocence. Your Lorcan, the Fae king's mighty right hand. I guess the Fae realm is just like the human realm, women are held to a different standard than men. Well guess what boys, that changes. I'm so stupid to think I would come here and my world would make sense and everything would be ok. That love would piece back together the gaps in my heart."

The dark forest shimmered and grew out two more feet. Everyone looked to it surprised.

"That's the most it's grown at once." Her father breathed out.

"Goddess I think it's reacting to your feelings," said Angrbora nervously. "You would do well to mind the goddess and show her the respect she deserves. You're upsetting her further."

Lorcan spoke in a whisper, "Goldie I'm sorry. I'm sorry. I love you. We need to talk about so many things. Please forgive me. I never wanted to be the one to cause your hurt. You know that. Feel my heart. Feel what I'm feeling."

Goldie shrunk back down to her normal size but kept glowing. She opened herself up to his feelings. He felt remorse, regret, fear, and most of all unconditional love. She then looked to her dad with pleading in her eyes. He nodded and she opened herself up to his feelings. He felt loss, regret, deep pain, and most of all unconditional love. She let her tears fall freely.

Where each tear hit the ground, a golden flower bloomed lighting up the ground of the black hill.

Angrbora said, "Goddess look." And put a hand on her shoulder.

Goldie looked down at the golden flowers around her feet. She smiled and said, "Out of my sorrow came something beautiful. It's not all for naught."

"Nothing is ever for naught. We learn from it. I've learned that I have a true leader to follow in you. You will make your people proud. Go talk to your father and your heart mate. Love can fix your gaps, because it's slowly fixing mine," said Angrbora placing a gentle kiss on Goldie's lips.

Lorcan and the king both gasped in shock. "I will see you for lunch," said Goldie to Angrbora before turning to face the two men she wanted to pummel.

Chapter 21

The two men stood with their mouths agape. Goldie just looked at them confused. She didn't say another word to them. She just whispered, "Speir." And this time she was prepared for the sharp pain that came with her wings and she embraced it.

She took flight in the morning sky. The two men followed behind her. Goldie let the wind wash over her. She waved at the Fae below bustling about who waved up at her.

"Goldie that Formari..." She cut a look at her father.

He cleared his throat, "Your moon sister showing that kind of connection and emotion is unheard of. Formorians do not kiss. They don't even kiss when they are intimate." He choked on the last word.

"That's so sad to think they have been treated so poorly, felt so unwanted that they don't feel deserving of a kiss. I kissed her first last night," said Goldie.

Lorcan choked on the air. "You kissed her?"

Goldie smirked at him. "What you afraid I'm trading you in for a giant woman?"

He looked at her flatly and with concern.

"It wasn't that kind of kiss, just one of tenderness and care. They've never been shown either of those things." Goldie said.

"You sound like a mother," said Lorcan before flinching at his word choice.

King Oberon spoke then, "And she may very well be after what you did last night. It was a full moon. I knew it was big possibility and I guess it outweighed the danger she was in. Lorcan are you ready to be a father? I mean really? You will have a lot of responsibility with a babe since your wife is part goddess and will be ruling this realm."

"It's a little late now for this talk. All I know is I love Goldie with every fiber of my being and I'll be the best father to our child. He or she will be the best parts of us and I had a really great father to show me how." Lorcan said looking at the king.

The king's face softened and he said, "I know you will. We all just have high emotions. This has been a trying time. We all just want the best for Goldie and the realm and forget how love can push us in crazy ways. I do want you two to pick a wedding date. If a seed did take hold, I would like you married before you get round." He directed the last part to Goldie.

"And the war?" Lorcan asked.

The king smiled. "It seems that my daughter already has an army. She will just need to learn to fortify her mind and wield some magic. If she's with child we will keep her out of the serious fighting."

They all just flew through the wall when they got back to the castle and they headed straight for the dining room. Beatha was already seated with a buffet out before them. She smiled as Goldie walked over and hugged her neck.

Beatha said, "I told them you'd come back and that you were ok. They didn't listen."

Goldie laughed. "It's ok. My goddess side came out and I almost blinded them. I was with my moon sister last night. I felt drawn to her and needed air."

Beatha nodded with understanding. "Next time, swim on the full moon and see how that makes you feel. Your Granna always swam on a full moon."

Goldie smiled and said, "I will."

Goldie laughed as she watched her father try waffles with butter and syrup for the first time. He didn't like much from the human realm but he did like the food. They talked and her father was talking about the wedding and how it would be good for the kingdom to see a happy union.

Goldie finally said, "Lorcan hasn't even asked me to marry him yet. Well not really. He hasn't proposed."

King Oberon looked confused.

Beatha chuckled. "In the human realm men get down on one knee with a beautiful diamond ring and ask the woman if they will marry them."

King Oberon looked even more confused. "Is that really necessary if they have a heart bond?"

"Humans believe in soul mates, but everything is choice. It's special for a woman to be proposed to. The man puts effort into picking out a perfect ring and in the end it's her choice to say yes or no. Not all human traditions are silly." Explained Beatha.

Oberon looked over at Lorcan and just said, "Good luck."

Goldie laughed. "I'm not sure that the proposal is necessary, you already know I'm going to say yes."

"Even after I hurt you?" Lorcan asked.

Goldie knew this had to do with more than what had happened that morning. She also felt sad that Fae didn't understand you could be upset and hurt by someone, but not give up or walk out on them.

"Lorcan from what I understand, we will be together for hundreds of years. This won't be our last misunderstanding. We have to learn to work through them together. My heart couldn't handle parting from you." Goldie said.

Before she could comprehend it, Lorcan had her chair pulled out from the table and was kneeling in front of her holding her hands in his. He reached his hands up to grasp her face and pulled her lips to his in front of Beatha and her father. She willingly kissed him and placed her hands on the back of his neck. When he pulled away he whispered on her lips, "I love you so much."

She smiled with tears in her eyes and said, "I love you more."

Lorcan took her left hand in his and rubbed circles on her ring finger. A ring appeared. It was platinum with a blood red diamond surrounded by small black diamonds. On either side of the ring were two white diamond filled bands.

Lorcan said, "Be the light to my darkness forever."

Goldie did the same to his ring finger and a golden band appeared with waves on it and she said, "I'll be the light in the dark if you promise to always find me."

Lorcan nodded and Goldie grasped his face and brought it back to hers and kissed him as if her father and Beatha weren't in the room. They only stopped kissing when her father cleared his throat.

"Well with the proposal cleared up, we need to pick a date. Beatha will you help Goldie with all that?" King Oberon asked.

Beatha put her hand to her heart and let the tears fill her eyes. "Nothing would make me happier."

Goldie blew her a kiss and Beatha winked at her.

"Lorcan will you go with me to the camp. There is much we need to discuss. I want to make sure we are on the same page before I step aside for you and my daughter to rule. There is much we need to finish first too. I want my grandchildren to come into a peaceful world without the threat of darkness." The king said.

Lorcan gave a nod.

Goldie spoke up, "Please call Angrbora to join you. She will be head of my personal army. She should know what's going on. Her team will need to be prepared too. We are going to give them a chance. I'm supposed to have lunch with her today anyway, so I can leave with her afterward."

"Very well," said King Oberon warily.

Goldie smiled and nodded. "I'm going to go take a shower. I'll see you later. I love you all."

In unison they said, "Love you too."

Goldie smiled at that.

Lorcan got up and said, "I'll accompany you to your room."

He took Goldie's hand and they walked out of the dining room and then he teleported them to her room. "Who said I was going to my room to shower?" Goldie asked eyebrows raised.

Lorcan laughed and said, "Oh?"

"I was planning to sneak into your waterfall shower and use all your soap." Goldie said mischievously.

"That can still be arranged," said Lorcan teleporting her into his bathroom.

Goldie giggled. "Why are you teleporting me?"

"Well I said I would accompany you. You know that takes a good while in this large castle to walk anywhere and I was hoping when I said accompany they would assume we walked. Now I have time to kiss you and tell you how beautiful you are and how much I love you," said Lorcan kissing her neck.

Goldie's body heated and her need for him rose. Lorcan's nostril's flared. Goldie looked at him curiously.
"Can you smell me?"

"I can smell your need and it drives me crazy," said Lorcan sniffing her neck and then stilling.

"Goldie I'm sorry about last night. I didn't know…I mean I've never had that happen before. I guess my father or heck maybe my mother had some blood Fae in them. I'm sorry. Do you still want to marry me?" He asked.

Goldie held his face in her hands, "There's nothing you could do that would make me not want to marry you. We are both learning new things about ourselves. We will work through it all together. You didn't hurt me, but I think I passed out."

"I passed out from the pleasure I think," said Lorcan.

Goldie snorted. He just looked at her with a goofy grin. Goldie closed her eyes and made her clothes come off. Lorcan's nostrils flared again and he looked at her. She smirked and turned to the waterfall that was already cascading.

"I'm supposed to go with your father," said Lorcan pained.

"Then you better get going," said Goldie looking over her shoulder at him while checking the water temperature with her hand.

It was perfect. Goldie looked at her handsome fiancée and smiled impishly. She wondered if she could get him naked with her magic or her thoughts. Her smile widened at her brazenness. She closed her eyes and before Lorcan could say, "What are you up to?" He was naked too.

Lorcan looked down and laughed. "Goldie…." He warned.

She fluttered her eyelashes and said, "Yes Lorcan?"

"You know I really shouldn't do this right now. Your father is waiting on me," said Lorcan trying to talk himself into leaving.

"Then I guess you should be going," said Goldie stepping into the water and letting it cascade down her body.

When she titled her head back and closed her eyes to get her hair wet, Lorcan was on her. He kissed her exposed neck and rubbed his body against hers. He groaned when Goldie reached down in between them and stroked him with water helping her hand glide along him. She smiled.

He kissed her mouth and asked, "Are you not too sore? I don't want to hurt you."

"If you say one more word about hurting me, I'm going to, ahhh…" Goldie moaned as he thrust deep inside her up against the stone wall.

He moved with purpose and vigor. "I'm sorry las. I want to take my time, but I can't. Hold on to me. This one is going to be hard and fast."

He pounded into her relentlessly and it did hurt her sensitive core that was sore from the night before. She didn't complain though, she had wanted this. She welcomed the pain and opened her legs wider for him to go deeper. He moaned and she kissed his neck. She felt Lorcan push his magic into her. She felt what he was feeling. He was so so close. She felt it. Feeling what he was feeling she knew he could make her finish with him with just his magic and thoughts. She smiled at him and he looked at her. She felt his pace get frantic and somehow knew she could help him get there. She bit his neck.

Chapter 22

Lorcan cried out as he exploded inside Goldie. She could literally feel the force of him. He went on and on for some time like that, until she was so full of him that it had nowhere else to go but out around them. Their magic pierced every corner of the bathroom and they rode the high together.

When Lorcan finally stepped away from Goldie they were both trembling and it wasn't until Lorcan whipped the smear from her mouth that she realized she had bitten down on him enough to make him bleed. When she licked his fingers clean of his blood, Lorcan's eyes glowed but this time showed more red.

He stepped into her space and kissed her forehead and said, "I love you more than you could know. I don't know how you did that, but you are perfect."

"I love you and I would like to do this every way imaginable with you. There are so many things to explore. Go my da is waiting for you. Hey he doesn't smell things like you do does he?" She asked.

Lorcan chuckled. "I don't think so. That's a new thing since you've come into my life. It seems the heart bond and mating brings out new things in me. But if he could smell like me, he wouldn't know where I ended and you began." He said and quickly kissed her.

Goldie swatted his arm and said, "Go. I still need to wash. I'll see you later. Love you."

Goldie took her time washing and enjoyed the hot water from the cascading waterfall. The warm water had the rocks heated up and she put her back against the rocks and sighed. She smiled as she washed her hair thinking of all the places Lorcan had touched her. She touched her lips and thought of him on them. Then she thought of Angrbora and pressing her lips to hers. She wasn't sure why she had kissed her but felt the need to like Angrbora was part of her.

She shook her head and finished up. She smiled as she noticed her towel from her room laid out for her. Lorcan must have called it over before he left. She reached out in her mind to him and whispered, "Thank you."

He whispered back in her mind, "No. Thank you."

She smiled and continued to dry off and picked up the little hand mirror to look at herself. She looked different. More golden again and healthier. She looked happy. Her happiness faded though, when she thought about her Granda. She missed him terribly.

"Bhaile?" Goldie called out.

"Yes Goldie Divine?" The ambiguous voice replied in her mind.

"If I write a letter to my Granda in the human realm can you get it to him?" She asked,

"I believe so. No one has asked that of me before. I do like these new challenges," replied the castle.

"I do like you Bhaile. One more thing, will you dress me to go to lunch with my Formorian people?" Goldie asked.

Bhaile answered and sounding happy, "It would be my honor."

In an instant Goldie was adorned in black leather pants, a tight leather corset, a red jacket, and her hair was braided back with black leathers. Red lipstick was on her lips and black eyeliner was around her blue eyes. She had throwing knives in the inner pockets of the red jacket.

"Bhaile I don't know how to throw knives." She said looking at them.

"These are special just for you. With your magic all you have to do is picture the target in your mind and throw. They will go exactly where you want them to." The castle explained.

"You're the best. Thank you for looking after me." Goldie said wishing she could hug the castle.

"It's good to have our princess returned home and a goddess no less. I wish I could hug you too. This is one of the first times I wish I had a body," said Bhaile.

"You can't make yourself one?" Goldie asked.

"No. I'm here to serve whoever is ruling the realm. That is my only job. You are the first to really talk with me. Have a good time at lunch Goldie Divine," said Bhaile with a smile in its voice.

Goldie blew a kiss at the room nowhere in particular but knew the castle got it when the room shimmered.

Before going down to meet Angrbora, Goldie went back to her bedroom and sat on her bed with a pen and notebook that was already waiting her. She really did love the castle. She wondered what all she could tell Granda and didn't want to put him in any danger. She thought with the pen in her mouth and then she began to write:

Dear Granda,

I miss you terribly. My new place is magical. I have a bathroom even you would love. It's different here, but I'm finding my way. It's not without problems, but hey is there fair winds every day? Lorcan asked me to marry him. I said yes. He really loves me. My father is larger than life. You will like him and you will love his favorite place. The food is different, but good. I have made some true friends here too and Mack is living in a tree with other raccoons. There's a little girl one there that he likes. I feel like I've changed a lot, but I'm still the same on the inside. I have a huge responsibility here, but because of how you raised me, I'm better equipped to handle it than others that have been here forever. I wish I could tell you everything, but I wouldn't have enough paper. I'm actually about to go to lunch with someone who is more of a sister to me than anything. I can't wait to introduce you to everyone. I love you so much.
See you soon!
Your Charm

Goldie folded up the paper and left it on top of her dresser. It wasn't necessary to say anything. She knew Bhaile saw it. Then she cringed to wonder if Bhaile saw what happened in the shower. She shook her head and walked through her door. She had wanted the door because that was what was normal to her and she honestly still liked the looks of it, but she didn't have to open it to get through.

Goldie made her way through the halls and down to get to the front room. She still didn't know how to portal. She needed to learn right away. She heard hushed voices as she got closer.

"Does the king know?" It was Angrbora.

"No. What was I supposed to tell him? Oh since your daughter and I banged until we passed out, I realized that I have blood Fae in me and I bit her." Lorcan said sarcastically.

"Do you have it under control?" She asked him.

"Well it's a very new development, but yes. I can't be that much. I think that it was just a full moon heart bond thing." Lorcan said breathing heavily.

"Oh so you'll only be biting her on full moons. Great," said Angrbora cynically.

Goldie cleared her throat and they quieted quickly. She turned the corner and walked in. Angrbora let out a whistle and Lorcan swallowed hard.

Lorcan said, "You look, you look…"

"Bad Ass!!" Angrbora finished for him.

Goldie smiled and did a spin. "I even have some really handy throwing knives made just for me."

"Sweet," said Angrbora.

Lorcan was still staring. "Wait. Throwing knives?"

Goldie nodded. "You never know. A girl's got to be prepared."

"I'm thinking you need to rain check lunch and go back to your room with me," said Lorcan, eyes starting to glow.

Goldie shook her head no. "I'm going to lunch with the head of my personal guard and meeting my people. I'll be back in one piece still in this outfit." She walked up to Lorcan and pecked his lips.

He groaned and pulled her to him and kissed her fervently. She pulled away and said, "You're going to smear my lipstick."

He shook his head no. "Not in Fae realm. You still look perfect. Have fun, but not too much. Angrbora take care of her."

"With my life," said Angrbora.

Angrbora and Goldie left the castle. They walked slowly along. Everyone stared at Goldie with the large Formorian woman. Goldie waved and talked to people as they went and introduced them to Angrbora as the head of her personal guard. People were shocked but didn't say a word, but when Goldie let her mind barrier down, she heard all kinds of nasty things from the thoughts all around her.

"How could she betray her father like that?"

"Formorians can never be trusted. She'll slit her throat in her sleep."

"Foolish girl. Just because she has goddess blood, doesn't mean she's all powerful."

"She's here to change our whole world."

Goldie quickly put her barrier back up. Angrbora noticed Goldie's pained expression. "You can hear what they think can't you?"

Goldie nodded.

"I will understand if I need to step down," said Angrbora putting her head down.

"Absolutely not. I'm not here to bend to everyone's will. I'm here to save our people and do what's best for the realm." Goldie explained.

"I'm proud to serve you," said Angrbora.

"Now with all due respect, if you'll get to goddess size, we can make it to lunch a lot faster." Angrbora said nudging Goldie.

Goldie laughed and visualized herself larger. She sprouted up. People around her gasped and she just smiled at them.

"Walk with more confidence and authority and people won't question as much," said Angrbora.

"I don't want them to fear me, just respect me and give me a chance," said Goldie in reply.

"Well, fear is easiest if I'm being honest. Respect takes time. You have to earn it." Angrbora said with a nod.

They made their way out of town and to the outskirts. They walked up the black hill that now had a spot with golden flowers on it and started down the other side. All Goldie could see was the dark forest.

"You live in the dark forest?" Goldie asked.

"Yes. It's safe for us here. No one comes searching in the dark forest unless they are desperate. Everyone is scared of the dark magic, but the dark forest isn't all bad. You will see. It's just misunderstood. It was created after all. Think about this, is it the creation's fault for being different and feared or the creator? Formorians have dealt with this from day one. We didn't ask to be created or born, but here we are and we are feared just because of what we are." Angrbora said thoughtfully.

"That's an excellent point. It's never really the creation's fault at least not a forest or an animal. However intelligent beings have the option to choose their paths. I don't think the whole sum should be judged by just what a few have done, but like you said, respect takes time. Changing people's outdated views takes even longer. Together we will do this." Goldie said.

"Now the dark forest is full of vines with thorns. It's meant as protection. There are safe places to walk. Close your eyes and feel the forest with your magic. It will light the way," said Angrbora.

Goldie did as she was told. The vines looked like tangled spaghetti in her mind, but sure enough like a path of stepping stones there was a lit pathway. She took the first step tentatively and then kept going.

As she walked along her mind map, Angrbora spoke, "The key to your safe arrival is trust. The moment you open your eyes and stop trusting the forest and your magic, you will get tangled up."

"It's like our castle walls, as long as you're welcome, you can pass right through," said Goldie.

"Yes more similar than you know. All magic has the same root. Just because something is dark, doesn't mean it has to be used for bad." Angrbora said, "Think about knives for example. They can be used for bad things like killing, but they also cut food and can be used as tools. My knife can start fires if need be, cut rope, cut food, and protect me. Just because the knife can kill, doesn't mean I have to use it for that."

Goldie mulled all that over in her mind. Everything just was misunderstood. She halted when the map in her mind stopped.

"We are here. Open your eyes Goldie." Angrbora said putting a hand on her shoulder.

Goldie opened her eyes and gasped at the view in front of her. There were lanterns hanging from all the trees to form a circle and lanterns dotted off to mark pathways. It was beautiful. The wooden buildings were huge. They looked like old Victorian style houses. They all had colorful trim and looked inviting. It was hard for Goldie to believe that people that had such beautiful craftsmanship, didn't feel loved or of worth.

"It's beautiful," said Goldie spinning in a circle to take it all in.

Angrbora smiled. "Follow me goddess. We are going to the tavern for food and drink."

Goldie followed her. Angrbora took her to far side of the circle and they walked into the biggest building. It was huge old school restaurant style pub. It was packed with Formorians. Goldie straightened her shoulder and smiled at everyone.

Angrbora shouted, "Get up and recognize our goddess! She has come to be among us!"

Simultaneously everyone stood and placed their right hand over their heart and bowed their heads. Goldie stood still and looked around. She was in shock. They revered her.

"Thank you all. Please be at ease. I just want to be one of you and part of you." Goldie said.

"It is us goddess that are part of you," said a huge blonde man.

Goldie's breath hitched in her throat when her light blue eyes met the light blue eyes of the tall blonde Formorian. Another chain clicked in place. She didn't know how, but she was bound to this man somehow. His eyes registered shock too. Angrbora watched the exchange.

The man walked over to Goldie, took her hand, and knelt in front of her and said, "Blood of my blood. You have come home."

Chapter 23

Goldie gasped in shock but she felt a familiar zing in her hand as he clasped it in his large one. When he stood, he looked down at her, even though she was in her taller form. She saw a resemblance in them. Her grandmother had looked like this man. She had seen the picture her Granda had.

"How?" Is all Goldie managed to say.

The giant of man smiled bemused. And took her hand and led her to a table in the back.

"I am your great grandfather, Godfrey." He announced as she sat down.

Goldie looked at him still confused. "My great grandfather Godfrey? You're going to have to fill me in, because I've just recently learned a lot about myself. I've thought I was human for well, my whole life."

He smiled at her. He had a wide mouth with straight teeth. He had no gap though. His blue eyes seemed to twinkle with golden light. He didn't look old enough to be her great grandfather. He at most looked forty. He wore a sleeveless robe that was cream with golden scroll work on it. He had a large golden sword at his right hip.

"I'm sure you didn't hear much about your great grandmother las. Our story was tragic like all the others. Two lovers stuck on opposing sides. Our love was forbidden. We met in secret. Formorians were a lot different in those times. Your great grandmother changed me with her love. Love really can change things. When I held your Granna for the first time, I knew I could no longer fight for the first king. I did get to see your Granna and I watched her from afar. If they would have known I was her father, they would have killed her. You resemble her. You have our eyes. You are beautiful young one." Godfrey said with an emotion hidden in his voice.

Goldie opened up her senses. She wanted to see what he was feeling.

 He smiled and said, "You must only ask. We hide those things to guard our hearts here." He touched his thumb to her forehead and she felt love. Yes love from an old Formorian. She felt pride and she felt hope. She also felt a deep seeded fear. She pulled back.

"What is giant of man like you afraid of?" She questioned.

His face sank and he said, "I promised myself I would hide no truths from you, because you my child are what your grandmother foretold. You should know it's not only our world you will have to prove yourself to, but the world of the Gods. They could decide you are too much of a risk. Formorians are not supposed to reproduce. We are not supposed to love. We are only supposed to go to war for whoever is ruling over us. Our human parents can't handle raising us and we are an abomination to the gods, but they won't kill their bastards, their love children in a twisted way. They watch us help to mold and rule the world with iron fists and anger."

Goldie shivered and for the first time felt real fear other than in a dream.

Godfrey continued, "You don't have that part of me. You only got the best parts. You will change the world for us. You are proof that Formorians can love and you are so much more powerful than your great grandmother and I could have ever imagined. It took the right bloodlines for you to be what you are. I don't know who your human Granda is, but he must be a great man of character for you not to be watered down."

Goldie softly smiled and said, "He's the best. I miss him terribly. He loves fully."

"I hope I can get to know you while you are here, but my beautiful, young one, you will have tread carefully. Come to me if you need anything. I will not hide in the shadows when it comes to you. I've hidden long enough. Young Angrbora has done well with leading our people in the light. I will join when the time is right." Godfrey said clapping a hand over hers.

Goldie felt the warmth of his love and his strength. He was old and strong.

"What should I call you?" Goldie asked the giant.

"Whatever you feel comfortable with. I know it'll take time to get to know me." Godfrey said understandingly.

"I don't know the Irish language well. What would you call your great grandfather if you had one? I call my grandfather now Granda." Goldie wondered aloud.

Godfrey smiled and said, "If I had one, I think I would call him Daideo'."

"Then that's what I shall call you. Daideo'." Goldie said smiling. "Am I allowed to hug you?" Goldie asked tentatively.

Godfrey's face lit with happiness and he said, "I should like that very much."

Goldie said, "Oh good because I am hugger." And she got up from the table and wrapped her arms around the huge man's neck.

He wrapped her up in his brawny, long arms and held her tight. She was pretty sure his arms could all but wrap around her twice. She placed her head on his chest and just sat there. She felt safe there. She knew without a doubt this man would do anything to protect her and it was a glorious feeling.

When she let go of Daideo', the pub was quiet and watching the exchange.

"They are not used to new ones coming in and wanting to show affection. We are so used to just being feared and disliked," said Angrbora as Goldie looked from face to face.

Goldie stood tall and smiled. "Would any of you care for a hug? They don't cost a thing and are pretty amazing."

The Formorians looked from one to another and shifted. They seemed to want to give her a hug but were afraid to step up. Goldie looked down at her Daideo' who was seated still. He shrugged a shoulder and said, "You all have my permission to give my granddaughter a hug if you'd like. No funny business."

There was almost an audible sigh and one by one, every single giant in the room came and wordlessly gave her a hug. One lady sighed at the contact. One shivered. One let a tear slide down their face. And one man held on a little too long and her great grandfather prodded him along. Angrbora hugged her last. "Moon Sister and Goddess you bless us with your presence and your gentleness towards us. We will fight by your side and for you."

The rest of the large men and woman but their hands over their heart and in unison yelled, "Aaroof!"

Goldie nodded at them and said, "It is you who bless me. Together we will forge a better realm for not only us but our children. I believe everyone should all be allowed to love, marry, and have families. You are part of my family. I have blood here and a moon sister. That will not be over looked."

After that they ate. The food was delicious. It was fire roasted boar and roasted potatoes and green beans. They drank dark ale and water. The conversations were lively. They talked about old wars and who they were. Goldie learned of the games they liked to play. They all introduce themselves to her and when the eating was over, the music started. It was a lot of flute type instruments and guitars. It was upbeat and lively. Goldie danced with everyone there. They spun in circles jumping and laughing. She felt like she was at a huge family reunion.

Before she left, she hugged everyone again. This time the Formorians weren't so stiff and welcomed the hug. They all thanked her and welcomed her back anytime. She promised to be back soon. Her great grandfather kissed her forehead and said, "Go in light and love young one."

Angrbora walked Goldie back through the dark forest, again with closed eyes and only using a mind map. The path was different this time. Goldie asked, "Does the map change every time."

Angrbora answered, "It does. Another way we are kept safe."

"You know earlier when I got angry and the dark forest grew, why do you think it did that? I'm having a hard time believing that it is bad when it protects you." Goldie asked her moon sister.

"I really don't know. The dark forest used to cover the realm, but it was malignant. It choked off other life and kept the world very dark. The only one I've ever seen grow it was the first king. He was so dark. He forced us into his army, but we liked war and glory then. We liked to be feared. The first king was part Formorian and part blood Fae. That is why your great grandfather is worried the gods might think you too dangerous. You are part of many things and are only growing in power." Angrbora answered her friend.

"There's just so many unanswered questions and I don't understand how my power keeps growing." Goldie stated.

"Even just a little god blood mixed with magical Fae blood can do many things. And you're here now. Our ground will only help you grow in power. The magic is living here. It flows from being to being and back into the Earth." Angrbora answered.

"So Formorians don't have powers?" Goldie asked.

Angrbora gave a sad smile, even though Goldie couldn't see it. "The gods didn't feel like we needed more powers other than being giant and crazy strong. They were afraid if we had magical powers paired with our war skills and strength that we would take over the entire world. In all honesty, we might have. We probably would have tried to take on the gods themselves. You see what the first king did with his power."

"My great grandfather hid his feelings from me?" Goldie said as a question.

"That is really not a magical ability per say. We all guard what we feel and our expressions on our faces as a way of protecting ourselves. We can hide our feelings but allow them out when we want. Your grandfather is the oldest of us, so he can project his through touch somewhat, but that's it. Most of us do have heightened senses though. We hear and see better than most." Angrbora explained.

Goldie nodded and then remembered they were walking with their eyes closed and her moon sister couldn't see her. "Ok. I'm just trying to take it all in. So during the wars, Formorians fought magical beings. How did they not lose? I mean sure the race is good at war and fighting, but magic would seem to be something that could harm you."

"Yes it can, but it takes much more to kill us. We are still part god, even if we don't have powers. And when the first king was in charge, he would have us armor and shields made that had magical defenses cast on them. We can't perform magic but we can be protected by it in things we wear or hold." Angrbora said.

"Ok I get it now I think. Thank you for teaching me about all of this. And thank you for trusting me to go to your home and meet our people. I can't believe I have a great grandfather." Goldie said breathlessly.

Angrbora laughed. "I had wondered when I saw you at first but wasn't sure. Seeing you with Godfrey though makes perfect sense. He has always been the most sensible of us and always seemed to possess something no one else did. Now we know it was love."

Goldie made her way to the castle. She told Angrbora she could fly the rest of the way. It would be faster. Goldie thought of everything she had learned and of all the fun she had with really what were her people. She was finding out that she really had part of all the creatures in her. She wondered more about her great grandmother now.

Lorcan's voice rang out in her mind. "My love are you getting close to being back home or did you trade me in on a giant?"

"I'm in the sky headed back. I had the best time and met some really great beings. I have so much to tell you. Meet me in the dining room with Da and Beatha please." Goldie said back.

Goldie sighed in relief when the castle was in view. She laughed to herself thinking about how quickly, just a day really, and this place felt like home. She eyeballed the walls and tried to figure out which one would directly into the dining room. She thought she knew where. She flew right into the wall and went through easily.

She didn't find herself in the dining room though. She was in a small dark closet. Even her enhanced eyes couldn't see much. She decided to feel her magic within to light up so she could see. Her body went warm and began to glow. Her breath hitched in her throat at the sight before her. What she thought was a small closet was just an entry way into an even darker room. She was in a torture chamber.

Chapter 24

Goldie didn't know what to do. She was curious and mortified. There were all types of instruments for torture; stretching board, shackles with teeth, clamps, whips with glass shards in the ends, hooks, pliers, and all sorts of sharp objects. She walked over to what looked to be a cabinet and opened the doors. She jumped back at the appalling sight before her. There were labeled jars, hundreds of jars; all filled with eyes.

There were eyes from every type of creature, including small animals and humans. She read the labels quickly, water Fae, Formorian, Sky Fae, Earthen Fae, Blood Fae, Selkie…She doubled over ready to vomit. She was scared to open the bottom cabinets, but she did. In there were jars filled with blood and all labeled like the eyeball jars. One of the jars of blood simply read, "Diedre."

"What? No!" Gasped Goldie grabbing the jar with shaking hands. "Why would this be in here?"

"Bhaile!" Goldie shouted. She didn't care if anyone outside of the room heard her. "Bhaile!"

"I'm here Goldie Divine," said the voice she had grown used to, but it sounded sad.

"Where am I Bhaile?" Goldie asked with a quivering voice.

"You are in the first king's private chamber. When he used his magic to make this room, he made it so that it could never be destroyed and never be found." Bhaile said.

"Then how did I find it?" Goldie asked scared to know of what the answer might be. She had found out she was connected to so many creatures here. She didn't want to be connected to that monster.

"You know how the magic works here, only those welcome may enter. Your blood must call out to the room. You are welcome here." Bhaile answered.

"Bhaile I'm not a monster am I? I don't want to be welcome here. Why is my grandmother's blood in a jar?" She asked in flurry of emotions.

"By now you know that the first king was a Formorian and Blood Fae. He drank blood to sustain his health and strength. He also performed blood magic. That's why he was so dark. He mind controlled those around him with their blood. There are things I will never repeat that happened in this chamber. I do not watch sleeping quarters when they are occupied, especially by lovers. But, their screams would haunt me and I would try to soothe them. But with no arms and hands, I wasn't much help. I was also under the control of the king who lived here. Even though my energy is ultimately good and made for creating things, I had to be dark with him." Bhaile sounded so distant now.

"This is a sleeping quarter. A room for torture?" Goldie asked.

Bhaile simply said, "Look around child."

Goldie gently set her grandmother's blood back on the shelf and stood to walk around. The only light was that from her glowing body. She saw a weird symbol in the floor and stood on it. It lit up golden and changed to red. Goldie didn't know what it meant. Then on a small table with a single light shining down on it, Goldie saw a black leather bound book. She walked over to it. It was written in a language she didn't understand. She opened it up and she knew immediately it was something to do with blood magic. The rituals, she assumed.

She closed the book back up and continued exploring. She shuddered when she found the bed in the furthest darkest corner of the room. There were chains and shackles connected to the black iron head board and foot board. Above the bed was a mirror and what looked like iron pokers. The sheets were black silk and there were no pillows. There was a single nightstand by the bed. It held a single black chalice and one picture.

Goldie walked over to the picture frame and picked it up. It was a picture of her grandmother standing in the middle of the circle with a large man standing behind her with his mouth on her neck. As she looked closer, she could see a trickle of blood coming from her grandmother's neck. The circle was lit bright red. Her grandmother's face just looked determined. She wasn't smiling or frowning, she just was there.

Goldie clasped a hand to her mouth and let the tears fall silently. "Granna what happened to you?" She whispered.

Bhaile whispered back, "She was the only one who wouldn't scream. It drove him mad. He did love her in a twisted way."

Goldie shuddered now. She cried out to Lorcan in her mind, "Lorcan please come get me."

Lorcan didn't reply. Then Goldie went still. She had shouted at Bhaile and no one came to see what was wrong and Fae had extra good hearing.

"Bhaile, why can't Lorcan hear me when I call out to him with mind?" She asked.

"This room is guarded by blood magic and it's also sound proof. No one can hear you here, except for me." Bhaile explained.

"I want to get out of here," said Goldie before turning around at something whispering to her.

"Come here. Come here," whispered an ominous gravelly voice.

Goldie searched to see what could be calling to her. The voice made her hackles rise. Her eyes darted across the room of horrors.

"Come here divine one." The voice spoke again.

This time Goldie registered where the voice was coming from. It was the magic book. Had she awoken something when she opened the pages. Against her better judgement, she crossed the room to the pedestal the black book was sitting on. She ran her hand across the cover of the book and it lit up gold and the writing changed to English. It was changing to fit her.

She drew her hand back and the book seemed to cry out. "What do you want?" She asked.

"Only to help you divine one. I can help you gain all the power of the realm. You just need open me and see the secrets I hold." The gravelly voice said.

"Are you good or evil? I will not do harm to those around me." Goldie said to the ancient book.

"I am neither. I am what you true heart wishes. If you wish to do evil, so it shall be. Sometimes you don't have a choice but to cause harm to protect yourself." The book said solemnly. "Diedre understood that."

Goldie's eyebrows raised in surprise. "My Granna?"

"Why yes divine one. She was much like you. She understood someone had to come to harm to make the cycle end." The book said.

"I don't understand," said Goldie.

"And why should you? You've never known real power. Just open the first page and place your hand palm down. I'll show you." The book said.

The idea intrigued Goldie, but although she was naïve, she was still smart. She understood that Bhaile didn't always say things. You had to ask. So, she did. "Bhaile, is this the truth? I'm feeling too nervous to just open this black book and give it my hand."

Goldie could hear the relief in Bhaile's voice. "Goldie Divine the gods blessed you with great discernment. Once you open that book and give it access to your being, you will be tied to it. It will call to any darkness you have within you. I will not lie to you though, as I can't. The book does hold great power and knowledge. But if you open it, it will change you forever."

Goldie nodded and turned to the book. "Great book there is much I need and want to know, but not at the risk of who I am. Thank you for your offer though."

You could hear the surprise in the ancient book's voice, "You turned me down. In all my years, you are the only one who found me to say no. The prophecy will be fulfilled with you. Divine one many hard things will come to pass, but you will rise to be a great leader. I will be here when you are ready to open my pages, because one day, you will be."

Goldie shook her head and gently tapped the book with one finger as to say bye.

"Bhaile, please help me get out of here," said Goldie pacing in a circle.

The book spoke up once again and said, "You know divine one, you are the only to voice Bhaile's name and hear the power so clearly."

Goldie didn't know what that meant. She just called to Bhaile again.

"Goldie Divine you must only walk through the wall. After you get out of this chamber, I can light the way to the dining room for you." Bhaile said patiently.

Goldie picked a wall and just went. She had to get out that room. It had hurt her heart, especially seeing the photo of her grandmother and jar of blood. That's something her Granda never needed to know about. As soon as she breeched the wall, she felt like she could take a good breath again. The dark room had stifled her. And just like Bhaile had said, small flowers along the corridors lit the way to the dining room.

When she got to the dining room, all three who were waiting on her were pacing in circles and Angrbora was there too. She was looking over a map. They all looked up when she walked in and relief immediately graced all their faces.

Lorcan spoke first, "Why didn't you answer me when I called you? I've been going crazy over here."

"He really has. He all but burnt down the dark forest to get to me, thinking we must have done something with you," hissed Angrbora angrily.

Goldie's eyes went wide. "Lorcan, that was wrong. Angrbora is my family. You know that. The Formorians are more of my family than any of you know."

"I know Goldie. I'm sorry. Something broke in me when you wouldn't answer. I freaked out. It was like you were cut off from me. It hurt." Lorcan said looking down.

Goldie crossed the room and grabbed Lorcan's hands to still him. She looked from face to face and said, "I was cut off from you. But I was here in the castle. You all aren't going to believe what I have to tell you."

Chapter 25

Everyone's mouths were agape as she told them of her unexpected entry into the dark chamber of the first king. She didn't leave anything out. She told them about the jars and her grandmother's blood and the picture. She shuddered at that part. But in her own mind, she struggled. Lorcan had bitten her and it didn't really bother her. He hadn't harmed her. She told them of the ancient book and its offer. She told them she turned it down, but it said she would be back.

King Oberon immediately left to try to find the room, even though Goldie told him he wouldn't find it. Only those welcome could get in. He wouldn't be welcome. Beatha hugged Goldie tight and told her how proud she was of her.

Angrbora simply said, "Tomorrow you learn to fight like one of us." Then she left after hugging her.

Goldie looked to Lorcan and he nodded. "There are magical powers here that we don't even know about or understand and they are all calling to you. You need to be able to fight. Angrbora will better at teaching you to fight than I will. I won't want to hurt you and honestly, you need someone who can set feelings aside for that kind of training. I can't. I will however, work with you on your flying and making portals. Beatha and your da need to work with you on your magic."

Goldie looked at Beatha who nodded. "Now child, go up to your room and get some rest. Tomorrow the real work begins. You my dear one has so much on your shoulders, but as always, I will be here for you every step of the way." Beatha walked over and kissed Goldie's cheek before disappearing.

"Lorcan when I called out to you and you couldn't hear me, it scared me. I hated it." Goldie said wrapping her arms around him tightly.

She didn't even feel him, portal them to her room this time. He rubbed her hair back from her face and kissed her forehead. "I love you more than I ever knew was possible Goldie. You know that right?"

Goldie nodded and kissed him softly. "I know that because I feel the same."

"I never knew you would come into my life and be all that I would need or want. You weren't part of my plan and now I can't see my future without you love," said Lorcan pulling her to him.

She hugged him for a long time and heard the water start in her bathroom. She smiled into Lorcan's chest. He was starting the bath for her. She smelled her bubble bath and sighed. In her mind she was sure to ask Bhaile to sound proof her room too. Her da had enough shocks for one evening.

Lorcan spoke to the top of her head, "I figured you could use a bath after all that."

"You know me well," said Goldie pulling from his arms and making her clothes disappear to head to her bathroom.

Lorcan watched her walk away. "Do you want to be alone?" He asked.

Goldie turned to face him and said, "I wouldn't have taken my clothes off in front of you if I wanted to be alone. Lorcan, I always want you with me. It's important we have lives outside of each other, but know I always want you with me."

Lorcan gave her a half smile and made his clothes vanish and he chased her to the bathroom. Goldie let out a shriek as he scooped her up in his arms and sat down in the water with her in his lap. Water splashed over the edge of her huge tub. It didn't matter though. Her seaweed style bath rug soaked up and seemed to get even bigger and softer.

Goldie settled in between Lorcan's legs and rested her back on his chest and leaned back. She let the water kiss her skin and sighed. Lorcan wrapped his arms around her and rested his head against the wall. He seemed restless.

Goldie asked, "What's the matter?"

"It's just what you saw down there. The jars of blood and the picture. Does it make you think I'm a monster? I would never hurt you on purpose. I didn't even mean to do it the first time, but Goldie I want to bite you so badly again it almost hurts. It's like I need your blood inside of me. You are a part of me now and I need you as much as I need air. I don't want to frighten you." He answered honestly.

"You don't frighten me Lorcan. I think it's sad that you may be the very last of the blood Fae. Maybe like the Formorians, they were just misunderstood. From what I learned tonight; the first king controlled many of the creatures with their blood using blood magic. I'm sure people just were scared of the power that blood can wield. You didn't hurt me. Do you think I'm a monster for biting you? I bit you this morning. I actually thought about all this earlier too. I can't deny my love for you any more than I can deny the bond that pulses through me connecting me to you. Lorcan bite me." Goldie said angling her neck away from him to give him access.

"I don't want to harm you. I don't want to be a monster," said Lorcan with his voice changing and his hardness growing under her.

Goldie turned to face him. She put her legs on either side of his and took his face into her hands. She saw the reason for his changed voice. He had fangs protruding from his mouth. She looked deeply into his eyes and said, "You are no monster. You are just learning who you are like me. I will sustain you, only me. I don't want you taking blood from anyone but me. I'm selfish when it comes to you. I only want it to be me. I love you and I give you my full permission to bite me." Goldie said kissing him with his fangs and all.

He kissed her back like he was starving and she thought he very well could be. He pulled away and looked at her, really looked at her. She looked back unashamed. Lorcan traced her face with his fingertips and Goldie closed her eyes at the gentle sensation.

Goldie let out a silent cry as Lorcan entered her in two ways at once. As he bit her neck, he surged inside her from below. There was a single sharp pain and then nothing but red-hot pleasure. Lorcan had opened his senses to her and let her feel everything he was feeling. He was in complete rapturous ecstasy. Goldie gasped and held on as she felt the gentle sucking at her neck and the pull from her core at the same time.

He only sucked on her neck for a moment longer before licking where he had bitten her. She felt no pain and just knew there would be no mark left behind either. He moved slowly inside her and Goldie stared at the man that could shatter her world. She watched him with racked breath. He let his eyes glow. His silver glow dotted with red now. He looked healthier and more vibrant. He put his forehead on hers and thrust his hips upward, stroking her from the inside.

Goldie's head fell back and Lorcan held her neck in one hand, supporting her. Goldie began to move now. She still wasn't sure what she was doing but she wanted to move. She knew by Lorcan's moan, he liked it. She moved faster and her breaths came out shallower. Her knees were starting to hurt from the bottom of the tub and she wanted to move to the bed. She rode him harder and thinking only a little of her pained knees and thought how much better she could move on the bed. In a blink, they were on her bed and she was still astride him. Lorcan's eyes registered shock and Goldie felt the shock too.

She didn't stop though. She kept riding him chasing her high. She opened up her feelings to Lorcan and let him feel what she was feeling. His face softened and he got a sly smile. He grabbed her hips on the way down and helped her to grind into him. Goldie cried out and Lorcan followed right behind her gasping and holding on to her. Goldie fell forward onto Lorcan and he wrapped his arms around her.

They stayed like that for a long time before Goldie asked, "Did I move us to the bed?"

Lorcan laughed and Goldie felt the jolt of him still inside her. Goldie sighed, "Mmmm."

Lorcan just raised one eyebrow.

It wasn't until after the third round of crazy love making that Lorcan finally answered her. "Yes, love you moved us from the bath to the bed. Your da would have a heart attack to know the first time you teleported was while I was buried inside you."

Goldie swatted at his chest.

"What were you thinking about when you moved us. It will help me help you to portal." Lorcan said.

Goldie blushed. Lorcan raised that eyebrow again and prodded, "Oh tell me. Now I really want to know."

"Fine," huffed Goldie. "I was you know…" She trailed off.

"Riding me hard," helped Lorcan with a smile in his voice.

"Yes, that and my knees started to hurt from the tub and I thought how much better it would be on the bed and then I thought I could…ride…you better on the bed and then we were on the bed," said Goldie quickly.

"You know my love; we will continue to explore each other very thoroughly naked. It's ok to say whatever you want. In fact, I'd like it if you'd tell me what you want. Next time say, Lorcan Baby, I want to ride you like I stole you, and I'll know exactly what you want." He teased.

Goldie hid her face under her pillow. "Lorcan, I thought we were going to talk about me teleporting us."

"Ahh yes. You teleported us out of necessity. Your knees were hurting. You thought about it and it happened. You will just have to think about what you need as a starter." Lorcan said. "It gets easier over time, but if we are going to battle, you need to be able to portal at a moment's notice."

Goldie fell asleep cradled in Lorcan's arms and she woke the next morning in his arms. She felt so loved and safe in his arms. She wiggled up and kissed his chin. His arms tightened around her and she felt him at the ready to bring her more pleasure. She shivered and Lorcan laughed.

"You are insatiable. But I love it," said Lorcan kissing her head.

"I can't help it. It's like you woke up something inside me. All I can think about is being with you," said Goldie wiggling some more.

"Then I better help you," said Lorcan maneuvering into place, when a knock came at Goldie's door.

Lorcan groaned and Goldie let out a huff of breath. They both quickly got out of bed and materialized clothing and Goldie went and opened the door. Beatha stood on the other side with her eyes wide.

"I didn't mean to disturb you…two," she said eyeballing Lorcan who ran a hand through his disheveled hair.

"You didn't really disturb us. We were up anyway." Goldie said standing to the side to let Beatha in.

Lorcan spoke into Goldie's mind, "Yes we were up."

Goldie cut her eyes at him and he just gave his goofy grin.

"Beatha do you need me as well or should I leave you two ladies to it?" Asked Lorcan.

"You can leave us. It seems like it's a good thing I came up here to do some wedding planning," said Beatha giving Lorcan a pointed look.

"Very well. I need to go check in with my men. Let me know if I can help," said Lorcan kissing Goldie quickly and nodding at Beatha.

"Goldie you are much changed child," said Beatha looking her over.

"Yes, I am. My power is still growing and I'm so in love," said Goldie smiling.

Beatha smiled back. "You do understand if you gave yourself to Lorcan on the full moon, you are probably with child. I know the pull was probably too much for you, but there is still so much you need to learn and do before bringing new life into the world."

"Lorcan and I knew what the possibilities were. I can live with them. That night, I wasn't prepared for what the moon would do to me. I literally hurt for Lorcan. He was the only thing that would make the hurt go away and I caved to it. I don't regret it. I love him and we are getting married," said Goldie boldly to Beatha.

Beatha nodded her understanding and said, "Well to have a heart mate is precious, so I don't blame you for wanting to fulfill the bond to the fullest. So, let's plan a wedding, shall we?"

Goldie nodded with excitement and looked down at the ring on her finger. She wanted both of them to be represented in their union, just like in her ring.

There was no trying on dresses. The perfect dress would materialize for her the day of. They did go over what kind of food they would be having and had to pick a date. The whole realm would be invited. Goldie also had to pick a place to hold the wedding. Goldie decided on the tree where Mack lived with his other friends. Beatha smiled at her choice.

"Bhaile, will you be able to come if I have the wedding at the tree?" Goldie asked aloud.

Beatha's eyes widened. "Child you talk to the castle?"

Goldie nodded. "I can hear Bhaile in my mind. I've grown so fond of it."

"And I have grown fond of you and just knowing you want me there would warm my heart if I had one. I cannot leave here. I have to stay to protect your home, but I will be with you in spirit and you can show me the whole day when you get back home." Bhaile said.

Beatha said, "You are the only one to hear its voice. You my child are so precious."

"We will marry on the next full moon, because what else would be the perfect date?" Goldie asked smiling broadly.

Chapter 26

Angrbora came and got Goldie after lunch to start training her on how to fight. She took her back to her home. Godfrey was waiting for them in battle gear and with a smile across his face.

"Blood of my blood you are home and ready to train?" He asked.

Goldie nodded yes.

"Then here young one, but on these." Godfrey said throwing a bag at her.

Goldie looked to Angrbora.

"We don't magically put clothes on. We have to make our own, but our battle garb is the strongest there is. Godfrey worked all night to finish yours for you." Angrbora explained.

Goldie felt warmth in her heart. "Daideo' thank you." Goldie said as she rushed forward to hug the huge man.

He wrapped his giant arms around her and picked her up off the ground. He hugged her fiercely and then sat her down. "Now get dressed and come ready to fight. You have much to learn."

Angrbora said, "Come with me. I'll take you to my place to change."

Goldie followed Angrbora to a Formorian sized apartment on the edge of the forest. Inside Goldie was shocked to see paintings of different flowers on the wall. They were beautiful. She looked at each one and stopped at the blue flower that her mother loved so much.

"That flower was made by the gods for their children." Angrbora explained.

"It was my mother's favorite," said Goldie reaching out a single finger to touch the painting.

"That makes sense now that we know you are her daughter. God's blood runs through the females in your family." Angrbora said.

"Did you paint these?" Asked Goldie.

Angrbora nodded and said, "We all get something from our lineage. I am from the bloodline of Brigid, The Goddess of Spring. It's deep within me to love Spring and flowers. I am quite good at growing plants and keeping them alive. In the dark forest flowers don't just grow, so I took up painting them."

"They are quite beautiful." Goldie said looking back to the paintings.

"You better get dressed before your Daideo' comes looking for you." Angrbora said nodding towards the bag Goldie was holding.

Angrbora walked back outside. Goldie's breath hitched and her eyes widened when she pulled out the battle clothes her Daideo' had made for her. They were the color of the deep ocean. They flowed and were light. Waves were sewn into the small metal mesh that would protect her heart and lungs. The leg guards had been pounded out by hand and were Damascus but also looked like waves. The shoes were made of leather that was stained to match her battle garb. Her name was etched across each of the arm guards and filled in with gold. There were places for her throwing knives. She had a leather skirt that went to her knees in pleats.

She dressed out and looked into a large full-size mirror. She looked like a goddess going to war.

Angrbora nodded her approval when Goldie walked back out. "Here let me do your hair. We always wear it in several braids and tied up not to get in our way," said Angrbora making quick work of Goldie's hair.

"Here." Angrbora said, handing Goldie a golden sword. "You will need this." She smiled at Goldie who now felt nervous.

Her hand felt warm where she held the golden blade. It didn't feel heavy either. It felt like it belonged in her hand. Goldie made her way to the center of the Fomorians homeplace in an open area similar to an arena. She had learned this is where they practiced. Her great grandfather was waiting on her, sword in hand. He motioned her out into the center of the arena.

Goldie walked out to the center and took a deep breath. She looked at her great grandfather and waited. He didn't say a word. He charged straight for her. Goldie's eyes widened and she moved left to miss his attack. Daideo' swung back around with his sword towards her head. Goldie ducked and threw her sword up and met his with a loud, powerful clank. Her shoulder almost buckled under his force.

"Good. Get up!" He hollered at her.

He didn't wait for her to get set. He moved at her again. Swinging his sword. Goldie dodged again and moved around him.

"Let your instincts guide you las. It's in your blood. Let the sword work for you. Listen to the hum in your veins. You are part Formorian. You know what to do. It's inside you," said Daideo' tripping her and putting his sword at her neck.

Goldie grunted and looked up at her great grandfather. He had a twinkle in his eyes. He stepped back and let Goldie get up. She dusted off somewhat, never letting go of her sword. She looked down at her hand

and the hilt in it. She closed her eyes and tried to feel the hum in her veins. It wasn't coming to her. She was getting frustrated. She heard footsteps coming at her.

Goldie didn't open her eyes, instead she listened. She could hear everything. The sand particles crunching under Daideo's feet as he came at her, his breaths coming out hard, his heart beating. Goldie's eyes flew open and Daideo' was at her with his sword raised. Goldie didn't know if time had slowed down or if she was just processing everything differently. It was as if she had all the time in the world to counter his moves. The sword felt like part of her and she moved it effortlessly to stop each blow that came at her.

She started to have fun with the sparring and realized it was like a dance. She just let Daideo' lead and she followed out of his reach and countered with effortless efficiency. She smiled and Daideo' did too.

"You feel it now. I can see it. You are a natural my las. The only way to learn is to do. Young one you will be ready when it's time. Look at you," said Daideo' in awe as he stopped his onslaught and bent to a knee.

Goldie looked down at herself, not only was her body glowing golden, but her armor and sword. Her sword was so bright it almost hurt her eyes. She felt her body get larger too as she looked around the outside of the arena to see everyone down on a knee with their hands at their hearts.

Goldie looked down to Daideo' and said, "Please get up Daideo'. You are my blood and I want you to just be a grandfather to me."

His eyes softened and glistened. He stood and put a hand on her cheek that was now level to his and placed his forehead on hers. Goldie felt the chain inside her clink again into place and the bond was set. She knew there would be no going back.

"Alright young one. Let's get you to spar with another young one that won't go easy on you," said Daideo'.

Goldie's eyes widened. "You were going easy on me? You didn't even say anything. You just came at me with your sword."

Daideo' laughed. "Well, the only way to learn is to get your hands dirty. You need to feel real danger for your body to react and the sword become one with you."

"Bres!" Daideo' hollered.

The crowd outside the arena shifted and a very large Formorian with bright red hair stepped over the arena fence. Goldie's breath hitched in her throat. He was huge. Even bigger than her in her Goddess form. He was actually beautiful. A lot of Formorians were thought to be scary, ugly creatures, but this one was flawless. His eyes were the color of the ocean depths and his strong jaw was masculine. He had on no armor. He wore no shirt and his white skin looked like marble and just as hard. He was so defined it defied nature. He had on brown buckskin pants and no shoes. His feet were large and slender.

When she made her way back up to his face, he was smirking. "Like what you see las?" He asked her with glee in his deep voice and his dimples showing.

Goldie shook her head and answered, "I'm just taking an inventory of who I will be fighting."

"Oh yes, las. We shall fight," said Bres smiling at her.

"Where's your sword?" Goldie asked him.

"I don't need one. I'll just take yours." He said with an eyebrow raised.

"What?" Goldie asked.

"I didn't stutter. I'll take yours." He said again, pinning her with a stare.

Goldie looked over to her great grandfather, who just shrugged. Daideo' said, "Bres is probably our best fighter but the least disciplined. He will be good to practice with. You won't find anyone stronger than him."

Goldie felt her heart bock at that, because in her mind Lorcan was the strongest man she knew. She didn't have time to dwell on it though, because Bres charged her. He was fast, even with her heightened senses. He moved in and out and she missed him with each thrust of her blade. He danced around her and she followed his movement.

She wasn't quick enough. As she swung at him with her sword, he dodged and punched her hard in the side. She had on armor so it blocked most of it, but it still hurt and she knew she would have a bruise. Before she could think on it too long, about how he could punch armor and still hurt her, he was behind her. He grabbed her by her braided hair and pulled her into his chest.

"Oh, I could get used to this." He whispered in her ear, just before Goldie elbowed him in the stomach.

He laughed as he let her go, for her turn around and face him again. Goldie could feel her cheeks starting to burn. She was getting angry. She was trying to learn and he was just playing with her. He wasn't taking her seriously at all. She felt her skin start to glow.

"Now las, going all goddess isn't fair." Smirked Bres.

Goldie gritted her teeth and ran at him. She went to swing her sword at his head, but at the last minute slowed her swing. She didn't really want to hurt him. But that was her fatal mistake. When she slowed her arm, Bres caught her wrist and squeezed it so tight she felt her bones crunch. She cried out as her hand shook and she tried to hold onto her sword.

"Las, I told you I would take your sword. You're not ready for battle yet. How about this," whispered Bres. "I'll let you keep your sword just for a little kiss." He puckered his lips towards her. He was just inches from her face holding her right wrist which was still barely holding her sword.

Goldie smiled at him. "Oh, just a kiss? That's all you want from me. You don't want to see what else I've learned here?" Goldie tried to sound sultry and raised an eyebrow at him.

Bres swallowed and smiled like he had won. "Las, I could teach you more, I'm sure. But I'll settle for a kiss to not take your sword. I do have you at a disadvantage here."

"Or is it an advantage for me? I mean kissing such a handsome man like you, hardly seems like a punishment. You saw me look at you earlier." Goldie said leaning in closer to him.

Bres smiled, knowing he had won his prize and leaned towards Goldie. She smiled back at him and leaned in towards him too. His grip lightened slightly on her wrist and she took a needed breath. Bres started to pucker his lips and when Goldie got within an inch of his lips she said, "You will never take my sword." And she swung her head back quickly and thrust it forward so fast to hit him in the face. The headbutt made her world go black.

Chapter 27

Goldie came to with Angrbora wiping her face with a cool rag and someone put something foul smelling under her nose. "Ugh." Goldie mumbled as she rolled to her side to sit up.

Angrbora smiled at her and said, "You still have your sword. Hope the headache was worth it."

"Definitely worth it. Did you hear what he said to me. That pig wanted me to kiss him to let go of me," said Goldie getting flustered again.

"That pig is right here las," a muffled voice next to her said.

Goldie looked over to see Bres rolling over to sit up, holding a bloody rag to his nose.

He had a twinkle in his ocean blue eyes. He took the rag off. Goldie didn't avert her gaze at his crooked bloodied nose. She almost felt bad for messing up his beautiful face, almost. Bres took his large hands and pressed them around his nose and cracked it back into place. Goldie didn't shutter like she wanted to. She just held his gaze. He smiled at her now.

"I have to say, I didn't see that coming." Bres said, wiping at the blood on his face.

"Of course, you didn't. Your lust and pride will be the death of you. You were so sure that just because you have a pretty face and I was a damsel in distress that I would kiss you to make all my trouble go away? Newsflash, women aren't just toys." Goldie said less than amused.

"So, you think I'm pretty?" Bres asked smiling even wider at her.

"That's seriously all you got from what I just said?" Goldie asked feeling exasperated.

Bres put on a straight face. "I do not think that you are just a toy. You are a beautiful toy and who wouldn't try to steal a kiss from you?

Goldie growled. She was getting to her feet with her sword in hand. Bres put his hand up and said, "I don't wish to go at it again. You need to understand though, fighting, really fighting isn't pretty. You can never pause for a moment or second guess yourself, or you will end up dead. You can learn all the fancy moves and techniques you want, but it needs to be instinct. I had a moment of weakness and you seized the opportunity. You do have some Formorian blood in you with that devilish move. Make a guy think he could get something he wants and then boom, lights out. But not everyone will stop and give you that option to have time to think or offer you something else in order for you to save your life. You did fight better than I thought you would."

Daideo' broke in. "Alright you two. That's enough for the day. Bres, you're lucky I don't get after you for pulling that stunt. I think I would cut your lips off if they touched my granddaughter."

Bres smiled at him. "Oh, you would love it if I were her man."

Daideo' pinned him with a sharp look and Bres ducked his head some. "Luckily I didn't need to do anything because she broke your nose on her own." Daideo' said starring the large, red headed Formorian down.

"That she did," whispered Bres.

"My las. I'm proud of you. You fight well for just starting. You will be a true Formorian Warrior soon. Now that we are your guard, we can come to you to practice at the castle if you wish." Daideo' said to Goldie.

"I would like that from time to time, but I also like being here." Goldie said getting to her feet.

Angrbora smiled and said, "We like you being here. You bring us such honor Goldie."

"I feel at home here and I'm pretty sure Lorcan would kill Bres if he knew what he just asked me to do," said Goldie looking at Bres.

Bres chuckled, "He could try. I would fight to have your hand."

"I said nothing about fighting for my hand Bres. You do understand that Lorcan is my heartmate, don't you?" Goldie said looking him over. His nose was already healing.

"And your Granna was Balor's heartmate, but she split and picked someone else. You could pick me if you wanted to." Bres said looking her in the eyes.

But Goldie only felt a cold shudder. "What?" Goldie asked quietly.

For the first time, Bres didn't look so cocky. He drew his eyebrows in together and studied Goldie for a moment. He asked, "You didn't know?"

"That can't be true. He wasn't her heartmate. My Granna was soulmates with my Granda. They loved each other so much. No. No way. I understand the heartmate bond. You couldn't just leave that person. That's not how it works." Goldie said looking away from Bres.

Bres just nodded and looked away. Everyone in the camp was silent. Goldie looked around, but no one met her eyes. She looked to her Daideo' and he titled his head to the side.

"Is it true?" Goldie said barely loud enough for him to hear.

Daideo' gave a sad smile. "No one is sure. But Balor went mad when she left. He would stare at the water for hours. It is said he even prayed to the gods to bring your Granna back. Your Granna never said if they were, but all we know is that in the end Balor realized that your Granna was special to him. That didn't make him a good or better man. He was just as ruthless. Your Granna realized she couldn't change him, so she did the next best thing, she left to give the people a chance. Had they had a child together, Balor would still be ruling and his bloodline would be just a ruthless and take over and with your Granna at his side, their child would have been too powerful."

"Their child..." Goldie said sadly and looked off and then she abruptly looked up.

Angrbora saw the distress in her eyes. "What is it my sister?" She asked.

Goldie looked nervously around at the two other men who were close to her. But then straightened her shoulders and said, "It was a full moon. Should I be fighting like this? I could be pregnant."

Daideo's eyebrows shot up and Bres blanched. It was an uncomfortable topic for sure, but Goldie wouldn't put her and Lorcan's baby in danger. Daideo' looked at Bres who shook his head. Goldie was confused.

Daideo' said, "You are not with child my young one. You will be a wonderful mother one day with the way you are already thinking."

"How do you know? Da and Beatha said that I would most likely because of the full moon and you know…" She trailed off.

Bres spoke up, "I would be able to hear the heartbeat. I can sense life. I don't know why or how, but it's one of my gifts. Maybe I'm not all Formorian like you. I also have the best hearing out of all the Formorians. It's one of the reasons I'm such a good fighter. I can hear your moves as you make them. Just the tiniest of sound as you shift your weight and the grains of sand shift."

Goldie studied him and nodded. She was intrigued and relieved. "So, we continue practicing. We can practice at the castle tomorrow. And seriously Bres, don't ever pull a stunt like that again."

"You have my word las. But for the record, I will kiss you if you ever feel the need arise." Bres winked at her.

"I won't," deadpanned Goldie.

"We will see," said Bres with his cocky smile returning.

Goldie didn't even respond to him again. She thought about needing to be home and needing a shower. She teleported herself back to the castle. She found herself in Lorcan's shower still in her battle clothes. She chuckled and shook her head. She stepped out of his shower, so she could at least let her family know she was home.

"Bhaile, will you take me to me family? I'm not sure what room they are in," said Goldie.

"Of course, divine one. Glad to see you are home in one piece." The ambiguous voice said into her head.

The hallway flowers lit up to show Goldie the way. Goldie followed the glowing path set before her. She stopped short when the lights disappeared through a wall. She would never be used to just walking through things. But she took a breath and stepped through.

She found the three she loved so much all bent over a large table looking at a map of the Hollow Hill with their heads together.

"It would seem that the darkness is spreading out from here on the East side. If I could just get in there and see," said Beatha tapping the map with a finger.

"No. No way. We just got you home. You cannot go there. I won't lose you this soon," said King Oberon, grabbing her shoulder.

"I'll go. I can take my most trusted men and go. We should only be gone two days." Lorcan said studying the map and nodding.

"No. You are not going." The command fell from Goldie's lips before her brain could catch up.

All three of them turned around to face her. A slow smile spread across her father's face and Beatha looked her up and down as if tracking to see where all her injuries were. Lorcan's face grew red.

"What's wrong?" Goldie asked looking at Lorcan.

"Who did that to your face?" He asked walking to her to cup her cheeks.

"I did." Goldie said as he placed a kiss to her forehead.

"What?" Everyone asked in unison, confused about her hurting herself.

"My Daideo' taught me the basics and we sparred. But then he had a huge Formorian named, Bres, come to fight with me. He said the best way to learn was to just fight. You should have seen this guy. I am in all my armor, oh and Daideo' made all this for me by hand. Anyway, I'm decked out in my armor and have my sword. This guy comes out in nothing but buckskin britches and no weapons. He said he would take my sword from me. I couldn't let that happen. He was a much better fighter than me. So, he had my wrist in a bone crushing grip and I was losing my grip on the sword. I had nowhere to go. He took a moment to speak to me and that gave me enough time to decide to head butt him. I knocked us both out. But I didn't lose my sword." Goldie finished cheerily.

"That's my girl!" Her dad said patting her shoulder.

"Let me look at you child," said Beatha turning her head this way and that to inspect the damage. "Looks like you fought hard."

"I did and I'm almost scared to say I enjoyed it. They are coming here tomorrow to practice with me," said Goldie.

"Is Bres coming?" Lorcan asked bitterly.

"I'm sure." Goldie sighed.

"What did he say to you?" King Oberon asked.

Goldie was silent for a moment. She couldn't lie, but she didn't want to say it either. Instead, she said, "He said something that put a fire in my soul. It was nothing I couldn't handle. He was drawing the fighter out in me."

Goldie looked up to Lorcan, who had his jaw set. She searched his face. He looked down at her and said into her mind, "I know Bres. He's a good fighter and he loves women. I could guess what he said."

"Then your guess would probably make it worse than it was. He said he would let me up if I kissed him. You see how that ended, I knocked us both out. I broke his nose if that makes you feel any better?" Goldie raised her eyebrows in his direction.

Lorcan's lips twitched and he smiled. He kissed her mouth softly.

"I take it you two just had a conversation of your own?" Beatha said.

"Yes ma'am. I was trying to leave further bloodshed out of the equation, but I can't hide anything from Lorcan. Bres tried to get me to kiss him to let me up. That's when I broke his nose." Goldie shrugged.

King Oberon busted out laughing. He laughed so hard that tears came to his eyes. "You are my daughter. You made this father's dream come true. If only every da could be lucky enough to hear his daughter say she broke someone's nose who wanted to kiss her."

The rest of them joined in the laughter.

"Your armor is so beautiful. I've only seen work like this one other time," said Beatha touching her armor.

"I love it. I was nervous it would be heavy and hard to fight in, but it's not," said Goldie smiling.

Lorcan asked, "Would you like me to walk you to the shower? I'm sure you're tired and ready to clean up."

Goldie smiled and nodded. "I really need a shower and I'm worn out if I'm honest. Would it be ok if I just ate something small in my room?"

Her father gave her a sweet smile and nodded.

Lorcan held her hand and walked her to his room. When they got through the wall, he gently helped Goldie get out of her armor. They used no magic. They didn't say a word. He started with her arm guards, tracing her name on each of them. He kissed each of her fingers as he pulled them off. He then gently pulled her mesh chest protector over her head. He bent and kissed her shoulder where a bruise was starting to show. He gently rubbed his hands down her back and unclasped her bra and slid it down her arms. He knelt and kissed each spot on her body that was now bruising from training.

Lorcan's lips danced across her ribs where bruises shown and down to her belly button. On his knees, he pickup up one foot, taking off her leather shoe and then the other. His deft fingers then moved to the leg guards and he kissed her calves as he pulled each one free from her. He looked up from his knees at her as his hands reached up to pull her leather pleated skirt down. He slid it slowly down her legs, never breaking eye contact. When it hit the floor, he continued raining soft kisses on her bruises. She had some on her outer thigh. Goldie's breath hitched in her throat when he pressed his nose to her panties and inhaled deeply.

"Lorcan, I need to shower." She said with embarrassment and lust filtering into her voice.

"You're perfect. I hate to see your body bruised, but am filled with such pride at the same time. I could worship you. I want to worship you, Goldie. Will you let me?" He asked filled with such emotion.

Goldie looked into his eyes and saw the sincerity. She didn't say a word out loud. She just nodded.

Lorcan smiled slowly and put his nose back at her apex and nuzzled her. Goosebumps sprung across Goldie's exposed flesh. She yelped when Lorcan nipped at her through her panties. He let out a satisfied chuckle and looking up at Goldie, he pulled her panties down. She stepped out of them and watched him with racked breath. When Lorcan placed a kiss on the top of her mound, her eyes went wide and she sighed. With her sigh, Lorcan pulled Goldie closer to him and he buried his face into her core.

Goldie cried out as he ravaged her with his mouth. He was like a starving man that only she could satiate. He was relentless. He lapped, sucked, and nipped at her until she was writhing on his face. Lorcan threw one of her legs over his shoulders and as his tongue dove deeper inside her, she let out a breathy cry. He let out a satisfied grunt and worked harder, as if he was trying to drink her. He pulled back just far enough to say, "You are the sweetest thing to ever touch my lips. I could do this forever; worship your body. I love you."

Through the pleasure haze, Goldie whimpered, "I love you Lorcan." She also felt, stronger. It was odd. Her body began to glow and light burst out from her as she climaxed.

He smiled letting his fangs show. A shudder went through Goldie. He went back to her center driving her senseless and when she came again, she didn't care that his teeth were penetrating her most sensitive area. He sucked and lapped as she came down. She looked down to see him literally eating from her. She wasn't turned off by the sight nor frightened. She smiled down at him as the aftershocks continued to pull from her body with each pull, he took from her. It was prolonging her ecstasy.

When he finally released her with a loud smacking sound, Goldie said, "My turn."

Chapter 28

Goldie woke early the next morning, feeling like a new woman after her new experiences the day before. She felt stronger and more in control of herself and her power. She rolled over to place kiss on Lorcan's bare chest. He smiled with his eyes still closed and wrapped an arm around her.

"Feeling ready to conquer the world I see," said Lorcan, opening one eye.

"Mmhmm," Goldie sighed into his embrace. "I feel stronger somehow and like I'm more in control," said Goldie as she drew hearts on Lorcan's chest with her finger.

Lorcan opened both eyes and looked at her, really looked at her. "You're all healed up and you still have a glow about you. You know gods get power by being worshipped. It is said that our old gods fell into a deep sleep because we quit worshipping them."

"Would you call what you did really worshipping me?" Asked Goldie thoughtfully.

"For me, yes. I worshipped every inch of you. I love you. In my mind and soul, I wanted you to feel that love and my faith in you." Lorcan said, lacing his fingers with hers on his chest and closing his eyes again.

Goldie looked at him and smiled. She was ready to conquer the day. She pulled his hand to her breast and nipped at his neck.

Lorcan chuckled. "Ok I'm up. Let's go down and have breakfast. It will be another long day. When is Angrbora getting here to practice with you?"

"Sometime this morning. It'll be my whole guard and my Daideo' will be coming. You will get to meet him." Goldie said smiling excitedly at Lorcan.

"And Bres?" Lorcan asked with a bit of grit in his tone.

"I'm sure he'll be coming too. He is the best fighter supposedly," said Goldie rolling out from under his arm and standing up.

Lorcan and Goldie got dressed and teleported to the dining room. King Oberon and Beatha were already there. Goldie smiled when she saw the waffles. "Moring Da. Morning Beatha." Goldie said smiling.

"You look well rested." King Oberon said looking her up and down.

"I feel rested." Goldie said cheerfully.

"You'll need it. You have a big work day today child. Battle workout with the Formorians and then magic with me." Beatha said sounding serious.

"I'm ready for it. I want to be tip top shape before I get married. I don't want Lorcan to be going off into battles alone. I will be there to fight too. I will do my part." Goldie said with a nod.

King Oberon smiled. "I know. You are my daughter and you are so capable. I can't wait to watch you fight today. Do you know who you will be sparing with?"

Goldie shook her head no, because she had a huge mouthful of waffles. Lorcan let out a chuckle next to her and she looked at him.

He spoke into her mind, "You're eating like you're starving."

"Maybe I am," replied Goldie in her mind while looking over to Lorcan.

He just chuckled again.

As soon as Goldie finished eating, her guard was walking through the gate. She met them out front. She hugged Daideo' and Angrbora as soon as she got to them. They were leading the group. King Oberon, Beatha, and Lorcan were quickly behind her.

"Da, Beatha, Lorcan, this is my Daideo', Godfrey." Goldie said excitedly making the exchange.

King Oberon's eyebrows rose in recognition. "I have met you once before. You were the fiercest warrior for Balor, until you disappeared."

"Love changes a man. I regret my time with Balor, but am grateful I have the chance to meet my great granddaughter. I will train her to be the best warrior. I have trained all the Formorians you see before you. They fight well as a team and independently. My granddaughter has great abilities. She will also be a fierce warrior." Godfrey said with pride.

Oberon shook his hand and said, "I have no doubts.

Beatha blushed looking at Godfrey, but then took his hand and shook it.

Lorcan was last. When their hands clasped Godfrey's eyes went wide. "You are part of us son." Godfrey said, his eyes searching Lorcan.

Lorcan didn't falter. He looked into Godfrey's eyes and stood tall.

Godfrey continued, "Your blood calls to mine. Someone in your family line has some Formorian in them. That's probably why you and Goldie connected so well."

"Well and we are heartmates too Daideo'," said Goldie.

"That you are. He seems to be a good match. Welcome to the family Lorcan," said Godfrey pulling the man into a hug. Lorcan laughed and embraced him back.

"Alright. Alright. Enough with all the fuss. I thought we were going to do some fighting." Bres said walking into the front of the group to stand beside Godfrey and Angrbora.

Lorcan stiffened. "Bres." He said flatly.

"Long time no see Lorcan. How's the castle treating ya?" Bres asked casually.

"It's well. I'm doing well with the woman I love," said Lorcan with deadly intent in his eyes.

Bres snickered. "I assumed something was up when you didn't make your way back to hang out with us at the pub. The girls have all been missing ya."

Lorcan's fist clenched and his face went red as his eyes narrowed.

"What? Our young goddess doesn't know about who you really are? How I'm not the only one the lasses love around here? C'mon brother. I'm upset with you." Bres said tisking.

"ENOUGH!" Goldie shouted and power shot out from her at the two men.

"That's new," said Bres looking Goldie over.

"I do not care nor want to hear about that. You will shut up or I will shut you up Bres." Goldie said dangerously teetering on the edge of something.

"That's right las. Get mad. Get mad at me. That's good. It will make you fight better." Bres said stepping towards Goldie.

Goldie's eyes blazed and Bres's widened in surprise. "I think you're ready to spar with me las. Get your sword and meet me in the training area." Bres said planting a kiss on her cheek too quickly for her to move.

Lorcan's hand shot up and grabbed Bres by the throat. Bres smiled at Lorcan. "You will not touch Goldie or so help me, Bres."

"So, help you what Lorcan? You're going to kill me?" Bres smiled seeming unconcerned that Lorcan had a hand around his throat.

"Boys that's enough!" Boomed King Oberon. "Lorcan, I expect much more than that from you son."

Lorcan let go of Bres and ducked his head. He looked over to Goldie, who wouldn't look at him. He knew she was feeling hurt. Bres grunted his acknowledgement toward Oberon and walked past them towards the training area.

Godfrey called after Bres, "Bres I love you like a son, but if you ever intentionally try to hurt Goldie again, whether it be word or deed, it won't be Lorcan you need to worry about. I will come for you."

Bres stiffened and gave a single nod.

Beatha moved around King Oberon to be by Goldie and place a much-needed hand on her shoulder. She spoke in her mind through their physical connection. "I haven't been here in many years as you know. Boys say stupid things when there's a beautiful young woman around. That's something that has never changed. Lorcan loves you deeply. You know that and so do I. Bres is trying to get under your skin. Don't let him.

You need to be clear headed and ready for battle. There will always be something hard trying to get your attention no matter what the fight is. Learn how to use that negative energy for good. I have all the faith in the world in you."

Goldie's body hummed and slightly glowed. Beatha's eyes widened and she smiled. She spoke in her mind again. "Careful Goldie. Your divinity is showing."

That made Goldie smile and she spoke back into Beatha's mind. "I love you. I don't know what I would do without you. I get stronger when people claim their faith in me or something. I am hurt though. I know Lorcan had a life before he knew me, but I don't want to hear about it. He's never spoke of it with me."

Beatha squeezed her shoulder and let go. Godfrey watched Beatha and Goldie. He had a small smile on his lips.

Angrbora spoke up. "I'm sorry about Bres, Goldie. He's just jealous. Even though he's such a ladies' man, he wants real love. Everyone does whether they admit it or not. Now go kick his ass in practice. Beg your pardon majesty." She nodded towards King Oberon.

He smiled at Angrbora. "I can see why you are my daughter's moon sister. I guess that makes you my moon daughter. Thank you for caring for my girl."

Angrbora smiled wide and said, "I will always have her back. Let's go get you ready Goldie."

Angrbora turned and faced the rest of the guard. "Royal guard, Guard to our Goddess Goldie, you will flank and keep your eyes on our queen. You're her right and left hands. You protect her at all costs. Spread out and learn the perimeters and meet the other guards. We will work with the royal army here together. We aren't sure what is coming in the future, but Goldie has made it clear; we will have a united future."

The Formorian guard all hit their chest plates and said, "Aaroof!" Then they marched in all directions with their eyes forward and heads high.

Godfrey smiled. "I'm happy to be here. Go get ready Goldie. Bres needs his butt kicked."

Goldie smiled and walked off with Angrbora.

Lorcan spoke into Goldie's mind, "Goldie I'm sorry. I don't know what to say. Do you want me to come help you?"

Goldie spoke back and said, "I have Angrbora to help me. There's nothing to say. You have a past before me. I'm going to have to learn to make peace with it."

"I love you." It sounded like a whisper in her head from Lorcan.

She turned and made eye contact with him and nodded with a sad smile.

Angrbora raised her eyebrows. "Is he already groveling?"

Goldie laughed softly. "Sort of. He's apologizing for his past before me and doesn't know what to say. The truth is there is nothing he can say. It hurts to know another woman touched him. He's the only one I've ever given that part of me to. I imagined I would only ever give that part of myself to my husband and I guess I had just hoped I would be his only too. It sounds stupid and I know I shouldn't be mad at him for something that happened before he knew me, but I am."

Angrbora nodded in understanding. "I get that. I've had many partners. Formorians just fill a need though. It's rarely about love. It's just about chasing the high and moving on. It's sad to say, but a lot of it's meaningless. I'm sure that's what it was for him. Especially if he was hanging out with Bres. Women just like to say they've had the best warrior. I know that doesn't make you feel any better. You were raised differently. The way you feel so deeply is something us Formorians envy.

You make all of us feel something. You hug us and care about us. You are opening up things inside of us we didn't know existed."

Goldie smiled. "I hope I bring peace and happiness. I do love our people. I feel awful for how you've been treated for so long. At least Bres is open about who he is. Lorcan has always been so so…"

"Chivalrous?" Angrbora interjected.

"Yes. I guess. He always seemed so mannered and like he wasn't the man whore type. I don't know. I just thought that maybe he had one or two girlfriends you know?" Goldie asked.

Angrbora nodded. "Bres is very open about loving all types of women and very confident in his skills. Lorcan isn't like him. Experienced sure, but not a man whore. I don't think anyway."

Angrbora and Goldie walked into Lorcan's room where her armor still was and Angrbora looked around and looked at Lorcan's armor. "He's got nice armor, but yours is better."

Goldie smiled. "Daideo' made me some beautiful stuff."

"That he did," said Angrbora helping her get suited up.

After she was suited up and ready to go, Goldie said, "Angrbora, hold on to me. I want to try something."

Angrbora never questioned her or wondered what was going on. With all the faith in the world, she just grabbed onto Goldie. Goldie thought about needing to be in the training area and fighting. In an instant her and Angrbora were in the center of the training arena. Bres jumped at their sudden entry.

Goldie laughed and said, "Oh did we scare the big bad Bres?"

"No. I was just caught off guard." Bres scoffed.

"I thought good warriors were always ready for anything," said Goldie stepping away from Angrbora to circle Bres.

"We are." Bres said flatly.

"But you weren't ready for me," said Goldie stepping into his space and pulling her dagger out.

Bres smiled. "Close warfare today then?" He asked eyebrows raised.

Goldie felt all the eyes on them. "Are you nervous Bres? These are my people. They want to see me kick your ass."

Bres laughed. "Nervous isn't in my vocabulary las. Let's see if you can kick my arse. I doubt it."

Bres again was just in britches and nothing else. It peeved Goldie that he was so cocky. But he was the best and for good reason. Goldie lunged at him and Bres side stepped missing her dagger but it gave Goldie the perfect angle to plant her foot solid on his butt. She kicked him and smirked at him.

"I just kicked your arse as you say it," taunted Goldie.

"You will pay for that one las," smiled Bres.

Bres lunged for her, but Goldie slid on the ground like she was coming into Homeplate fast and slid in between his legs and as she went under, she let just the tip of her dagger cut the seam of his britches. Bres quickly grabbed for his junk.

"I could have aimed higher Bres," said Goldie looking at the red Bres.

The crowd was roaring then. "Get him Goldie!" "Show big Bres who's boss!" "Cut his balls off!" A woman shouted. Goldie winced at that and Bres took the opportunity to go after her.

He grabbed her hand that held the dagger and pinned it over her head and got nose to nose with her. "I saw your face las. You want me to keep my balls."

"Believe it or not, I really don't care about your balls," said Goldie rearing her head back to head butt him.

"Oh no las. I learned my lesson from yesterday," said Bres flipping her around to where her back was against him.

He squeezed her wrist so hard that she dropped her dagger. Her eyes were spotting from the pain.

Godfrey spoke up, "Las use the pain to make you focus. He's vulnerable. Think it through and strike."

"Still need your coaching I see. I like this side of you. You feel nice and smell nice. If I wanted to, I could have you here in front of everyone." He whispered so that only she could hear.

Goldie saw red. But Daideo' was right. He was vulnerable. Goldie arched her back into him, making her butt rub against his sensitive groin. Bres let out a breath and Goldie said, "You like that don't you?"

Bres thrust his pelvis towards her and Goldie could feel he was quite impressive. As she purred into his touch and rubbed herself on him, she spread her legs wider and Bres took that as an invitation. When he went to put his leg in between hers, Goldie used her leg to trip him and flip him over her back. He landed on the ground hard and with a thud. While he was still trying to regain his lost breath, Goldie retrieved her other dagger from her other arm guard and put it up to Bres's throat with her knees on his chest and with her other hand, she shoved it in the cut she had made along the seam of his britches and took a tight hold of his balls.

Bres's eyes went wide and he made a strangled noise as he turned red. Goldie squeezed tighter, enjoying the pained sound that left Bres's mouth. She smiled at him and got nose to nose with him, dagger still at his throat.

"I think I like this position baby. I literally have you by the balls." Goldie smirked at him.

Bres's eyes showed defiance but still had a twinkle. Even with the dagger at his neck, he leaned his head up and his lips just grazed Goldie's as he said, "You want to kiss me right now. You like what's in your hand."

"Oh, you think so?" Goldie asked squeezing even harder and adding a twist.

Bres sucked in a deep breath and the pain shown on his face. Through gritted teeth he said, "Unless you want me to puke on you, let go of me."

"Do you give?" Goldie asked.

Bres gave a small nod and Goldie grimaced at the streak of blood she saw trail down his neck. Goldie loosened her grip on his balls and slowly removed her dagger. There was a streak of red across his neck.

"Las, you're still holding my balls. I'd like to have them back. Usually, the prospect of being groped would excite me, but I still feel the need to throw up," said Bres almost pleading her to let go and move.

Goldie shook her head and moved her legs to straddle his chest instead of having all her weight on him. Goldie cocked her head to the side as she thought about what just happened. She still had a gentle hold of him now. She whispered to Bres, "I want to try something ok. Just lay there."

Bres looked scared but nodded. Goldie closed her eyes and her body began to glow. Heat emanated from her hand and to his balls and then she placed the other hand on his throat where she had cut him. She imagined healing his cut and taking the pain from him. She pushed love and happiness into him and warmth and healing.

When she opened her eyes, Bres was looking at her with wonder. "You healed me."

Goldie didn't have time to say anything, she leaned over to the side and heaved. She threw up. Bres quickly sat up and cradled her as she threw up all her breakfast. He pulled her hair back and rubbed her back. No one from the crowd moved. They just watched with racked attention. Bres's eyes went wide when Goldie finally looked at him. She had a small cut along her throat and healed so quick that he almost didn't see it.

Bres pulled her close to him and whispered, "You took my injury and pain into you. Why would you do that las?"

"Because I did that. I really didn't want to hurt you. I was just mad." Goldie barely whispered.

"I deserved it. I taunted you so you would fight hard. I hurt you too. Maybe not with my hands but with my words. I am sorry. I didn't deserve to be healed," said Bres kissing the top of her head without thinking.

Chapter 29

"Let go of her now," seethed Lorcan through gritted teeth.

Bres looked up with tears in his eyes and Lorcan was taken aback. Bres stood up holding a now unconscious Goldie in his arms. He slowly walked to Lorcan.

"What did you do to her?" Lorcan asked starting to feel panicked.

"She kicked my arse and then the crazy girl took my pain and injury into herself. She healed me and I didn't deserve it. She filled me with more than just healing strength. I feel more things." Bres said looking troubled at Lorcan.

With shaky arms he gently handed Goldie to Lorcan and knelt. "Lorcan go take care of my queen."

Everyone was silent. This was a huge moment. Bres acknowledged Goldie as his queen and bowed. Lorcan nodded and in a blink disappeared from the crowd as he teleported Goldie to her room. Beatha flashed behind them. King Oberon stayed for a moment longer to talk with the guard and give instruction.

Lorcan laid Goldie gently on her bed. She moaned as she hit it. "Las wake up. I love you. Please wake up for me." Lorcan said grabbing her hand and kissing it.

Beatha was behind and said, "Move child. I need to lay my hands on her."

Lorcan stepped out of the way and Beatha moved in. Beatha ran her hands along Goldie's body and stopped at her head. Goldie moaned. Beatha's soothing magic swirled around Goldie. When Beatha pulled her hands back, Goldie didn't move.

King Oberon was now in the room. "Beatha, why isn't she waking up?" He asked sounding concerned.

Beatha rung her hands. "It is her battle. She unleashed a power she wasn't ready for. She is stuck in her own mind. She needs to go somewhere she feels at home."

King Oberon paled. "She is home."

"Fionn, I said where she feels at home. She needs to be set back at peace." Beatha said.

"What do you mean at peace?" Asked Lorcan.

Bres spoke from the doorway, "She is internally conflicted with what she did. She is having a hard time with the violence and wanting to take care of people. She hurt me after I provoked her, but then healed me. Her mind cannot handle both worlds right now."

Lorcan's head whipped around. "What are you doing in here?" He asked angrily.

"The door was open and I needed to check on her," said Bres looking down at his large bare feet with Angrbora on heels.

King Oberon looked to Beatha, "What do we do for her?"

"She needs her Granda and home I guess to feel safe and feel at home," said Beatha wrinkling her brow.

Godfrey walked through the door. "Can I take her somewhere? I know of a place her ancestors loved. You know she loves the water. Let me take her to her family's water."

Beatha's face softened. "I think I know where you want to take her. I'm coming with you."

"I didn't agree to anything," said King Oberon.

"She loves the water more than land. Look at her bed and her bathroom. Ask Lorcan about her in the ocean. This makes the most sense." Beatha said grabbing Goldie's hands.

"I am going too," said Lorcan.

"I am too," King Oberon said.

Godfrey picked Goldie up and her head lulled from side to side as he carried her through the castle and out of the royal grounds. Bres still followed with his head down, even though Lorcan stared daggers through him.

"Angrbora, you're in charge in our absence," said King Oberon to Angrbora.

Angrbora straightened her shoulders and said, "I will not take it lightly. Thank you for entrusting me."

"Well, my daughter trusts you, so I will too." The king said turning to wait to see what Godfrey was doing.

"Can we not just teleport there?" Lorcan asked.

"No son you cannot. This place is special and it is protected by magic from magic. Even when the world was dark and led by Balor, this place was still light." Godfrey explained as he kept walking.

They followed him along the dark forest's edge and over four big boulders. When he turned around, you could see water that seemed to come out of nowhere traveling through the middle of the four boulders and it seemed to disappear.

"This water is the same water that leads up to the castle. This was the same stream that Goldie's grandmother, my daughter, made her way out of the Hollow Hill. It will lead out into the ocean if you know where to go. Only those who have the power of the current in them are accepted through the boulders. Some of you may not be able to pass through." Godfrey explained.

Godfrey's outstretched a hand and penetrated an invisible veil. It shimmered blue and opened like a curtain. He motioned for them to follow him. King Oberon, Beatha, and Bres made it through. The curtain slammed shut before Lorcan and he was stuck outside.

Lorcan stopped abruptly and felt his heart ache as he felt Goldie getting further away from him. He tried to put his hand where Godfrey did, but he felt nothing. He sat on a big boulder and put his head in his hands. How was he supposed to protect Goldie if he couldn't even be with her?

The darkness lit from within as Godfrey walked further into the cave the water went from ankle deep and got deeper as they went. It looked like glitter everywhere. Ocean blue glitter coursing across the walls and it was alive. The lit glitter moved as if in waves like the current of the ocean following the group that passed.

Bres took a deep breath. "I've never seen anything like this."

"Because there is nothing else like this anywhere in the world lad," answered Godfrey as the water got waist deep.

Godfrey started to sing and when he got to the last stanza:

"As I walk I can feel him,
Always watching over me…
His voice surrounds me,
My Spirit of the Sea.."

He sat Goldie gently down in the water and let her go. Beatha went to grab her as she sunk to the bottom.

"No Beatha. You must let her be. She has to let the water heal her and she has to want it," said Godfrey holding Beatha back.

King Oberon took a deep breath and his eyes went wide as the water surrounding Goldie started to shine brightly. It was like the blue glitter on the walls had descended to cover her body.

"Blessed be," Bres breathed out as they watched Goldie's clothes disappear.

"Avert your eyes lad." King Oberon hissed at Bres.

But none of them could take their eyes off Goldie. Her fingers started to twitch and became webbed. Her nails grew into fine points and were the color of the caps of waves. Her hair gained a blue streak. Her feet disappeared into a single fin and her breast ended up being covered by her hair that was now a good two feet longer. Goldie opened her eyes that now glowed bright blue with a golden rim and sucked in a breath. Not a regular breath but a breath under water.

At first, she looked like a goldfish opening and closing her mouth. She looked confused like she wasn't sure what was going on. She looked up out of the glowing water to Godfrey and he smiled at her.

"You're beautiful las. There hasn't been a true mermaid in the Hollow Hill for a long time." Godfrey said.

Goldie looked up confused and then it registered. She lifted what would have been her feet and saw an enormous flipper. It was glittery blue, green, purple, and had golden accents. She smiled, but now all of her teeth were sharp points. She looked at her hands and flipped them through the water. She looked around and saw her Da and smiled at him. She saw Beatha with a hand over her mouth and she saw Bres with his mouth open wide.

Confusion struck her again. She opened her mouth to speak and her words sounded like music, but they couldn't hear her. She felt stupid when she realized she was still under water. She went to sit up and accidently breached the water. She laughed when she plopped back in the water. She landed on her butt. She sat there and looked at everyone. She could see their magics swirling about them. She tilted her head when she looked a Bres. He should only have one color and it be the color of the God which contributed to his DNA, but he had three colors. She looked at Godfrey. His color was hidden but she knew it was blue.

When she spoke this time, she was above water. It was still musical and everyone but Godfrey started to walk out to the water to her. "Where is Lorcan?" She sang.

She looked again in confusion as they walked out to her. Godfrey answered her unspoken question. "Your voice calls out to them to come to you. It's a siren's call. Think about what you want your voice to be used for before you speak. Luckily the water isn't deep here, but if it were, they would walk to their deaths."

Goldie's eyebrows shot up. She cleared her throat and thought, "Normal voice. Do not harm."

When she spoke again, she was composed. "What happened and where is Lorcan?"

Bres spoke up with his voice cracking a bit. "You took my pain and injury and it was too much. You hurt yourself. It was my fault. You should have never healed me. I'm so sorry. I liked getting a rise out of you, but not at risk of truly hurting you."

"Oh, so he does have a heart in there," said Goldie smiling with her wicked teeth and then her mouth began to salivate. She put a webbed hand up to her mouth to cover it quickly.

"Ouch!" She said pulling her hand back to realize she was bleeding after grazing a tooth. She carefully ran her tongue over her teeth and went wide eyed.

"Da?" She asked.

He smiled and said, "You are beautiful my dear, but you are hungry. You need to replenish yourself after using so much power on Bres."

"My mouth started watering when I mentioned Bres's heart. Is something wrong with me?" Goldie asked feeling horrified.

Beatha smiled and said, "Child, you are a mermaid-siren being. They eat flesh. Don't you know the stories. Most of them just stuck to fish, but some went dark and would carry sailors down into the depths, have their way with them, drown them, and then eat them. Mermaids come from a siren mating with a human. You seem to be both which is unique. You are just full of surprises. One being to unite us all I suppose."

"Try out your fins and swim. If you go that way," said Godfrey pointing to the back of the glittering cave, "you'll be out in the ocean. Go catch you a fish las."

Goldie beamed and looked where her Daideo' was pointing. She turned on her rump and dove down and took off almost too fast for her family to see. She disappeared to what looked like the wall, but it was just the magic.

Goldie revealed in the freedom of the ocean. She smiled and breathed in the salty goodness of the sea quite literally. She swam with dolphins for real now. She kept up and even breached the water with them and played. When they worked together to herd some fish, she worked alongside them and took one for herself when they all attacked their food. At first her stomach whirled at the thought of eating a still wiggling fish raw. But then again, sushi. Her whirling stomach soon turned into a growling one and holding the fish tightly with her sharp nails digging into it so it couldn't escape, she bit down.
Goldie moaned as an explosion of taste hit her mouth. She could taste where the fish had been. She could almost see the ocean pictures in her head. She devoured it, bones and all. When she finished eating, she turned to the dolphins and said, "Thank you for letting me tag along."

She almost jumped out of her skin when the largest said in her mind, "It was our pleasure, Goddess." Then the pod swam off. Goldie felt her heart ache and she rubbed her chest. Something was missing. She felt so free and almost didn't want to go back. "Lorcan," she whispered as his face was all she could see in her mind.

She turned and swam even faster back to the hidden magical cave. She marveled as the water lit around her body as she entered the cave. She popped up out of the water to find Godfrey, Bres, King Oberon, and Beatha all seated along the cave walls waiting for her.

"How was it las?" Daideo' asked with a twinkle in his eyes.

"Everything I could ever imagine." Goldie said.

She looked from face to face, not seeing the one she wanted still. A smell hit her nostrils and her stomach let out a loud growl.

"Still hungry I see," said her Da chuckling.

"Something smells so good in here. Do you see a fish?" Goldie asked spinning in the water and searching.

Beatha said, "There are no fish here child."

Goldie sniffed the air again with her eyes closed. When she opened them, her eyes locked on Bres's.

"Las what is it?" Godfrey asked.

"He smells so delicious." Goldie said still looking at the very flushed Bres.

Beatha ruffled. "Child you can't eat Bres. What in the world? Is it the Siren in her?" Beatha asked looking at the men with a worried look.

King Oberon looked at Bres thoughtfully. "She healed him with her magic. Maybe she smells that."

Godfrey said, "Or maybe it's his blood calling to her senses. Sirens were part of the blood fae family. They needed more than meat to survive."

Before Goldie knew what she was doing, her voice went lyrical as she looked at Bres. "Come to me Bres," sang Goldie. "I want to taste you."

Chapter 30

Bres blinked his eyes rapidly as if trying to comprehend what Goldie had said. His feet started to move toward Goldie on their own. He looked down confused and over to Godfrey.

Godfrey said, "Bres you're a Formorian, you don't have to go to her call. Think about it lad. You have the blood of a God coursing through your veins. If you go out to her, it's because you want to."

Bres abruptly stopped. Goldie cried out in frustration. Bres looked at her thoughtfully and asked, "What is it that you want from me las?"

Goldie blinked as if she was coming back to herself. She looked Bres in the eyes and said, "What I already said. Something about you is calling to me. I need to taste you." Goldie put her hand up over her mouth and her eyes went wide at her own truthfulness.

Bres cracked a half smile. "So, you do want me las? Do you want to hurt me? I'm not going to come out to you if I'm going to have to fight you or hurt you to release me. I won't hurt you."

Goldie scrunched her eyebrows together and said, "I don't think so."

Bres started back towards her. He was still only in britches. King Oberon spoke up, "Is this such a good idea? I don't know that we should allow him to go to her."

"I think she needs this," said Bres. "I will feed her if that's what she needs, especially after she healed me."

Bres was in the water and as he got closer, Goldie tingled with anticipation. Goldie smiled showing her sharp, pointed teeth. Bres didn't falter. He walked straight to her. He stood right in front of her. As Goldie sat in the water, Bres's crotch was right in her face. She closed her eyes and took a deep breath. As her nostrils flared, she licked her lips. Bres's eyes heated when she opened hers and looked at him.

"I'll just sit las. I don't think I want your teeth that close to my manhood," said Bres.

Godfrey let out an amused sound. King Oberon frowned and Beatha covered her mouth.

"Are we going to let her do this?" Beatha asked. "What will Lorcan think?"

"This isn't up to anyone but me," said Goldie looking around Bres and at the people watching her. "Something in him calls to me and I must find it."

"I've never let anyone take my blood before las. How do you want to do this?" Bres asked Goldie.

Goldie reached out a trembling hand and ran it down Bres's neck. He shook under her touch and his eyes went wide. His blood glowed where she touched him. She trailed her finger down to his chest just above his heart. She laid her hand flat on his chest and felt the beating underneath and smiled. Bres watched her closely. He put his hand over hers and their eyes met. Hers glowing blue with a golden rim and his blue. Her eyes widened.

Goldie whispered, "Don't move," as she leaned in close to him.

 Bres sat stark still. Goldie smelled down his neck and to where their hands were still joined. She moved their hands away and licked him. Her tastebuds ignited and she had to bite. She thought about not wanting to hurt him though and she got a panicked look in her eyes.

"It's ok las. I'm not afraid of pain. Bite me." Bres commanded her.

With that, Goldie sank her teeth into his chest above his heart. She moaned as his warm blood filled her mouth. It was the most decadent thing she ever had tasted. Bres shuddered under her and moaned too. Suddenly, her mind was filled with what she could only describe as a film real. She saw Bres's life played out in her head. Every moment training with Godfrey and his secret moments of longing for parents. She felt the rush of lust as he saw her the first time in her armor. She felt his joy at taunting her and pride when she landed a blow. She saw and felt his fear as he had held her earlier while she lay limp in his arms. She felt love. God, she felt love.

Goldie opened her eyes and released him quickly. As she did, she felt power running through her veins. The power shot out from her and lit the cave, making it a kaleidoscope of colors and shooting out of the entrance. Bres looked at her in awe. She licked at the wound on his chest from her. It looked like a perfect baby shark bite. As she licked him, he healed and his breathing became labored. Goldie looked up horrified at what she had just done. She came back to her complete self and jumped back from Bres. As she did, she saw the hurt in his eyes at her sudden push away.

Goldie felt a pain in her chest and realized that it wasn't her own pain, but Bres's. She was now irrevocably linked to him. Taking his blood created a bond between them. Her eyes widened at the implications. She felt her tail morphing back into her legs. It didn't hurt, but felt like the pins and needles you get when your leg falls asleep. Her hair at least didn't change so her naked breasts were still covered, but Goldie shrieked in alarm when she realized her nakedness. Bres turned his back to give her privacy.

"Goldie," soothed Beatha. "Use your magic child. You can use your magic to make clothes."

Goldie took a steadying breath and thought about what she needed. It came easy this time as her body buzzed with more magic than she thought she could handle. She ended up in black leather pants and a black tank top and of course no shoes. She padded out of the water and looked around at where they were at.

"Where are we? This place is amazing," whispered Goldie reverently.

"This my las is where your ancestors have come from the beginning of Hollow Hill to escape to the water. This place is magical. Only those who are worthy can enter," said Godfrey.

Goldie scrunched her eyebrows in concentration. "Then where is Lorcan?"

She felt a pang in her heart and knew it was from Bres. She felt a little guilty. Had she been able to control her hunger, she would have never taken blood from him. She hurt thinking about what Lorcan would feel when he found out. Goldie tried to bite back her next comment, but failed. "But he is worthy. He's my heartmate."

This time she rubbed at her chest and hissed.

"What's wrong child?" Beatha asked coming to grab her.

Goldie looked up to Bres and his eyebrows rose in understanding. Beatha looked at the exchange and nodded.

"You two are now bonded as well. You healing him and the blood he gave you willingly bound you." Beatha said her face etching in concern.

Bres looked at Goldie and said, "It's ok las. Don't feel bad for me. I'm the maker of my own problems not you. No one has to know. You saved me and I tried to repay the favor. It was nothing."

Goldie nodded but they both knew that was a lie.

Godfrey still saw the concern on her face and said, "Lorcan probably just wasn't allowed in because he has no ties to the water. It's not that big of a deal. Only a select few can get in. Usually only our bloodline. You know by now we love the water. You may be strong enough to alter the magic so he can pass if you wish."

Goldie said, "I'm ready to go home."

King Oberon smiled and said, "Let's go."

Goldie closed her eyes and thought of Lorcan. She wanted to portal to where he was. When she opened her eyes, she was still in the same place. Godfrey had a twinkle in his eyes.

"This place is magical las. There's only one way in and one way out on foot. We have to walk the old-fashioned way." Godfrey explained.

"Lead the way Daideo'." Goldie said.

Daideo', Beatha, King Oberon, Goldie and Bres filed a line to get out of the cave. Goldie felt Bres's eyes on her and she tried not to think about it. She tried not to think of her animalistic side that had come out and how she felt not herself. She tried not to think about the power that now coursed through her veins when her siren was awakened. One question kept running through her mind, "What am I?"

Then clear as if she had asked the question out loud, Bres answered her, "You are everything."

Chapter 31

Everyone stopped abruptly and turned to face Bres.

He looked puzzled. He asked, "What?"

"Who were you talking to lad?" Godfrey asked.

"Didn't you hear Goldie? She kept asking the same question." Bres said looking confused.

Goldie turned and faced him completely. "Bres I didn't ask it out loud. You heard my thoughts."

"I don't want to hear your thoughts las. Unless they are dirty ones about me." He tried to joke, but Goldie could see the pleading in his eyes. He didn't want to hear what she was thinking when she was reunited with Lorcan.

"I will try to block them from you. I think I can if I concentrate." Goldie said straightening her shoulders.

Bres just gave her a nod.

They kept walking. Goldie marveled at the way the glitter moved on the walls. She couldn't help but touch it. When she did, the walls glitter emerged and entered into her. Her body lit up like the glitter and the current danced upon her skin. Goldie's eyes widened in shock.

Bres took in a deep breath and the three leading the pack turned around to see what happened. Beatha's eyes bugged out and King Oberon took in a breath. Daideo' just smiled.

"What's happening?" Goldie asked with a shaky voice turning her hands over to see the current ripple through her.

"You my grandchild, have been gifted your ancestors' magic. This place is special. You now will have the power to control who comes in and out and the power over the water in the Hollow Hill. You ancestors found you worthy. You are who will heal us. You were foretold las." Daideo' said.

"But how?" Goldie asked.

"Your great grandmother was somewhat of a seer. She knew love would be the downfall to Balor and so did your grandmother. You are a result of that love tenfold and now you return love to us all. You are part of us all. You bring us all together. You're not just one type of fae or have just one type of power. You embody them all." Daideo' said walking back to her and putting a soft hand on her cheek.

Goldie's eyes met Beatha's. "It's ok child. You can handle this. You will learn how to control it all with time, but for now think about how your magic works. It always comes out when you need it to. Think about what you want to happen this very minute." Beatha said soothingly.

Goldie nodded and closed her eyes. She thought of the magic within her retreating into her body and leaving her skin back to its normal complexion. When she opened her eyes, her skin was back to its normal hue, although she felt a new hum inside her. She felt so powerful and it frightened her a little.

They kept walking and made their way out. Goldie was shocked to realize that it was now nighttime outside. Time felt differently in the magical cave. Her breath hitched in her throat when she saw Lorcan sitting on the ground just waiting. She wondered how long he had been there.

When he saw her coming his eyes lit up and she knew hers did too. He got up and was on her in an instant. He crashed his mouth down on hers and kissed her passionately. When he pulled back, his nostrils flared.

"Why do you smell of Bres?" He asked eyes flashing.

Goldie looked down and away. Lorcan stepped back and looked at Goldie.

"You seem much changed. Your hair is longer and do I see blue? You feel and smell more powerful too. But what I don't understand is why you smell of Bres." He said again.

Godfrey and King Oberon took a step forward to be by Goldie's side. Lorcan's eyes went wide.

"Lorcan, I..I am much more yet again. When I awoke in the water I woke as a mermaid with a tail and all. I was so hungry. Daideo' told me to swim out to the ocean and eat. I did. I ate a fish. I felt better, until I got back into the cave. You weren't in there and I was still so hungry. Apparently, I'm part blood fae too because the siren in me called out to Bres. He smelled so good.I...."Goldie trailed off.

"After what she did for me, I offered her my blood. She needed the nourishment and I wouldn't let her go without." Bres said trying to defend Goldie.

Lorcan's eyes went wild. "You drank from him? From him? I would have fed you! I would give you anything!" He hollered.

Goldie whispered, "I know Lorcan. I was not myself. I couldn't help it."

"Couldn't or wouldn't? I know how powerful and strong you are," said Lorcan shaking with hurt and fury.

"Lorcan that's not fair! You weren't even in there. You didn't see me or what happened. I don't love Bres. I love you damnit!" Goldie shouted feeling angry.

Goldie doubled over in pain and hit the ground after letting those words leave her lips. Everyone ran forward to grab her. She was holding her chest when they rolled her over.

"What's wrong?" Shouted Lorcan.

Goldie opened her eyes and looked past Lorcan to Bres. Lorcan followed her line of sight to the huge red headed Formorian standing still wide eyed.

"What is she looking at you for?" Lorcan asked through gritted teeth.

Bres moved closer to Goldie and knelt beside Lorcan. He reached his hand out and grabbed Goldie's.
"You blocked your thoughts, but you can't block the words you said out loud. I hurt you again and I don't mean to. I'm sorry las. I have to go." Bres took off running.

As he got farther away, Goldie's chest began to relax. Slowly she sat up and took deep breaths.

"What does all this mean Goldie?" Lorcan asked looking scared.

King Oberon spoke up for Goldie who was still trying to collect herself. "When she took Bres's blood, she bonded to him in a way. She feels his pain now."

"But why would she be feeling pain? There was nothing wrong with him," said Lorcan looking at Goldie.

Godfrey whispered the answer this time; "Because he loves her lad."

Lorcan shot up to a standing position and anger coursed through him. "What?" He bellowed.

"It's not his fault. It's mine. I shouldn't have chosen him to spar with her, but he is the best. I mean really, do you blame him lad? Goldie is the first royal being to acknowledge Formorians as more than tools. She chose to show us compassion and friendship. She showed the younger ones true care. He couldn't help but love her. Bres will work his feelings out. Give him time," said Godfrey with a look of sadness in his eyes for the young lad.

"As long as his time means he's no longer close to Goldie," said Lorcan going stiff.

"Lorcan," whispered Goldie, "Look at me."

He did.

Goldie spoke out loud for everyone to hear. She understood he needed affirmation of her love in front of everyone. "I love you with my whole heart Lorcan. I can't explain nor do I understand everything that happened tonight. I do know that when I came back to myself, you were who I asked for. I'm wild at heart and I am one with the sea and it's a great feeling, but I understand how my grandmother would have given it up for my Granda. I love you that much."

Lorcan's eyes finally softened and knelt to the ground in front of Goldie. He took her hands in his. "I love you with my whole heart too. His scent on you drives me insane, but I'm not mad at you. I'm a jealous, selfish bastard that wants you to only be mine. That's just not possible since you are our queen, but I don't like the idea of another man nourishing you. The idea that you have a bond with another man tears at my heart."

"And the thought of you having shared your body with other girls before me tears at my heart Lorcan. We just have to trust that our love and bond is strong enough to pull us through these insecurities. We have to remind each other that we are heartmates. We have to fight for each other daily. I wake up and choose you Lorcan and had you been in that cave, I have no doubt who I would have wanted." Goldie said squeezing his hands.

Lorcan leaned in and kissed her gently and then rested his forehead on hers. "I still need to get his smell off you."

Goldie laughed and said, "Well then get it off of me."

Lorcan got a wicked smile and in an instant teleported he and Goldie away from everyone. Goldie laughed when they landed in her bathtub, clothes and all. She shrieked. She closed her eyes and with a thought had both of their clothes gone. She noticed after the cave her magic came a lot faster and easier. The water began to run and Goldie's body shimmered with the blue glitter currents.

Lorcan's eyes widened and he said, "That's new." He rubbed his hands along her arms and watched the currents move with his touch. "It's beautiful."

"This is how my ancestors' magic manifested to me. My Daideo' said I'm worthy and that I am the one to heal the land. It seems crazy to me. I just always thought I would be on a shrimp boat my whole life." Goldie said.

"Now you're here with me," said Lorcan grabbing the soap and creating suds.

Lorcan gently washed every part of Goldie's body. He left no place unwashed or untouched. He kissed the side of her head as she leaned back into him after he finished washing her. Goldie hummed her approval. She wanted Lorcan to feel how much she loved him. She wanted him to have no doubts, so she concentrated and radiated it though her body to him.

Lorcan sucked in a breath in shock at the sensation from her magic licking his body. He felt warmth and then gasped as it sunk into his skin and he had a light blue glitter sheen shine.

"I love you enough to give you everything I can," said Goldie.

"You don't have to share your magic with me. I know you love me and I love you. I'm sorry I got so angry earlier. I just..You're it for me Goldie." Lorcan said kissing her again.

They got out of the water and dried off and didn't bother with clothes. They would cement their bond again. They both needed the closeness of one another. They needed to reconnect in the most primal way to feel secure again. Lorcan found Goldie's mouth with his.

She sank into the kiss with her mind, body, and soul. She felt Lorcan let go too. It deepened to the point where she felt like she was drowning in him, but she breathed it in as she had the water and her senses opened up to him tenfold. They shared a completeness together. They felt and heard the thoughts of the other and their magics wrapped around them like a blanket and pushed them together.

When the magic pulled Goldie up off the ground, she didn't question it. She just wrapped her legs around Lorcan and let the magic and their bodies push their efforts along. She sighed in pleasure as her body sank onto his and his eyes looked at her in wonder. Their arms were still wrapped around each other. Their magic was leading the way. Goldie's colors lifted her up and down and Lorcan gasped and Goldie took the opportunity to push her tongue back into his mouth. She moaned as he nipped her lip with his teeth.

She didn't have to speak for Lorcan to hear her say, "I love you." And Lorcan didn't have to answer, because Goldie already felt it. The pace wasn't blazing but it was working and with the magic caressing and pushing them together it was more intimate than anything they had done.

Goldie groaned as her release got closer. The magic lit up from around her. As she came her glitter bounced off her. Lorcan's eyes went wide and he gasped as her magic filled him in the most unexpected way and he came with her name on his tongue. He felt his fangs lengthen. He didn't have to ask permission because he knew she wanted him to bite her. As his fangs slid into her neck, Goldie came again, wringing even more from him. As he pulled from her vein, Goldie's teeth changed into her little shark like teeth and she sank them into his shoulder.

Lorcan cried out, but not from pain. He released even more inside her and her magic pushed at him. They lapped at each other and then both went still, when they realized they were both hovering off the ground. Their combined magic held them off the floor and together. Goldie's blue glitter permeated the room. She giggled when she looked. Lorcan got a hooded look.

Their magic gently caressed them once more before slowly laying them on the waterbed. Lorcan didn't even bother pulling himself out of Goldie. He just held her tight, hoping that his magic and scent would stay with her all her days. Goldie didn't try to get him to leave her or let go. She simply went to sleep in his arms and relished in all that was him and the magic she could feel filling them both.

When Goldie awoke, it was with Lorcan kissing her neck and growing hard again inside her. She giggled and wiggled into him. Lorcan chuckled and rolled her onto her back still deep within her. Something had changed in their relationship. They were connected by so much more than just the heartbond; blood and magic now intertwined them like they were one.

Lorcan kissed her softly. "I love you so much. I don't deserve you and I think you know that after my display last night."

Goldie smiled and said, "I love you too. We don't have to talk about that again. You do deserve me my love. I've given you all of me and my magic flowed freely from me to you last night. Do you think I would have been able to share my magic with you if you were not worthy?"

Lorcan kissed her again and made love to her. No magic this time, just him showing her she was his world.

Chapter 32

When Goldie made it down to breakfast with Lorcan, Beatha and Da were already eating. They looked up and their eyes went wide at the sight of them.

"Lorcan, you seem to shimmer," said King Oberon with a slight grin.

"Yeah, uh, Goldie did that." Lorcan said sheepishly.

"I guess the wedding will just be a ceremony. You two have bonded more completely than anyone ever has," said Beatha nodding her approval.

"There's something more serious we need to discuss," said Daideo' walking in the dining room unannounced.

King Oberon's face showed concern. "What is it Godfrey?"

Godfrey answered, "I don't think it's necessarily bad, but I think when Goldie received the blessing of her ancestors' magic or maybe when she hit the sacred water and the power radiated from her, or..."

"What happened? What did I do?" Goldie asked feeling panicked.

"Well, the dark forest retreated a lot. More of the Hollow is light now. Your magic I suppose pushed through the darkness and more of our realm is back." Godfrey said scratching his chin.

Everyone looked at him open mouthed.

"Well child, perhaps the war doesn't have to have bloodshed. If you can pulse your power outward in a burst, it can heal the land. It's worth trying." Beatha said thoughtfully.

"I still don't understand who I'm fighting," said Goldie.

"We don't either, but someone is controlling the darkness. If there wasn't, it would have dissipated almost completely by now." King Oberon said.

"But is the darkness all bad. Angrbora and I had a conversation when we first met. Maybe the dark and light need each other. A balance of each seems important." Goldie said.

Lorcan kissed her cheek and said, "You are smarter than the rest of us."

The full moon was upon them. Goldie had continued training with her fighting, but just with Angrbora and her Daideo'. Bres still hadn't come back around. She knew he had to keep his distance for both of their sakes. She hated that he was hurting but her heart was Lorcan's.

She did wonder where he was though. She tried to reach out in her mind to him; "Bres, I don't know if you can hear me. This may be all for nothing, but I hope you are somewhere safe. I'm sorry for what I did to you. I didn't mean to bond you to me. I'm sorry I'm a curse on you. You shouldn't have to stay away from our people for my sake. If you come back, we will find a way to fix this Bres."

All she got in return was silence.

She didn't take any magic training. She didn't need it with the amount of power she had anymore. She only had to will things to happen and they did. But Beatha and Da made her practice wielding it more quickly. Her thoughts on what to do had to be second nature. She could use all the elements at her disposal but especially water and water was strong. She could even throw power balls. When they burst or hit their target, her blue glitter flew everywhere.

She learned that when people praised her for doing something well, she grew a little stronger. The goddess part of her was growing stronger. She tried her magic at a part of the dark forest and she could in fact make it retreat, but she wasn't sure if it was what she should be focusing on. The darkness would slowly creep its way back towards where it had been. They needed to find the cause of the dark magic. Lorcan never went on the two-day mission to find out, but Goldie had made the decision they would go together after they were married.

The wedding was planned as much as you plan a magical wedding and Goldie was ready to be united with Lorcan in this last final way in front of everyone. The night before the wedding Lorcan stayed in his room and she stayed in hers. She took an extra-long bath and soaked in bath salts. She washed her hair a little longer. She closed her eyes and breathed in the comfort and relaxation. She did miss Lorcan though.

She reached out in her mind to her love. "Lorcan what are you doing?"

She heard his warm chuckle in her head. "I'm lying in my bed las. You can't handle it can you?"

"Like you're handling it well." Goldie teased.

"I'm not. It's been a long time since I've slept without you." Lorcan said into her mind.

Lorcan asked after her silence, "What are you doing?"

"I'm soaking in the bath." Goldie answered in her mind with a smile on her lips.

She heard his groan. He replied, "You always think about me while you're in the bath. I approve."

"I can't help it. I miss you being next to me too. I love you," said Goldie through their mind link.

"I love you too my light. I'll see you at the tree tomorrow," said Lorcan with the sound of excitement in him.

"I'll be there. See you tomorrow," said Goldie and then sank back lower into the water.

Beatha and Angrbora walked through the door first thing in the morning. Goldie popped up happy to see her favorite women. They both came over to her and hugged her tightly.

"Good morning child. I'm so happy for you. I know you Granna would have been happy to be here. I know she's proud too." Beatha said with tears in her eyes.

"I'm just honored to call you sister and friend and feel privileged to be here with you," said Angrbora squeezing her tightly.

"I love you both so much!" Goldie exclaimed.

"I'm not sure what all we have to do, since our magic takes care of everything?" Goldie asked her eyebrows raised.

"Sure, we don't have to do too much, but we will enjoy normal girl things," said Beatha pulling Goldie to her feet and putting a white robe on her that says bride.

Goldie giggled and let the ladies lead her down the hall to the dining room that was set up with an elaborate breakfast. There were frittatas, waffles, muffins, bacon, sausage, fruit, and mimosas. She smiled and hugged the two ladies again.

They dug in talking animatedly and Angrbora devoured all the new foods with gusto. They ate and enjoyed each other's company and then after that, Beatha painted Goldie's fingernails and toenails the old-fashioned way. They were of course sparkly blue. Angrbora fixed Goldie's hair half back in multiple braids. Her blue streak she left alone and curled down to hang by the side of her face.

Before Goldie completed the look, she found her little rouge on her dresser and dotted her cheeks and lips. Beatha got teary eyed. "How about some jewelry?" Beatha asked.

Goldie hadn't thought about that. She would have to wear her crown she knew, but she didn't think about the rest.

"How about your Granna's pearls?" A voice she knew better than her own said from her doorway.

Goldie let the tears fill her eyes as she spun to find her Granda in the doorway. She ran to him and wrapped her arms around his neck. She let the tears fall onto his shoulder.

"Come now my Charm, don't let me spoil your day." Granda said.

"You didn't spoil it. You made it perfect. I'm so happy to see you. I've missed you so much." Goldie said holding on tight.

Granda pulled away and kissed her cheek and Goldie lit up golden. Granda smiled with his eyes and said, "May I?" Holding up the pearls.

Goldie turned around and held her hair up for him to clasp the old pearls around her neck. Once they were in place her fingers trailed to them and a single tear ran down her cheek. She turned and hugged her Granda again and using his calloused thumb, he wiped her tear away.

"How did you…when did you get here?" Goldie asked him.

"Lorcan made sure I got here. He sent one of his men to get me here. That portal thing is tough on an old mortal man like me," said Granda scratching his head.

"I wouldn't miss your wedding las. I met your father. He seems to be a good man. I guess I can learn to like him, even if he got your mother pregnant out of wedlock. He did give me you," said Granda smiling softly with sadness in his eyes.

"I got you Granda. I wouldn't be the woman I am without you. Because of the way you raised me, I'm making a real difference here." Goldie said looking into his eyes.

On his weathered face, she saw herself reflected in him. She smiled. "Granda I've got so much to tell you and so much to show you. I'm not a selkie, but I did turn into a mermaid or a siren or both the other day. I can swim so fast. I also have wings and I get taller when I'm angry or feel threatened. Granda, I have no clue what I actually am, but they say I am part of everyone. I get the best of all the worlds I guess."

He smiled at her. "You have time to tell me las after the wedding. You have to get ready. I will be here after your married and the honeymoon. Your da said I can stay as long as I want."

Goldie smiled brightly letting her gap show with no reservations. She turned to Beatha and said, "Well?"

Beatha's eyes twinkled with amusement. "How about a dress?"

Goldie's eyes went wide and she looked down at her robe covered body.

Angrbora laughed. "Yes, my sister, you need something other than a robe."

Granda's eyes shot up. "My sister?"

"Yes, this is Angrbora, my moon sister. She is so important to me. She is also head of my council and my army." Goldie explained smiling.

Granda walked over to the woman who was a foot taller than him and gave her a hug. Angrbora's shocked face quickly grew to one of happiness and she hugged him back.

"I see where Goldie gets her hugging from," laughed Angrbora.

"I always wanted another granddaughter. You can call me Granda," said Granda smiling at the huge woman.

Angrbora's face went soft and she said, "I think I will like that. I've never had a Granda before."

Then everyone turned to face Goldie as the castle's magic and her magic fused together around her, sending a shimmering affect. Goldie giggled as her robe disappeared into a beautiful wedding dress. It was a sweetheart neck that was form fitting and pressed her breasts up. It was form fitting all the way to her calves until it fanned out to look like a mermaid tail. From the bottom of the dress up to her waist line was beautiful blue and turquoise beading to look like the most elegant waves. On her arms were golden bands. She still wore no shoes, but on her second toe was a gold toe ring curved to look like waves and on top of her head sat her crown perfectly in place. She was a queen; a goddess. Goldie spun in a circle and everyone's eyes moistened.

"You look beautiful," said King Oberon from the doorway.

Everyone turned to face him and he said, "It's time."

Chapter 33

They didn't teleport to the tree. They walked through the village. Everyone was outside their homes smiling and throwing flower petals on the ground before Goldie. The towns' children ran before her laughing and throwing flowers in the air. The rest of the Fae people followed behind Goldie, Da, Granda, Beatha, and Angrbora.

Angrbora still looked formidable. She was dressed in her warrior garb, but dressed her face with a smile. Beatha wore a light blue dress that went down to her knees and her hair up in curls on her head. King Oberon wore his kingly dress that Goldie had seen the first day she arrived. Granda had on his Sunday best. She loved him for it. It was just a simple tweed coat and his khaki pants. She just wanted him to be himself and he didn't disappoint.

Goldie smiled when she saw Mack's tree come into view. She saw the dark form of Lorcan waiting at the tree. Her breath hitched when his eyes found hers. His eyes filled with water and he smiled at her with longing and pride.

"You look beautiful." He said in her mind.

"You are handsome beyond words." Goldie said back in his mind.

Lorcan was in his warrior dress too, but more formal. He had his dark hair slicked back and his black leather braid that he wore on his head, now had a single golden thread in it too. His eyes seemed to be lined in dark liner and they stood out brighter as they glowed. He stood tall with his shoulders straight. He had a secret smile on his face just meant for Goldie. His swords were gleaming at his sides and his black bands on his arms only defined his muscles.

As Goldie got to what would be considered the top of the wedding aisle, the ground shook. Coming from the dark forest beyond the tree, her personal Formorian guard marched up. They looked magnificent, all-in warrior form and with their weapons. They stood tall and proud. They stopped in a semi-circle behind the tree. Goldie smiled and acknowledged each one and felt a pang in her heart when she didn't find Bres's face among her guard.

King Oberon kissed Goldie's cheek and said, "This is where I leave you las. I will marry you off to Lorcan this time.

She smiled at her da and nodded as he took off down the aisle first. Everyone in attendance hit a knee as he walked past. When he got to the front he said, "Please rise and remain standing for your new queen as she enters into her bond with her heartmate. Behold her beauty and grace and remember this day when our land was united and reignited with love and hope."

Goldie looped her arms through Granda's and Beatha's and began the slow walk down the aisle. Angrbora kept close in step behind her, keeping her eyes open for any threats. Goldie laughed when she saw Mack climb out of the big tree and run down the aisle to her. He carried a single blue flower in his hand. He climbed up her body and placed the flower in her hair and licked her cheek before scampering back to the tree to take a perch on a branch just above her father.

As Goldie walked past the crowd of onlookers, they lowered their heads in reverence. She smiled and made eye contact with as many as she could. Flowers grew behind her as she made her way forward to the tall, dark man waiting for her with a smile. Goldie smiled at him and let her feelings radiate to Lorcan. His eyes went soft and he said in her mind, "I've been waiting all my life for you."

King Oberon nodded at Granda and Beatha when they reached Lorcan. Each one of them took the hand that was on their arms and placed Goldie's hands into Lorcan's large ones that were waiting. Granda and Beatha each kissed Goldie's cheeks before sitting down in two chairs waiting for them in the front row. Angrbora took her place behind Goldie.

Goldie and Lorcan's colors swirled about them as they locked the union in place. The crowd gasped and Goldie and Lorcan only saw each other. They smiled brightly at one another. Lorcan didn't wait for the ceremony to truly begin. He bent his head and kissed her. Light shot out from Goldie and it splintered into glittering bits of magic flowing down on the crowd. Her happiness radiated from her.

King Oberon laughed and said, "My children come now. Let's make this official." He turned his attention to the crowd. "My people, my family, today we are here to be witness to these heartmates becoming one. I believe had not the heartmate bond pushed them together, they still would have chosen one another. Today they say their own words from the heart to one another."

Lorcan nodded at Goldie and said, "Ladies first."

Goldie chuckled and nodded. "Lorcan, you literally walked into my life and I had no clue what you would bring me. You've brought me fun, happiness I didn't know existed, confidence, and a love so strong it holds me together. You've seen me though many things in our short time together and you protect me in ways I didn't know I needed protecting. I know without a doubt your heart is my heart and I can't live without you. I'm still learning about our people and this place, but I feel secure knowing I will have you beside me for it all. I love you so much."

Lorcan smiled softly and brushed a kiss on her forehead. "Goldie I've said from the beginning that you are my light. You keep me grounded and you fill my heart with so much love that sometimes I don't know what to do with it besides pour it all back into you. You've taught me the meaning of friendship and second chances. When I watch you work with all the people and go to them with open arms and building new relationships, I beam with pride. Knowing that you are mine is enough to keep me going forever. Seeing how you operate and love, it makes me want more with you. I want it all baby. I want to watch you rock our children and teach them to be light just like you. I love you so much."

King Oberon smiled and said, "With that you are now one in the realm's eyes. Now Lorcan kiss your wife."

And oh did Lorcan kiss her. He kissed her like a whole realm wasn't watching. He deepened it to the point that Goldie felt heat pull at her core and she held onto him desperately. When she opened her eyes, she realized they were hovering off the ground. She smiled at him and he smiled back, inhaling deeply and his eyes going dark with want.

A single loud clapping was heard at the back of the aisle and everyone turned around as a darkness crept in. King Oberon went stiff and Angrbora stood taller. The dark form loomed closer hovering off the ground. When he lifted his hooded head, Goldie gasped. "Balor." She breathed out.

He smiled an evil smile and had he not been so evil, he would have been handsome. "Oh sweetheart, it warms me you know my name. It's been so long since a beautiful pet has said it."

Goldie felt her insides quake as she looked at this man that had tormented her Granna and harshly ruled her people. He looked too familiar. Her eyes widened as he came closer.

"I'm so upset I didn't get the invite to the wedding. I see the apple doesn't fall far from the tree." He said looking at Goldie.

She shivered and he smiled. Lorcan straightened next to Goldie and pulled her closer to him. Goldie reached her arm around Lorcan for stability.

Balor's smile grew even more wicked. Goldie held onto Lorcan for steadiness. She saw Angrbora put her hand on the hilt of her sword. Then Goldie paled, Daideo' wasn't here. He never showed. She felt guilty because in her rush to marry the man she loved, she had left and didn't think twice.

She reached out to Lorcan in his mind, "Daideo' isn't here. I'm afraid something terrible has happened."

Lorcan didn't respond. He just squeezed her tighter.

King Oberon's voice boomed. "Balor you are not welcome her nor do you rule over this land. It is time for you to go."

"Really because I think the fun is just getting started. You really didn't think that you could kill me on your own, did you?" He sneered with some sort knowledge behind his eyes that terrified Goldie.

Balor looked to Lorcan now. "You surprise me. I didn't know if you had it in you, son."

Find out what happens next in Book Two- Goldie Divine: Going to War